The
Uncertainty Principle

The Uncertainty Principle

BY JOSHUA DAVIS & KAL KINI-DAVIS

Penguin Workshop

PENGUIN WORKSHOP
An imprint of Penguin Random House LLC
1745 Broadway, New York, New York 10019

First published in the United States of America by Penguin Workshop,
an imprint of Penguin Random House LLC, 2025

Text copyright © 2025 by Joshua Davis and Kal Kini-Davis
Boat illustration copyright © 2025 by Kal Kini-Davis

Title page illustration by Feifei Ruan

Penguin Random House values and supports copyright. Copyright fuels creativity, encourages diverse voices, promotes free speech, and creates a vibrant culture. Thank you for buying an authorized edition of this book and for complying with copyright laws by not reproducing, scanning, or distributing any part of it in any form without permission. You are supporting writers and allowing Penguin Random House to continue to publish books for every reader. Please note that no part of this book may be used or reproduced in any manner for the purpose of training artificial intelligence technologies or systems.

PENGUIN is a registered trademark and PENGUIN WORKSHOP is a trademark of Penguin Books Ltd, and the W colophon is a registered trademark of Penguin Random House LLC.

Visit us online at penguinrandomhouse.com.

Library of Congress Cataloging-in-Publication Data is available.

Printed in the United States of America

ISBN 9780593660300

1st Printing

LSCC

Design by Jay Emmanuel

This book is a work of fiction. Any references to historical events, real people, or real places are used fictitiously. Other names, characters, places, and events are products of the author's imagination, and any resemblance to actual events or places or persons, living or dead, is entirely coincidental.

The publisher does not have any control over and does not assume any responsibility for author or third-party websites or their content.

The authorized representative in the EU for product safety and compliance is Penguin Random House Ireland, Morrison Chambers, 32 Nassau Street, Dublin D02 YH68, Ireland, https://eu-contact.penguin.ie.

For All Those Who Turn to Face the Wind

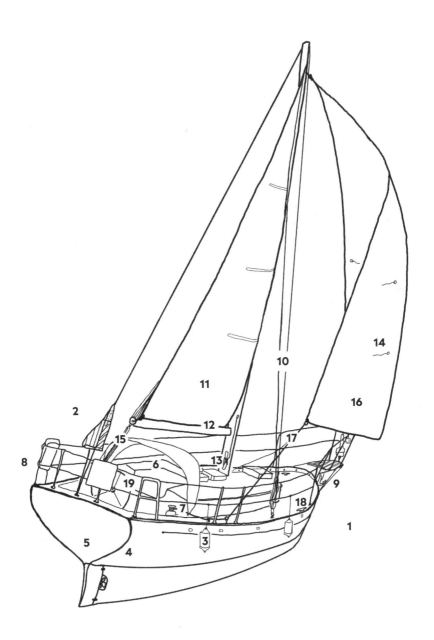

Sailing Glossary

1. **Starboard**—The right side of the boat when facing forward.
2. **Port**—The left side of the boat when facing forward.
3. **Fenders**—Plastic bumpers used to protect the side of the boat when docking.
4. **Hull**—The watertight body of the boat.
5. **Transom**—The back span of the boat.
6. **Cockpit**—The area where the crew steers the boat.
7. **Winch**—A device used to tighten lines on a boat.
8. **Stern**—The rear of the boat.
9. **Bow**—The front of the boat.
10. **Shrouds**—Rigging that holds the mast side to side.
11. **Mainsail**—The primary sail of a ship.
12. **Boom**—A pole that extends from the mast to hold the bottom of the sail.
13. **Halyard**—A rope used to pull a sail up.
14. **Tels**—Snippets of cloth on the sail that indicate if the sail is properly trimmed. Also known as telltales.
15. **Mainsheet**—The line that controls the angle of the mainsail.
16. **Jib**—A triangular sail that sits ahead of the mast.
17. **Jib sheet**—The line that controls the angle of the jib.
18. **Cleat**—A metal or wood protrusion used to tie off a rope.
19. **Helm**—A wheel for steering a boat.

Chapter 1

A sharp whip of salt water lashes the bow of the dinghy and smacks Mia hard in the face. With her free hand, she wipes the water from her eyes, blinking furiously to see through the warm rain. She knows she shouldn't be out here, certainly not on a battered ten-foot inflatable dinghy. The storm is quickly transforming the blue Caribbean into angry, darkened waves. She needs to turn back now, head for the safety of the French West Indies behind her.

Instead, she twists the throttle and accelerates into the storm.

Up ahead, she sees nothing but sheets of gray-black rain and waves that rise like terrible, shape-shifting creatures. Her dinghy, with its puny six-horsepower outboard motor, is like a puppy lost in the wilderness. She is already half sunk, with the pummeling rain and the boat's floorboards sloshing with seawater. The only upside: The water on board adds weight, holding the boat down so the violent gusts don't flip her like a pancake.

Sheets of mist streak off the tops of the waves, giving her only brief glimpses of what's ahead. With each rise of the swell, Mia unconsciously holds her breath, hoping to spot her. But then the dinghy drops into a trough and Mia's heart falls.

I've lost her, she thinks, the tears welling up.

Six months ago if someone had said she'd end up racing into a tropical storm on a rescue mission, she would have laughed. She thought high school in Duluth would just grind on forever, an endless succession of awkward days. She could never have imagined this, battling through nine-foot waves on a small rubber boat in the Caribbean.

The salt water pours down her sun-streaked brown hair and stings her eyes, turning them bloodshot, and she laughs through the tears. She must look truly insane: red-eyed, hair blowing wildly, bouncing across the surface like a skipping stone. If kids from school saw her, they'd probably think she'd lost her mind.

Which isn't far from the truth.

Ahead, a wave sweeps toward her, getting bigger until it looms like a mountain and begins to wobble. The wave must be at least fifteen feet. She tenses as the white crest crumbles and turns into an avalanche of water.

A jolt of panic courses through her—if the wave hits her, she'll be crushed. She instinctively jams the engine hard over to dodge the onslaught and eyes the angle of the swell, the push of the wind, and the speed of the dinghy. She might make the shoulder of the wave. The far edge hasn't broken yet. If she can get there in time, she can get up and over before the wave reaches her.

She twists the throttle harder, knowing that the engine is already maxed out. But every bit of power matters now as the boat begins to rise up the wall of water. She keeps the side of the boat to the wind, using the surface like a sail to gain any extra distance.

It doesn't help. The boat loses speed as it rises up the wave, and Mia realizes that this could be the end, the roar of the wave growing louder, only seconds away now. And, for the first time since leaving Duluth, Mia screams in fury, letting all the anger and fear boil out. She stands precariously and rages against everything with a primal, wild war cry—a warning to the wave, to the sea, to the world—that she's not giving up.

And then the wave hits her.

Chapter 2

Two Weeks Earlier

A light wind ripples the perfect blue of the Caribbean. In every direction, the water is flat and calm. Mia glances up at the tels on the sail of her forty-three-foot sailboat. The little snippets of nylon flutter loosely. Barely enough wind to make headway. Mia estimates they're moving at two knots bearing south by southwest. She squints over the bow. The sky is dotted with dollops of white clouds. On the foredeck, the dinghy is lashed upside down, looking like a baby napping on its mother's chest. Everything is quiet and almost pleasant.

Kaden doesn't even notice the soft breeze ruffle the pages of his plastic-wrapped copy of *Captain Underpants*. He's gotten so used to the boat, it's like he doesn't remember their life before. *It's easier for a ten-year-old*, Mia thinks. Her little brother has pretty much forgotten Duluth.

It'd be cold there today, she thinks. March in Minnesota meant parkas, scarves, and breath billowing like smoke. If she were home, she'd be doing her best to fit in: wear the right clothes, say the right things, or at least not say the wrong things. With green eyes and a wide, angular jaw, she is strikingly pretty, but she tends to say weird things about engines and radio waves. With other kids in Duluth, she had a blazing intensity that left little room for small talk. People at school thought she was odd and kept their distance.

It hurt and made her wonder if she just wasn't cut out for high school. Maybe she deserved to be where she was now, piloting a battered sailboat in the Caribbean instead of attending her junior year back home.

A gust of wind hits them and heels the boat over. The thing is nearly an antique, a forty-three-foot sloop built in the '70s. It's about the same size as a yellow school bus and it used to freak her out when the boat rolled with the wind. It felt like they were going to tip over. Now, she leans automatically as the boat rolls. She keeps her hands on the wheel, the gust whistling through the shrouds, and after a moment, the boat slowly lumbers back up.

Her overalls have long since been pushed to the bottom of the cabinet in her berth. Carhartts feel like thirty-six-grit sandpaper on your skin when they're soaked with salt water. In their place, she's got on her Caribbean uniform: a threadbare black sports bra, blue polyester shorts, and cheap sunglasses that are so scratched, it's like looking out of a cloud.

If only Sadie were here, things would be better. She'd be like, *What the hell are you wearing?* and then tell her exactly what to do and say. Sadie always knew what to do.

Sadie. That is the hardest part, being away from her best friend. Her only friend, actually. She can picture what they'd be doing right now. They'd be on opposite sides of some class with their laptops open. The school gave each kid a computer and said they were empowering the students to make good decisions. Nobody did. Their favorite game was to start a video chat in the middle of class. They turned the sound off and took turns making their faces ugly with filters. Whoever laughed first lost, and usually got busted by the teacher.

Overhead, a cloud passes across the sun, darkening the sea, and Mia feels a tightness in her chest. If she could just talk to her friend, maybe they could work things out. Instead, it's been nothing but silence since The Incident.

The memories of that day start to crash through her mind like a demolition derby. The school cafeteria. The splat of yogurt and then chicken potpie as Mia hurled them against the wall. She couldn't even hear herself screaming, she was so angry.

The flapping of the tels on the sail brings her attention back to the boat. The wind has picked up. Mia cranks the mainsail winch, bringing the boom in. Her forearms and biceps are thicker now—she can see the muscles ripple as she turns the crank. She smiles at the thought of what Sadie would say. She'd call her a brute.

Mia spins the wheel lock, holding their position, and moves past Kaden to an array of silvery glass squares strapped onto the starboard railing. She unclips the boat's old handheld radio—a waterproof walkie-talkie for calling nearby ships—and detaches the back.

For months now she has been completely isolated and cut off. Her cell phone is stuffed away in her cabin because there's no cell network out here and the radio's battery is dying. The thing can barely reach nearby boats.

But she hasn't given up hope. If she can keep the dying battery powered up and dial in the right frequency, it might be able to connect with one of the eighteen amateur radio satellites orbiting the earth and patch her through to Sadie's cell phone.

Mia connects an alligator cable to the glass squares and uses a multimeter to measure the current. The glass squares are an improvised portable solar panel she built herself. She could plug in to the onboard power, but she doesn't want to be tied to the suffocating boat. She wants to be able to go ashore—even if it's a deserted island—and call her friend in private. There's no privacy on a boat.

"Gotta be the electrodes," she mumbles, noting that the wattage is still too low. Kaden looks up but he's gotten used to her talking to herself and goes back to his book without saying anything.

"It's not the electrodes," Lene says. She's sitting cross-legged above the hatchway that leads below deck and is wearing her usual beige turtleneck and baggy, pea-green suit jacket. It's a ridiculous thing to wear on a boat, particularly in the muggy Caribbean, but Lene doesn't care, in part because she's a world-renowned physicist. Also, because she is Mia's imaginary friend. The real Lene Hau at Harvard has no idea that Mia exists.

"You should try a different substrate," Lene says helpfully. "Because what you're doing now really isn't working."

"I know, Lee," Mia mutters. The correct way to pronounce Lene's name is "Lee-nah," but when Mia gets frustrated with her friend, she sometimes says just the first part.

Kaden looks up again. He can't see Lene so Mia's strange mutterings can sometimes confuse him. Mia ignores him and stays focused on her homemade solar panel. It's made of five glass squares and each one represents a different idea about how to maximize electrical production using naturally occurring things. One is made out of wild berries, another from harder-to-get titanium dioxide.

She's been at it for months now, slowly improving the power generation. When they're anchored, she spends her days shuffling around the boat's small kitchen, boiling concoctions and mumbling with her imaginary friend. Eventually, she'll have a completely mobile communication system, the castaway geek version of a cell phone.

"This is one of the rare things your mom and I see eye to eye on," Lene says. "You're definitely becoming a weirdo."

Mia wants to argue but realizes it would only confirm the point.

THE UNCERTAINTY PRINCIPLE

After all, if your imaginary friend and your mom agree that you're weird, you probably have a problem.

Mia feels a pang of tension just thinking about her mom. Her dad's soft snoring has driven her mom out of the forward cabin and Mia can hear her tossing fitfully on the banquette below. They had a long passage last night and Izzy left Mia in charge so she could sleep. These moments on deck without her parents are one of the few times she can relax.

Normally, her mom is badgering her to read a book or study for an AP test, which is ironic because Izzy pulled them out of school to do something called "unschooling." Izzy had read about it in a book and it basically means they can do whatever they want. The book said that unschooled kids start by goofing off until they get so crushingly bored, they decide that studying sounds great. The approach was supposed to help a student discover "inner motivation" via intense boredom. But, after six months, Mia is still goofing off, at least as far as her mom is concerned.

Mia nibbles a stray piece of skin on her index finger and winces when it comes off. The sharp, fleeting pain is a distraction from the sound of her parents below. She can hear every snort, burp, and fart. Reason 147 why this was a bad idea: You never want to be jammed in this close with your parents.

They were in their kitchen eating breakfast in Duluth six months ago when her mom said she had some news. Kaden barely paid attention, more interested in his Frosted Mini-Wheats. Ethan, her dad, was fidgeting uneasily with the kitchen faucet, which had a slow leak. It was a week after The Incident.

Mia knew something was brewing because her mom had been scrubbing the counters incessantly, staying up after everyone went to sleep. Her mom was obsessed with cleanliness but this was worse: The laminate countertops were rubbed through to the particleboard underneath.

Mia figured her parents were getting divorced. Everything seemed to be falling apart. Mia had essentially been expelled. They asked her to "seek an educational setting more supportive of her mental health." At the same time, her mom was going to pieces, washing her hands till they were cracked and raw. She vacuumed their stained carpeting nonstop and yelled at the landlord, who refused to replace it. She'd gotten fired from her waitressing job at a steak house. It wasn't good when the waitress's hands looked like raw meat. Her mom always had trouble with what she called "goddamn germs," but this was something else. She needed psychiatric help.

Instead, she announced that they were going sailing.

There was a hush in the kitchen. The fluorescent lights hummed.

"Like for the day?" Mia asked.

"Longer."

Mia looked back and forth between her parents. For years, her dad had been refurbishing a broken forty-three-foot sailboat named *Graceland* in the parking lot of their apartment building. The boat was a never-ending argument. Any time her dad got carpentry work, he put the money into buying engine parts or new winches. It was like he had a mistress and it made her mom furious: She pointed out that there were a million other things they could do with the money while the damn boat just sat there, taking up their two parking spots.

So it was surprising to hear her mom talk about actually sailing somewhere.

"We're getting rid of everything, and we're going to sail to the Caribbean," her mom said, the words coming out in a rush. Mia was stunned. It seemed like her mom was drinking. When she'd had a few

THE UNCERTAINTY PRINCIPLE

glasses of wine, she liked to talk about how much better life was anywhere other than Duluth.

"So you want to go sailing for the summer?" Mia asked, trying to understand.

"No," her dad said. "We're not coming back."

She thought she heard him wrong. *We're not coming back?* It sounded like a death sentence.

Her mom tried to spin it as a great thing. They could leave everything behind and do whatever they wanted. Izzy said that unschooling was every kid's dream. She imagined that Mia would spend month after glorious month reading Shakespeare and teaching herself calculus. Izzy also pointed out that Mia wouldn't have to deal with *social pressures*, a coded reference to her meltdown.

Mia tried to argue with them. Sure, she had an issue in the cafeteria. But that was because Sadie was hiding something from her. And just because Mia freaked out once, it didn't mean they needed to move onto a boat, particularly one that hadn't been in the water for years. And it seemed pretty clear that running away wasn't going to solve their problems.

"You're not going to get away from your phobias if we leave," Mia pointed out angrily.

"This isn't about me," her mom said calmly. "You're not doing well."

Mia flushed with anger. "Are you kidding me right now?" she snapped. "*You're* the one that's a wreck."

"You covered the wall of the school cafeteria with food," her mom said, her voice rising.

"It was Sadie's fault," Mia shouted back.

"Sadie didn't throw food and forks and plates and trays at people," Izzy said, getting exasperated. "You did that."

"I had a reason."

"And look at your hands."

Mia shoved her hands into her overalls, refusing to give her mom any advantage. But what she wanted more than anything was to pluck a piece of cuticle off.

Initially, she just started picking the skin at the edges of her fingernails. It delivered a small jolt of pain that gave her something to focus on while everyone around her talked. Eventually, her hands looked a lot like her mother's.

Mia knew it was weird but didn't really want to stop. She wished she could be like everyone else and make small talk and laugh. But she couldn't, even after all the coaching from Sadie. Picking her cuticles distracted her from the fact that she didn't know how to be normal.

"If we had any money, we'd get you a shrink or send you to a program like the school counselor says," her mom said. Izzy was amped up with a surge of nervous energy. "But I'm out of options. Your dad is useless. I got fired and all we got is this shitty boat. So this is it. This is how we're going to fix you. We're gonna take what we got left and get the hell out."

"I don't need you to fix me," Mia said defiantly.

"See, that's it," her mom said, irritated. "At least I know I've got issues. You don't even know it. That's why we have to leave. I'm doing this for you."

Chapter 3

Mia's mom pokes her head out of the hatch and blinks in the bright sunlight.

"Everything okay?" she asks.

Mia glares at her mom. It's been six months, but Mia is just as angry as she was the day they left. Of course everything isn't okay. There's no way for Mia to learn to talk to other teenagers because they've been actively avoiding human contact ever since they left. They anchor off desolate islands for weeks until they run out of food or water. It's like civilization has disappeared and they're the only people left on the planet.

What makes it worse is that her mom actually looks good, the salt water making her black hair thick and wavy. Her mother's grandparents came from southern Italy and the constant sun at sea has brought out the olive hues in her skin. Even her mom's hands have healed and look normal.

"You going to say something?" Izzy asks, an edge in her voice.

"Everything's fine," Mia mumbles, not wanting to talk. Sailing is only bearable when she's alone on deck, or at least alone with Kaden and Lene, neither of whom really counts as a real human. Mia has actually come to like the roll of the sea and the wind in her face but being anywhere near her mom ruins it.

Her mom climbs into the cockpit and looks around. Low-lying

islands have appeared in the distance and stick up like small bumps on the horizon.

"A few hours more," her mom says, walking back to the hatch and shouting down. "Ethan! It's you now."

Her dad appears a moment later, yawning. He's lost weight over the past few months. His brawny carpenter's arms have thinned and bronzed and his eyes bug out of his head a little. He was never a sharp dresser but now his clothes don't really fit so he just goes shirtless and wears the same grease-stained pair of shorts. The shorts are cinched up with a length of electrical wire and he's given up on shaving so he has an explosive red beard, a remnant of his Viking roots. He looks like a wild animal.

Every couple of months, they pull into a port somewhere to resupply, and he hustles for work around the harbor. Izzy hates it: She dumps a bucket of salt water and soap on his head to disinfect him at the end of every day and insists that the kids scrub the boat constantly to fend off the germs. But his meager income is what keeps them going.

Once they're out at sea though, Izzy relaxes again. "The salt water," she says. "It cleans everything."

Mia pulls at her hair; it's knotted and tangled. The salt water certainly isn't doing much for her. Her mom can pull off the swashbuckling look—she's blossomed into her role as captain of the high seas—but Mia feels like a freak.

"Why don't you give me a hand?" Izzy asks hopefully, trying to connect. She points to a pile of rope next to her and starts coiling, the equivalent of tidying up on a boat. "You can tell me how the past few hours were."

"No thanks," Mia says, and looks away to show that she's not going to do an ounce more than the bare minimum. Mia was forced onto the boat, supposedly for her own good, and she wants her mom to know that it isn't working.

Her dad glances between his daughter and his wife, unsure what to do. His dream of sailing the world came true, but not in the way he imagined.

It was only five weeks after The Incident that they lowered the *Graceland* into the water and pushed off into Lake Superior. Her dad kept a solid grip on his copy of *Sailing Made Easy* and flipped through the pages whenever something unexpected happened, which was pretty much all the time. The lines got tangled, the mainsail halyard came loose, dropping the sail onto the deck, and the boom smacked her dad in the head, cutting a gash on his forehead. At one point, they found themselves going backward for reasons no one could explain. Her dad had crewed racing boats on the lake and supposedly knew how to sail, but he was always following orders. He was never the skipper.

To make matters worse, her mom was seasick and spent the first day leaning against the railing, throwing up into the lake. The whole thing was a disaster.

By the second day, her dad seemed to recognize that they had made a mistake. "You know what, let's forget the sailing for now," he said, flipping the switches to start the *Graceland*'s thirty-eight-horsepower diesel engine. "We can just motor."

"Perfect," Mia said sarcastically. "This has been really fun and now we can just go home."

That's when her mom spoke up.

"If we motor, we spend more on gas," she said, trying to tamp back her nausea. "We've got a sailboat so let's sail the damn thing."

Mia was used to her mother complaining. For years, she had come home from work and gone on about the managers at the restaurant, how people never tipped enough, about the germs on the cash she had to touch, and how the world was stacked against people who worked for hourly wages.

But now her mother sounded different. She had read *Sailing Made Easy* too and started telling everyone what to do: grab that rope, wrap it clockwise, now pull. Between commands, she'd dry heave over the railing and then, just by force of will, keep barking orders. Mia hated every moment of it but couldn't help but be impressed.

"And you," Izzy said, pointing at Mia's dad in exasperation. "Crank, for god's sake. People have been sailing for thousands of years. We can do this."

From that moment on, Mia's mom was the captain. Her dad became the first mate. It didn't matter that he had spent years lovingly refurbishing the boat or that he had actual sailing experience. Now he was crew on his wife's boat.

In fact, they were all crew on her boat.

Chapter 4

Scrub Island comes into sight in the midafternoon and it's a picture of paradise: a sliver of blindingly white sand topped with a fringe of low-lying scrub. Mia looks up briefly from her collection of little solar panels. Just another useless, deserted Caribbean island.

"Yeah, this sucks," Lene agrees, looking around skeptically at the gorgeous setting. "I don't think I can take much more of it."

"Just deal with it," Mia mutters.

They're sitting by the mast away from Izzy, who has the helm. Mia carefully notes down the results of the latest round of solar sensitizer tests. The panels have to be small enough to fit into a backpack, but powerful enough to fast charge her radio. It's a difficult challenge.

"It's too hot here," Lene says, pulling at her collar.

"You're wearing a turtleneck."

"It helps me think."

At first, Mia was happy to have an imaginary friend. She needed someone to confide in and was fascinated by Lene's online videos. Mia had come across them while trying to figure out how to repair the boat's crappy solar panels and loved reading that Lene was so smart, the Carlsberg beer company helped pay for her education. It made her think that the Danes must be really cool if beer companies gave scholarships to young girls who liked science.

In her videos, Lene seemed like a very strange person in the kind of way that Mia was. Lene talked about building complex machines at her lab in Boston. The main difference between the real Lene Hau and Mia was that Lene Hau appeared completely comfortable and confident in the world, while Mia felt the opposite.

Lene also looked beautifully strange. She wore a mishmash of ill-fitting clothes: an oversize, pea-green men's jacket and a purple scarf. She had a strong, square jaw and a mole above the left side of her mouth that made her look like a fashion model, albeit a fashion model who rummaged through free clothing bins and was a Harvard professor. In one interview, she talked about how she was once so deep in thought, she got into the shower with her clothes on.

Mia first met her as the water drained out of the Beauharnois Lock, a massive water elevator in Canada that lifts and drops cargo ships to and from the Great Lakes into the Atlantic. Mia was paying out the guide ropes feeling like she was entering an entirely new universe as the *Graceland* descended into the concrete basin. As the gray walls surrounded her, she felt like even Sadie wouldn't know what to do anymore. And then, suddenly, Lene was standing there, looking otherworldly and a little miffed.

"It's like we're getting flushed down the toilet of life," Lene said with a slight Danish accent. Those were her first words. She just appeared and expressed exactly how Mia was feeling.

As far as Mia could tell, Lene's job at Harvard was to make odd things. She was famous for building microscopic tweezers that could grab a single shard of light and hold it like a miraculous, glowing gem. It was the first time in human history that someone had stopped light. Out of 225 Nobel Prizes in Physics, only five had gone to women. Lene was at the top of the list to be the sixth.

But, over the months of sailing together, Mia has come to realize

THE UNCERTAINTY PRINCIPLE

that Lene usually says whatever Mia doesn't want to hear. It turns out that having an imaginary friend can be pretty annoying.

"You know what your problem is?" Lene says, interrupting Mia's effort to rewire one of her solar experiments.

"I don't really want to talk—"

"You don't understand quantum entanglement."

At the back of the boat, Izzy waves. "What are you doing up there?" Izzy shouts. "We're getting close."

Mia ignores her. Obviously, they're getting close: She can see the island dead ahead. Her mom doesn't have to tell her.

"We used to think that two things that are far apart can't be connected," Lene says. "But now we know they can. We just can't explain why."

"I'm connected to nothing so thanks for making it worse," Mia says, packing up the solar array before they drop anchor.

"You're connected to Sadie and she's not here," Lene says. "That's entanglement."

Mia looks out to sea and exhales, like someone punched her in the gut. Lene is right. Mia has known Sadie since kindergarten. They grew up together and shared everything. When they got to high school, Sadie helped her crack the code of the new social scene. She told Mia what to wear (crop tops when it was warm, Brandy Melville sweaters when it was cold). She told her how to talk ("Just smile and say 'cool' a lot"). To Mia, it all seemed foreign and awkward, but with Sadie's help, she could almost pass for normal.

"Without her, you don't even really know how to act around other people," Lene says sadly.

"Will you leave me alone?" Mia snaps, cracking under the truth of what Lene is saying.

"I barely said anything to you," Izzy snaps back, thinking that Mia was talking to her.

"I wasn't talking to you."

"Then who the hell are you talking to?" Izzy says, looking at her daughter with wide-eyed astonishment. "It's just us on deck so either you were talking to me or there's something really wrong with you."

Izzy looks at Mia with a taunting expression, daring her to answer. It's almost as if she wants Mia to be crazy. It's part of her mother's madness to push everyone else over the edge and then claim that she's the only sane one.

"Just tell me where we're dropping anchor," Mia says, trying to avoid the argument.

Izzy glares at her, but they're above the patch of water that Izzy wants to anchor in, a crystal-clear stretch of turquoise in a protected bay.

"Here's good," Izzy says at last. "Take the helm."

Mia takes the wheel and her mom walks to the bow.

"Ethan, Kaden," she shouts. "Get up here."

Izzy scans the water around them as Mia starts up the diesel engine and turns into the wind, bringing the boat to a standstill. Kaden and Ethan pop up on deck to lower the sails while her mom drops the anchor, the chain rattling noisily.

Mia throws the boat into reverse and waits. As the boat backs away, the anchor chain rises up out of the water and tightens, digging the anchor into the sandy bottom below. The boat shudders, straining against the chain as the prongs of the anchor grab hard into the sand.

"It's holding," her mom says and Mia rolls her eyes. It's obvious that the anchor is holding but it's like it's not real until her mom says it. "You can switch—"

"I know," Mia interrupts testily, killing the engine.

THE UNCERTAINTY PRINCIPLE

Her mom pauses and looks at her daughter, deciding whether to make an issue of her tone. She decides to shelve it.

With the engine off, there's almost no sound. Small waves break onshore two hundred yards away, sending out a gentle whoosh as they froth into a momentary bubble bath. The water beneath them shimmers turquoise, emerald, and a deep, sparkling blue, as if somebody threw handfuls of jewels into the water. A school of fish darts left and right.

"Well, this certainly isn't Duluth," Lene says.

~

By late morning, they're all on their knees scrubbing rust off the boat's stainless-steel railing. It's a weekly task: The seawater corrodes anything that's metal, even if it's stainless steel. It's the one cleaning task that Mia actually likes. There's something cathartic about polishing a small area with an old toothbrush, dipping it into a halved plastic Coke bottle of baking soda and steadily brushing away the brown flakes of oxidation until the railing is gleaming again.

Mia glances over at her mom. Izzy leans under the wire to get the underside of the starboard railing. Her shiny black hair dangles over the side of the boat like a dark waterfall. Mia is still amazed at how different her mother is now that they're at sea. So much happier and more self-assured.

Mia glances down at her fingers. The skin around her nails is already picked raw but she manages to pinch a thin sliver of cuticle and pull it free. A stab of pain courses through her body and she takes a sharp breath of humid air. A thin line of blood emerges from the cut and the wound starts to sting from the ever-present dusting of salt on her hands. It hurts but it also distracts her from thinking about how well her mom is doing.

"You've got to stop doing that," her mom says, a touch of concern in her voice. Mia didn't realize she was watching.

The last person she wants advice from is her mom. Mia packs up the toothbrush. "Leave me alone," she says, and trundles below to the calm safety of her solar experiments. She keeps everything in a plastic tub and unpacks the collection of glass squares.

"Interesting," Lene says, sitting down beside her at the banquette and checking out the latest results. "You might even break the Shockley–Queisser limit."

Sometimes Lene says nice things. The so-called SQ limit is the maximum efficiency of a solar cell. These two old guys named Shockley and Queisser said a solar cell couldn't convert more than 33.7 percent of the sun's energy into electricity. Mia thinks it'd be kind of fun to prove them wrong. And maybe she would prove her mom wrong too.

"But even if you break the SQ limit, you still have to figure out how to autopatch into a satellite," Lene adds unhelpfully.

Mia groans and retreats to her cabin with the plastic tub of experiments to put some distance between her and everyone. It's a ridiculously small space below the back deck of the boat but it's all she's got. The cockpit where she steers the boat actually juts down into her "room," creating a sort of tunnel for the mattress. To get into bed, she has to shimmy her feet into the tunnel. It is basically a cave with a door, which she shuts as Lene is about to say something more about satellites.

But when Mia turns around, Lene is already lying in the bed. Unfortunately, you can't really shut the door on an imaginary friend.

"Let's put aside the technical problems for a second," Lene digs in. "Even if you could figure out how to call her, Sadie probably doesn't want to talk to you."

"I need a new friend," Mia mumbles. The problem is, she doesn't know how to get rid of Lene now that she's here.

Mia fishes her old cell phone out of a plastic grocery bag. On the rare occasions when they're docked and she's able to find an open Wi-Fi network, she downloads science articles and scrolls through Instagram, which is painful. There are always photos of Sadie having fun with other people, looking like she's living her best life without Mia.

Now, trapped in her bunk room without Wi-Fi, the phone is a bittersweet reminder of what she used to have. She clicks the photo album open and scrolls through pictures of Duluth. There's a photo of her and Sadie at Dunn Brothers, a log cabin that houses their favorite coffee shop. As freshmen, they started going there after school and it felt so grown up, like they were entering a new phase of their lives and friendship. Sadie told her what to order (Nitro Vanilla Iced Nirvana) and how to flirt with the cute cashier ("Ask him why he has a tattoo of a squirrel on his arm").

The next photo brings a cascade of memories. It's of Mia wearing one of Sadie's dresses. They were just messing around in Sadie's room, rummaging through her closet. Sadie kept handing Mia clothes to try on. The dress was green, with a plunging V-neck, a fitted waist, and a hemline at the thigh.

"Oh, your ass looks so good in that," Sadie said in awe.

Mia felt the blood rush to her head. She didn't like wearing dresses—they weren't practical at all—but she liked the look on Sadie's face. It made her stomach feel like she was jumping on a trampoline, in that moment between rising and falling when everything floats.

"You wear that to a party and every boy is going to want to talk to you," Sadie said, coming close and pulling Mia's hair off her shoulders. "It matches your eyes."

"It's only going to match my eyes in this light with a bulb that's probably about three thousand kelvins," Mia said, babbling a little.

Sadie stepped back, held Mia by both shoulders, and looked at her. "High school is a puzzle, and you are the smartest person I know. You just have to solve the puzzle and the first step is to not say stuff like that. It's better to not say anything."

Mia liked the idea that socializing was as simple as taking a diesel engine apart. If there was a code, Mia figured that her personality didn't matter. She just needed to do certain things like not talk and the world would open up for her. And she wanted Sadie's help. She wanted to go to parties with her, but mostly just to watch how easy it was for Sadie to talk to people. It made Mia smile.

The next photo is of Mia and Leif outside of school. Sadie took the picture, and it is one of Mia's most prized possessions. Leif was a lug of a guy who dressed like a lumberjack. He was sweet, like a gentle giant, and always seemed open to listening to Mia talk about photons and solar cells.

Because Mia told Sadie everything, Sadie knew that Mia had an enormous crush on Leif. When Mia slept over at Sadie's house, they would stay up late talking about what their lives would be like when they settled down with husbands. Sadie wanted to know how many kids Mia wanted to have ("Two?" Mia said, wondering if that was the right answer) and where Mia imagined living with her husband (a mansion in Endion near the university). It was so nice to snuggle with Sadie, talking about a beautiful future.

The photos only make Mia want to talk to Sadie more but then that feeling crashes into the memory of what Sadie did and Mia's insides turn to knots. Her heart starts pounding in her ears like it did in the cafeteria and she quickly scrolls forward, banishing Duluth behind

THE UNCERTAINTY PRINCIPLE

endless shots of water from the *Graceland*'s deck. The steely gray of the Great Lakes turns into the navy blue of the Northern Atlantic before sliding into the vivid greens and blues of the Exumas. Besides a couple shots of Kaden, there are no more people.

Mia's throat tightens and tears well up again. She's hunched over in a cramped, dark tunnel that reeks of mildew and engine oil. If she could just call Sadie and talk it through, maybe things would be better. Maybe she could come back to Duluth and they could forget about what happened. Just go back to being uncomplicated friends. Instead, it's like she's being held hostage on this boat.

"That's exactly it," Lene says from behind her on the bunk. "You've been kidnapped by your own parents."

Mia is overwhelmed by the feeling that she has to get out, to get away, but there's nowhere to go. In a rush, she grabs her binoculars, hangs them around her neck, and heads back onto deck.

Her mother is sitting in the cockpit, reading, and looks up. Mia looks at her and feels a rising panic mixed with anger. They stare at each other for a moment.

"Say whatever it is you want to say," Mia finally blurts.

Her mom looks at her for a second, then with a falsely concerned tone says, "All you do is talk to yourself all day and play around with a bunch of junk."

"You told me I could do whatever I wanted," Mia nearly shouts.

"But you're doing nothing," Izzy fires back.

"I'm inventing things."

"Really? Because you've been at it for months and you've got nothing to show for it," Izzy says, sighing. "I just wish you would use this time to learn something useful."

"I'm trying to talk to my friends."

"What friends?"

"I'm trying to fix things," Mia says, feeling more and more pathetic. "You're just making it impossible."

"When I was your age, I was waitressing and working my butt off but you're slipping right back to being a child."

That stings for about a dozen reasons, all of which flood into Mia's brain. "You think I'm a child?" she says icily.

"You're not growing up."

"You won't let me."

"We're doing this for *you*," her mom says, her voice tight.

"Stop saying that," Mia yells, raising her voice.

"The whole point was to give you time to get straightened out."

"Whoa, whoa, whoa," her dad says, walking over from the railing with a toothbrush covered in flakes of rust. "What's the—"

"This is such bullshit," Mia shouts, pointing at her mom. "Do you realize how terrible it is to be trapped with her?"

"I thought you liked sailing," her dad says.

"It's literally hell," Mia says, regretting it a bit when she sees the hurt look on her dad's face. But it's the truth. "You two think this is all fine and normal but it's not. Mom needs medical help, not a boat."

"I'm actually getting better," her mom says sharply. "You're not even trying."

"The reason I'm not getting better is you," Mia says, deciding that it's not worth pretending she's okay anymore.

There's silence and then Mia says exactly what she's feeling.

"My problem is you."

The words hang in the air. Izzy starts scratching at her hands. "Don't blame your shit on me."

"You're the worst thing that ever happened to me," Mia says with as much venom as she can.

Her mom starts to cry and nobody says anything. Mia wanted to hurt her mom but now that she has, it doesn't feel very good.

"Look, I've been thinking," her dad says, breaking the silence.

"It's better when you don't," Izzy lashes out.

"I'm just thinking maybe we could talk to Uncle Paul."

"I don't think anybody—"

"Let me talk, Izzy," her dad cuts in and it's one of the few times he's ever interrupted her mom. Izzy is surprised but doesn't say anything. "My brother said he'd take Mia at any point. She could live with him and go to a high school in Tennessee. It'd be a more normal teenage experience."

"She had that," Izzy says. "It didn't work." Izzy wipes away her tears and looks at Mia, who tries not to show hope, but it is hard to contain. Uncle Paul lives in Tennessee with his wife and twin five-year-old boys. He is a financial adviser and is basically the opposite of her parents. He is normal, stable, and can pay bills.

"We won't be there to help you," Izzy says. "I won't be there."

Mia understands what her mother is getting at. Izzy thinks she's the only one who really understands Mia because she's the only one who feels what Mia feels. They're the same, in a lot of ways. But even if that's true, it doesn't mean Izzy can help. So far, it's meant the opposite.

Kaden appears on the steps coming up from below. Lene stands on the steps behind him. Everybody is watching Mia now.

"I think it might be better for everyone if I left," Mia says slowly and deliberately.

She glances at Kaden. He looks like someone punched him.

"You're leaving?" he asks, his voice breaking.

"I think Mia might just take a little time off the boat," her dad says, trying to sound totally fine but his voice is thin and strained.

25

"I'll be back for the summer," Mia says, even though she's pretty sure she never wants to come back. She feels a lump rise in her throat and she's suddenly confused. Her family is like a disease but they're still her family.

"Okay, we'll give Paul a call and talk about it," her dad says. "There's an inhabited island southwest of here. We can make arrangements there. How's that sound?"

He looks at Mia with tears in his eyes and Mia is flooded with grief. But then she's pissed all over again that they've put her in this situation. Why is she the one who has to make sacrifices? All she wants is a normal life. Why can't they back down and stop this boat thing? It's totally unfair.

"Yeah, let's call him," she says coldly and spins away, heading for the mast to hide her feelings.

She reaches the bosun's chair, a seat attached to the mast by a pulley. It's normally used to make repairs but Mia thinks of it as her personal space. In a minute, she has hauled herself up the mast until she's fifty feet above the deck and breathing heavily from the exertion.

It's the only place she can really be alone. Up here, above it all, there's no talk, no voices, no parents, no brother. There's not even enough room for Lene. If anybody were watching, it would look ridiculous. She's swaying side to side in a little hanging seat like she's gotten stuck at the top of a tree.

She has a better view of the island from up here. It's not much to look at. Just another low-lying strip of white sand in the emerald sea. But then something catches her eye.

She swivels in the hanging seat and sees a catamaran out at sea. Surprisingly, it is headed toward them, and it looks even more beat up than the *Graceland*. Mia focuses the binoculars and sees a couple bicycles lashed to the railings, a small windmill on a steel pole, and surfboards tied to the canopy over the deck. The sail is spotted with multicolored patches, and the hull along the waterline is blotchy with black fiberglass as if it ran ashore at some point. A deeply tanned middle-aged guy mans the helm. He looks like he's been sailing the boat since the 1970s.

Mia scans the front of the boat, and it takes her a second to realize what she's looking at. There's someone standing there. He's younger and has sun-streaked brown hair. With a start, Mia realizes that he's holding binoculars too and he's looking straight at her.

She abruptly lowers her binoculars, as if she's been caught snooping. She can feel her face redden. She swivels back to the island as if she doesn't care at all about the incoming catamaran and pretends to scan the shoreline. After a minute of looking at nothing, she casually pans back to the catamaran. She's deflated to see that the guy isn't looking at her anymore. He's opening the anchor hatch but it gives her a moment to check him out.

He appears to be about her age—she'd guess sixteen or seventeen—and he's wearing board shorts with no shirt, showing off a tanned, slender torso. It looks like he's never eaten an ounce of fat; he's sinewy, like the cross-country runners at school. His hair is a messy tangle tumbling down to his shoulders and he's got some kind of bandage across his forehead. He looks like a cross between a hippie and the survivor of a shipwreck. She spots the boat's name: the *Exodus* from Sydney, Australia.

He shakes out the anchor chain and she can see his lean muscles ripple. The catamaran tacks into the wind a quarter mile from the *Graceland* and Mia loses sight of him behind the sail. After a moment, he reappears and drops the anchor, plunging it into the translucent water. They're close enough that she can hear the chain rattling. Her heart is beating faster. She's not sure if it's because she's spying on him or that the guy is good-looking in a strange, offbeat way.

With his anchor down, the guy stands and looks around, his gaze settling on Mia's boat. She lowers the binoculars before she's caught again and realizes how ridiculous she must look sitting in her swing at the top of the mast. She suddenly feels childish and flushes with anger at the thought of her mother's accusation.

It only takes a minute to lower herself back down to the deck where her dad and mom are discussing what to do.

"We gotta say something," her dad protests.

"We literally have no idea where they've been," her mom says. She sounds panicked. "We just disinfected everything and we're going to mess it up for what? Just to say hi?"

Mia slips below deck to drop the binoculars and put on a sports bra that's slightly less grease stained. She can still hear her parents arguing above.

"They're gonna think we're smugglers if we don't say anything."

"Us? Look at them! They're the smugglers. Their boat looks like it's infested."

There's a burst of static from the ship's radio just outside Mia's berth and they hear a charming Australian accent. "*Graceland, Graceland, Graceland,* this is *Exodus.* Looking a lot like paradise, eh?"

Izzy and Ethan fall silent up on deck. "You know what that is?" Lene says, popping her head into Mia's berth. "That's the universe talking to you."

Mia steels herself. Lene is right.

Before anybody can do anything, Mia steps into the cabin and picks up the mic.

"*Exodus,* this is *Graceland.* Glad to have you here," she says.

THE UNCERTAINTY PRINCIPLE

"Mia!" her mom shouts from above and rumbles down the ladder into the galley.

"Listen, mate, you and yours want to join us for some mahi tonight? We got more than we know what to do with, over," the Aussie says.

"Tell him we're feeling sick so we should keep our distance," Izzy orders.

Mia holds her mom's gaze and nods. She presses the talk button. "We'd love to come over." Saying it feels really, really good. She lets the button go as her mom lunges for the handset.

"Goddammit, Mia," Izzy hisses, trying to grab the handset, but Mia stiff-arms her like a football player.

"What can we bring?" Mia asks quickly.

"We're not going over there," Izzy says, but Mia has already released the talk button so they can't hear her.

"No need to bring anything. We've got it covered," the Australian says as Mia wrestles her mother off. "Just come before sunset and we'll see you then, over."

"You don't get to make decisions like this," her mom says.

"Copy, copy," Mia says, struggling to keep her voice level as her mom jostles her.

"All righty, see you soon, over and out," the man says.

The radio falls silent and Izzy takes a step back. Ethan and Kaden stand in the hatch, looking down at the two of them, surprised at the tussle.

"I don't know what you're thinking," Izzy says. "We're not going."

"We haven't seen anyone for months. It's literally child abuse."

"You're leaving anyway, what do you care?" Izzy snaps. Mia gives her mom a look that says, *I don't care about you, I'm going.*

"I can take her and you could stay," Ethan says, trying to appease both of them.

29

"That doesn't solve the problem."

They all know the problem. If they go, Izzy will obsess about their germs. She'll insist that they spend the next few days disinfecting everything on the *Graceland* and will scrub her hands raw for a week. Even if Mia goes by herself, her mom will be convinced that she's bringing germs back.

Lene sidles up to Mia. "Think like your mom," she whispers in Mia's ear. Mia breaks into a smile. "What if we swim over?" Mia says. "The germs will all wash off."

Her mom hesitates. Any normal family would motor over in the dinghy and arrive nice and dry. But, according to her mom's theory, if they swim, the salt water will kill any germs. "Who shows up to dinner soaking wet?" her mom says, not wanting to go but unable to avoid the logic.

"We do," Mia says assuredly. "That's the kind of messed-up family we are."

Her mom looks at Ethan.

"She's right," he says with a shrug. "That's the kind of family we are."

Behind him in the cabin, Mia sees Lene doing an awkward dance, celebrating their first win in a long time.

Chapter 5

What do you wear to dinner on an Australian catamaran when you have to swim there? It's a question Mia has never faced before and it worries her. To make matters worse, she has a limited set of choices. She rummages through the small cabinet in her berth. It contains the sum total of her wardrobe: nylon shorts, tank tops, some plain T-shirts, a bunch of underwear, some socks (which are useless on a boat), sports bras, a pair of khaki pants, a pair of black jeans, overalls, and, at the bottom, a brand-new bikini with the tag still on it.

She holds the bikini up. It seems like a small amount of fabric but she's not much of a judge. Back home, she sometimes wore girlie stuff, but only because Sadie told her to. It was part of "cracking the code" of high school. But she never wore a bikini.

It was her mom's idea. They got it at Target on the last shopping trip before leaving. Mia knew that her mom wanted her to be a normal girl who didn't dress like a car mechanic but Izzy wouldn't just come out and say it. Instead, she said they should get it because you never know what kind of situation you might find yourself in.

At the time, Mia laughed. What kind of situation requires a bikini? Basically nothing. But maybe now it makes sense. It'd be easy to quickly pull pants and a T-shirt on once they're there.

When she emerges onto the deck, her parents gawk at her. "Are you okay?" her dad says, concerned. He's never seen her in a bikini.

"You look really weird," Kaden says unhelpfully.

"Leave me alone," Mia says sharply.

Ethan shakes his head and wraps a strip of silver duct tape around a plastic bag with their clothes. "Okay, we're good," he says. He ties the bag onto a life vest so it'll float. Izzy is wearing her normal frayed one-piece swimsuit, but Mia notices that she's put on some lipstick.

"You look good," Mia tells her, surprising everyone. Since she has made the decision to leave, this might be one of their last family dinners together. She might as well make it as nice as possible. Plus, the prospect of talking to another teenager is exciting. For the moment, her anger at her mom has cooled.

Her mom smiles and pulls Mia's bikini top straight. "You look like a space alien abducted my daughter and returned a slightly different version of her," she says. Mia feels the goodwill melt away.

"You were the one who wanted me to get it."

"No, it looks nice. Just don't talk about science the whole time and freak them out."

Ethan can see Mia about to explode and grabs her arm. "Let's get going," he says, corralling them to the transom.

Mia tries to ignore her mom's warning as she slips into the sea. Without Sadie around to lead conversations, Mia isn't sure what to talk about with other kids. She tries to remember Sadie's pointers about how to talk to boys: *Ask them questions about themselves, ask if they play sports, ask open-ended questions like what they think of Taylor Swift.*

Her dad swims up beside her, pulling their clothes on the life vest. He notices the look of concentration on Mia's face. "Just have some fun," he says, smiling kindly. "There's no pressure."

"Remember, on the swim back, everybody has to dunk underwater," Izzy says, breaststroking toward the catamaran. "Otherwise this doesn't work."

"I'll go underwater now," Kaden says, diving down and trying to make Izzy happy.

They swim in a nervous pack. Kaden anxiously chatters away about Captain Underpants to distract himself from his fear of sharks. Ahead, they can see a family of four standing on the stern deck, waiting for them. They look a little wild. The mom has half her head shaved; the dad's hair is thick and matted. Both parents are covered in tattoos. There's a boy about Kaden's age and his hair is close-cropped except for a snippet on the back that hangs down past his shoulders. The older boy is the only one who looks halfway normal, though he's still got a bandage on his forehead. As a group, they look like a band of postapocalyptic punks. Mia is relieved; they look stranger than her family.

"Dinghy problems?" the dad asks as they swim up. "I could have picked you up."

"We just thought it'd be nice to swim," Ethan says, trying to sound nonchalant, as if it was the most normal thing in the world to swim to dinner.

The Australian dad doesn't know if Ethan is being sarcastic, though Ethan's cheerful tone suggests it isn't a joke.

"Uh, well, let's get you all up here," he says, flipping the swim ladder into the water. Mia climbs onto the main deck feeling wildly exposed in the bikini. Now that she's here, she realizes that she's made a terrible mistake: She's essentially naked in front of all these strangers. Her only hope is to quickly get her clothes on but her dad is still in the water with the dry clothes.

As she looks back at her dad, the teenage boy steps up and sticks his hand out. "How ya going?" he says with an Australian accent. "I'm Alby."

She can see that his eyes are a grayish blue. They look good against his tanned skin and the beginnings of a blondish beard. He's wearing a bunch of tattered leather bracelets and a necklace of a star. He's got on a short-sleeved button-up and she can see a tattoo of a wave circling his left biceps. She's surprised: He seems young to have a tattoo. Up close, he looks less like a hippie and more like a pirate.

"Mia," she says, shaking his hand but looking back at her dad in the water. Alby seems confused. She's shaking his hand but looking backward. Mia has no interest in talking to him until she gets some clothes on.

Mia sees her mom start up the ladder. The Aussie dad offers a hand, but Izzy doesn't like touching strangers so she ignores it and steps on deck, keeping her arms tightly by her sides. Izzy immediately focuses on the boat's deck cushions, which are busted open in places, the yellow foam poking out. Each cushion is like a giant, dirty sponge, and Mia knows that her mother is about to have a meltdown and ruin everything.

"You're fine," Mia whispers to her. "Everything's fine."

The Australians are looking at them with alarm and Mia realizes that they heard her whispering. In fact, she probably wasn't whispering. She's not used to being quiet and abruptly understands how they must look to outsiders. She's wearing a bikini for the first time, shifting uncomfortably from foot to foot, and trying to convince her mom not to freak out. She hasn't met anybody in forever and the first people they come across think they're raving mad.

And then a second thought hits her even harder: Maybe her family is actually raving mad.

"All righty then, welcome aboard," the dad says slowly, trying to roll past the strange behavior. "Wanna swap your swimmers in one of our rooms?"

Mia doesn't want to wear the bikini a second longer. She rips open the clothes bag as her dad climbs out of the water, rummages through, and pulls the pants and shirt on in a hurry in front of everybody.

"We're all set," she says, and then sees all eyes on her shirt. She looks down. The bikini has soaked through, outlining her boobs and crotch in wet splotches on the surface of the pants and dark shirt. Her face starts to burn and she feels nauseous.

"Thank you so much for inviting us," her mom says loudly. "We're happy to be here."

Her mom sounds like she's acting—Mia knows with certainty that she is not happy to be here—but she feels a rush of gratitude as the conversation veers away. *Maybe she does love me*, Mia thinks.

There's a round of introductions and the adults shake hands. Even her mom shakes hands, which Mia knows she's doing to keep the attention off her daughter.

"This is a beautiful boat," her mom says, deliberately lying to buy Mia time. Luckily, the warm air is drying everything and the outline of her private parts is fading. "You've been sailing awhile?" Izzy adds, after a subtle glance at Mia's clothes to gauge the drying time.

"Oh, we've been out a good long time," Garrett, the dad, says. "Five years or so now?"

"Hard to keep track really, isn't it?" says Leah, the mom, laughing.

"Damn," Izzy says. "Five years is amazing."

Garrett explains that they're street musicians, performing on sidewalks in whatever port they pull into. They supplement their income by working as translators. He speaks French and Leah is fluent in Mandarin. After living the city-bound life in Sydney, they decided it'd be more fun to sail away from it all and play music, even if it meant they'd make less money.

"You got the right boat for it," Ethan says, impressed by their catamaran. It's like going from a bathtub to an Olympic-size swimming pool. The catamaran is basically a platform spread across two hulls and each hull is roughly the same size as the *Graceland*. It might be falling apart but it's big.

Garrett proposes drinks and soon the parents have plastic glasses filled with rum and guava juice. The kids get plain juice and Flynn, Alby's younger brother, sticks his finger in his cup and flicks it at Kaden, who smiles like he just met his soulmate and flicks juice back.

"Well, here's to coming across another family," Garrett says, looking relieved that at least the adults drink alcohol. He raises his glass and everybody clinks, though it's plastic and doesn't sound right.

While everyone takes a sip, Mia glances down at her pants. Fortunately, the wet spots have almost faded and she regains a little bit of confidence.

"It's not too often we meet other kids," says Leah. "You and your brother want a proper tour of the boat? Alby and Flynn can show you around."

It's better than standing in an awkward circle with the adults so Mia says sure and follows the Australian boys into the main cabin, which is set up kind of like a living room. Lene pokes around the kitchen and sniffs the counters, which is weird but seems like as good a way as any of sussing these people out.

"I think you should start dancing," Lene says, and she starts waving her arms over her head and twirling around the cabin. Mia shakes her head. She's pretty sure that's not the thing to do. She tries to discreetly pull down her bikini bottoms, which have bunched into a wedgie.

"This is so uncomfortable," she mutters.

"What's that?" Alby asks, looking at her strangely. She realizes with a start that she was talking out loud.

36

THE UNCERTAINTY PRINCIPLE

"Oh, I was just talking to myself," she stammers and decides it's time to deploy some of Sadie's socializing techniques.

"Uh, so what do you think about Taylor Swift?" she asks.

"Taylor Swift?" He's even more confused, and Mia realizes that maybe it's too soon in the conversation to ask that question. Sadie just threw out a bunch of possibilities but never told her what order to go in.

"I guess she's all right," Alby says. "I can get down with the Swifties."

"Oh, okay," Mia says, racking her brain for the next question in the series. Should she ask about sports now? Is that the next step?

"Uh well, this is the main cabin," he says, trying to make things less awkward by barreling ahead and Mia is silently thankful.

She looks around the space. There's an L-shaped couch built into the wall on one side with the kitchen across from it. In the middle, there's an island topped with a well-used piece of butcher block. Lene wipes her finger across the counter and then licks it. Mia cringes.

"Yeah, I know," Alby says. "It's pretty beat up."

"No, it's not that," Mia says. "It's much bigger than our kitchen."

Kaden and Flynn are already babbling easily about Captain Underpants and ninjas. The boys are having no problem talking. Flynn says he has Legos and they disappear down a stairway, leaving Alby and Mia alone.

"Well, I don't have any Legos so I won't invite you to my room," Alby says.

"That's too bad," Mia says, and it comes out sounding a little sexy, like she was hoping to go to his room. She flushes and grasps for something else to say. She already asked about Taylor Swift. She notices the bandage on his head and motions to it. "What happened?"

His hand goes to his forehead. "Oh, yeah, we were surfing and I endo'd and hit my face on the coral."

She doesn't really know what he's talking about but his Australian accent is nice. She realizes that he's looking at her, expecting her to say something.

"Yeah, ouch," she says. She sounds like an eight-year-old. It's clear that he doesn't know what to make of her. If there's any saving grace, he seems nervous too.

"Well, Flynn's got all the cool toys, but I can show you around anyway," he offers.

She nods and follows him down a steep set of stairs into the starboard hull. It smells like engine oil, which lends the space the vibe of a cargo ship. But she's used to that now: Her cabin smells the same.

"How long have you been out so far?" Alby asks.

"Six months now."

"Newbies," he says, looking back over his shoulder and smiling. "You liking it?"

"It's the worst thing that's ever happened to me," Mia says with a dark laugh.

He chuckles too. "Yeah, that's how I felt at first."

"You don't anymore?"

"I guess I got used to it."

They turn into a narrow hallway with a few doors. The *Exodus* is much bigger than the *Graceland*, but the passageways are still cramped and dimly lit. She's used to that. But she's not used to being in such tight quarters with a boy. The passage forces them to stand close, so close she can smell some kind of coconut sunblock on his skin. His shoulders are broader than she realized and he seems to fill the space. He's tall and has to hunch down so his head doesn't bump the low ceiling. She tenses a bit. She doesn't know him at all, certainly not well enough to stand this close to him. He could be dangerous; maybe they're a family of criminals. He could attack her.

Instead, he opens a door and she sees Kaden and Flynn sitting on a bed building a Lego city. The room is a disaster. There are crumpled clothes everywhere, toys, towels, books, crayons, broken clay pottery, and a piggy bank on the floor. Hand-drawn cartoons are taped to the walls and it smells like mildew and dirty socks.

Both boys are silently building their own Lego creations. They're deep into it but seemingly in parallel universes, neither talking to the other. It occurs to Mia that maybe the boys don't know how to talk to each other either. She can tell that Kaden is a little stunned by the sudden playdate. She feels a twinge of sympathy for him.

"This is Flynn's room," Alby says. "He's a feral little animal and all I can say is I apologize."

"Go away," Flynn says, flinging a Lego at Alby. The throw goes wide and smacks Mia in the cheek.

"Ow," she blurts, grabbing her face.

"What is wrong with you?" Alby shouts and turns to Mia. "Are you okay? I'm so sorry."

"I didn't mean to hit her," Flynn says by way of apology. "I was aiming for you."

"I'm going to bash you," Alby says, pointing his finger at his brother and banging the door shut.

Mia dabs her hand on her face. "It's fine," she says.

"Hey, I'm really—he's just a messy beast of a child," Alby says.

"I heard that," Flynn shouts from behind the door.

"He's also a bludging bogan," Alby says, raising his voice so he can be heard even better.

"And you're a bloody galah," Flynn yells back.

"All right, this isn't going anywhere," Alby says. "Let me take you to some light."

He leads Mia down the darkened hallway into a cabin slightly larger than Flynn's. It's got surfing photos on the wall mixed with posters for bands she's never heard of: Cat Empire, the The, Spy v Spy, Midnight Oil. By normal standards, the room would feel small but by boat standards, it's huge. It's way nicer than Mia's room. It even has a skylight.

"We can see a little better," he says, flipping the lights on and bending down to look at her cheek. "There's a spot of red. It didn't get you in the eye, did it?"

They're face-to-face and Mia feels her cheeks get hot, likely concealing whatever mark there is.

"It's fine," she says, turning away from him. The proximity is overwhelming. It's like she's been in solitary confinement and is now surrounded by blaring music. She glances around, hoping to redirect his attention. "This your room?"

"Yeah, needs a bit of a tidy up I guess," he says, turning to look at it. "But I'm a step ahead of that hoon down there."

"Hoon?"

"A little hooligan."

"Right."

"You get on with your brother?"

"We don't really talk much," she says.

"Probably for the best, the rats."

They lapse into a silence. Mia tries to think of something to say but Sadie didn't prepare her for this. Sadie taught her about the different cliques at school. She showed her where the jocks sat for lunch, where the debate kids ate. But here, on this boat floating in the middle of nowhere, there's no social order. It's just Mia and this strange boy.

"You know what?" Mia says, finally giving up. "I haven't actually talked to anybody for a while so I have no idea what to say to you."

To her relief, he laughs. "I'm a tad nervous myself," he says. "It's just the four of us and it's all fine and everything but it's not like I know how to talk to girls."

"Are you supposed to talk to girls differently than you talk to boys?" Mia says, half curious and half teasing him. She feels like an actor who's gotten to the end of the script and there are no more lines. Now she's just winging it.

"Oh, well . . . ," he stutters. "I guess not?"

There's another awkward pause. Mia notices a shelf full of books beside her. They're big, leather-bound books with gold and red text in English and languages she doesn't recognize.

"What's all that?" she says, hoping it'll be something they can talk about.

"Just my books," he says, turning red.

Mia feels a burst of pity for him: This is as hard for him as it is for her. The books appear to be religious: a Koran, a Bible, and a bunch she's never heard of. Mia picks up one written in a foreign language. "What is this?" she says.

"It's about the Bible," he says.

Mia tries to remember what Sadie taught her about people who liked the Bible. In the cafeteria, she pointed out where the church kids sat. They looked like nice people but Sadie said they weren't cool so Mia never talked to them. Sadie called them "Jesus freaks."

"Wait, are you super into Jesus?" Mia asks impulsively.

"Would it be a problem if I was?" he says, taken aback.

Mia thinks about it for a second. Sadie never explained what the problem was with the church kids. It's just that they weren't cool. But Mia wasn't cool either so that didn't seem like a reason to dislike them.

"I don't think it's a problem," Mia concludes.

To her surprise, he laughs.

"What?" she asks, alarmed.

"It's just that you really had to think about it," he says. But he's smiling and looks relieved that she's not judging him.

"So what's it about?" she says, flipping through the pages of the book.

"It's a bunch of people a thousand years ago talking about the Bible," he says as if it was the most natural thing in the world.

"For real?"

He looks at her sideways, worried that she's going to mock him. "Yeah, that's really what it is."

"And what are they saying?" Mia says, running her finger across a page of Hebrew text.

Alby steps beside her to read and she realizes that she's inadvertently invited him to stand very close to her. His shoulder touches her in the tight space and she feels a sudden thrill. While he scans the words, she looks up at him and notices his scruffy jawline and the light freckles on his slightly sunburned cheeks.

"It's about the rituals that bring God into our life," he says.

"Like what?" she says, her voice softer because something has shifted. It's like they're having a real conversation. Mia is pretty sure that Sadie would say that this guy is an oddball but Mia kind of likes the strangeness of it. She's never talked to anyone about God before.

"Like this," he says, tapping a small tube glued on his door frame and kissing his fingers. "It's a little prayer that welcomes God into the room."

Mia looks around the cabin. "So God is here right now?" she says, a little uncomfortable.

"Yeah, definitely." He brightens, energized that she's not trying to steer the conversation to something more conventional.

"I don't see anything," Mia says.

THE UNCERTAINTY PRINCIPLE

"You don't see radio waves but they're there," he counters.

Mia is about to say that you can detect radio waves pretty darn easily but nobody has ever dialed into God's frequency. But then she remembers her mother's warning: *Don't talk about science.*

"Sadie probably wouldn't like him," Lene says over Alby's shoulder. She's lying on Alby's bed, looking up at the skylight. "But I think he's kind of cute."

It's hard to disagree. He *is* kind of cute.

An idea starts to form. After The Incident, maybe Mia shouldn't trust Sadie's advice. She was clearly lying about everything. But that means Mia has nothing to go on, no idea how to socialize in Tennessee by herself. Or here.

"I'm actually headed back to the States to go to a regular high school," Mia says, teeing up a proposal.

"Oh?" he says, surprised again by the turn in the conversation.

"So I need to figure out how to talk to people after six months on the boat. And you're a little rusty too, right?"

He nods, unsure of where she's going with this.

"Well, why don't we practice with each other? You can teach me how to talk to boys and I can tell you how to talk to girls. We can figure it out together."

He looks confused. "Like a class or something?" he says.

"Yeah, a class," Mia says. "We won't ever see each other again so we can just be super honest about everything so we know what's good and what's bad."

He doesn't look so sure but he nods again. "All right, when do we start?"

Chapter 6

The adults take the table on the back deck, leaving the kids inside. Flynn and Kaden scarf down dinner at the kitchen counter, which means Mia and Alby have a table to themselves. It feels like they're on a first date. They've got two plates of mahi-mahi, some boiled carrots, and cans of a grapefruit soda called Ting.

Mia takes a bite of the fish and notices Alby looking at her hands. Her cuticles are streaked with raw, red wounds. She slips her hands below the table and he looks away, scratching the back of his neck awkwardly.

"So who goes first?" he says.

Lene raises her hand. She's sitting on the countertop with the boys. "I want to," she says. "I know how to do it."

"You go," Mia says quickly to Alby.

Alby nods. He cuts a bite of fish and pushes it around the plate, thinking. "Okay," he says at last. "Maybe ask a question about something you know the other person is interested in."

Mia lets one hand out from under the table and spears a carrot, thinking about what she knows about him. Something religious maybe?

"Why do you have all those old books?" she asks.

"I want to teach religion," he says, eating the bite of fish finally.

"For real?" Mia blurts, surprised.

He laughs. "You make it sound like a bad thing."

Mia flushes. She doesn't want to make him feel bad.

"I mean, how did you come up with that?" Mia says, trying to smooth it over.

"I guess I think that's what God wants me to do," he says simply.

Mia nods but she is baffled. "You think God has like a whole big plan for you?" she asks.

"Yeah. For all of us."

Mia stares at him intently. She's never thought much about God. But if there is a God, and if she, they, he, or it has a plan, then she just has to figure out what it is and follow it. Then she'll know what to do.

"So what does God say about high school?" she asks.

He smiles. "Well, the Koran says you should take all the AP classes you can manage and try out for the volleyball team."

"Really?" Mia says, surprised all over again.

"No, of course not," he says, laughing at her gullibility. "It doesn't say anything about high school."

Mia's heart plunges. The conversation was a trap and she fell into it.

"See?" Lene says from across the room. "Sadie was right. Your mom too. You shouldn't say anything. It never works out."

Alby sees the pain on her face. "I'm sorry," he says. "I was just making a joke."

"It's okay," Mia says glumly, looking up at the light bulbs overhead and wondering what temperature kelvin they run at. Machines are always easier to deal with.

"You know what, maybe there is something," Alby says, trying again. "There was a king in the Bible, a guy named Nebuchadnezzar."

Mia is guarded but she's listening.

"And the king wanted everyone to bow down to this weird gold statue and pretend it was God. Which, you know, is kind of like high school a bit. There's always some kid who says what's cool and everyone is expected to agree and bow down."

He doesn't seem to be making fun of her anymore and Mia finds herself opening up a bit to him.

"And anyway, these three guys say no thank you, not gonna bow. So the king throws them into a fiery furnace."

"Rough," Mia says, thinking of the fiery furnace of the cafeteria.

"Well, but here's the thing," Alby says. "These three blokes land in the fire and just start walking around like there's nothing going on."

"Okay," Mia says, intrigued.

"Turns out God was protecting them because they wouldn't just do whatever they were told to do."

Mia likes the story. She likes the idea that maybe Sadie and her mom don't know everything. They think they know everything, but they certainly don't know her very well. It would be nice to tune them out and just listen to God but Mia isn't sure how to do that.

"So the lesson is no bowing in high school?"

"Yeah, exactly. When you get to Tennessee, don't bow."

They both laugh and Mia feels a spark of excitement. She's having a real conversation with a real person.

His dad walks into the kitchen. "Hey, Alby, let's get the guitars out," he says, shoving a bottle of rum under his arm and grabbing two guitars from the corner of the cabin. He hands one to Alby, who takes it reluctantly.

"I don't think—" Alby begins to say.

"Get over it," his dad cuts him off, walking out to the back deck strumming a couple chords.

That leaves Alby and Mia alone again, though Alby now has a guitar.

THE UNCERTAINTY PRINCIPLE

"Isn't it your turn now?" he says, trying to deflect attention from himself. "You're supposed to teach me how to talk to girls."

Crap. Mia forgot about that part of the bargain. She's really not sure how a boy is supposed to talk to a girl. She tries to remember what Sadie told her. Mostly it was that Mia was supposed to listen and not say anything about what she was really thinking. Conversation topics that were safe were school, sports, and how bad the teachers were. But here, on this boat, there isn't any school, sports, or teachers. With nothing to go on, Mia decides to improvise.

"Okay, here's your first lesson," she says, giddy to be making up her own rules. "Start by singing a girl a song."

Chapter 7

Alby's dad starts strumming on the aft deck and they hear the parents debating what to sing. Ethan asks if they know any Grateful Dead; Izzy groans and asks if they can do classics like Cyndi Lauper or the Pixies. Mia can tell her mom is tipsy and, surprisingly, having a good time. *I guess we've all been starved for company*, Mia thinks.

"I'm gonna warn you that we make up for talent with enthusiasm," Garrett says, topping up the adults' drinks with a splash of Mount Gay.

"The rum helps, I'm sure," Izzy says, laughing.

Alby starts plucking out a song at the dining table next to Mia. The adults aren't paying attention; they keep arguing about what to play: Pink Floyd, Paul Simon. They're all over the place. Mia watches Alby mess around with the guitar. It doesn't seem like he really knows what he's doing.

"Okay, so then this one's for you," he says, looking straight at Mia.

She was kind of joking about singing a song, but it seems like that's what he's about to do. He focuses on the strings and bites his lip. He's trying really hard.

"Here I am again on this mean old boat . . . ," he starts singing, looking up and flashing an anxious smile.

Outside, the adults quiet down. In a second, the only sound on the boat is Alby singing.

"And you're so far away from me."

THE UNCERTAINTY PRINCIPLE

His voice is rich, with a hint of his Australian accent. She was ready to listen politely and say something encouraging just to be nice, but he isn't fumbling around. He really knows how to play and she realizes she's smiling.

Outside, Alby's dad starts strumming along and the effect is magical, the two guitars distant but playing together as the boat rocks slowly back and forth. In the kitchen, Lene starts to dance her strange, boxy-armed dance.

It's one of those moments when a song makes you feel something so strongly, something that was inside of you but you didn't know was there. The song is about being alone but ready for love. It's somehow both tragic and optimistic at the same time and it matches exactly how she feels right now, with this strange Australian singing to her.

The adults walk into the cabin and Mia is surprised to see her parents singing. Mia doesn't recognize the song, but her parents know every word. She's never heard them sing but everything about this night feels different. Her dad stands behind Izzy, wraps his arms around her, and they sway together.

Alby ends the song with a smooth downstroke. Mia doesn't want it to end; she wants to stay inside the song, to feel the delicious combination of possibilities with this strange boy and the rhythm of the boat and music.

But it's over and they're back to reality.

"Oh my god, Dire Straits," her mom says. "That was a great end to the evening."

Wait, what? Why does the night have to be over? They've literally got nothing to do, ever. But her dad is already shaking hands with Garrett and everybody is saying goodbye and thanks and how nice it was.

"Maybe we'll catch up on some other island," Garrett says. "We've got more '80s songs."

49

Mia's stomach clenches. "Where are you headed?" she asks Alby, the concern obvious in her voice. She's been on a roller coaster tonight. Just a second ago, she was as happy as she's been in months. And now it's already over.

"We've got some repairs to do on Saint Martin," Garrett says. "But I'm sure our paths will cross soon."

"Saint Martin isn't too far," Alby says with a note of pleading. "We'd be fine another day here, wouldn't we?"

Garrett looks over at Leah, who shrugs. "We could stay another day I guess," she says.

"Then maybe we can check out the island in the morning?" Alby asks, turning to Mia. "I heard Pablo Escobar built a runway here."

"Sure," she says, a glimmer of hope reappearing.

"Well, I'll give you a ride back in our dinghy," Garrett says. "It'll be tight, but I think we'll make it."

"You know what, I think we're probably all ready for a little after-dinner swim," Ethan says, looking to Mia for support. "Aren't we?"

"Yeah, totally," Mia says immediately, trying to make it sound like no big deal. Though she doesn't understand why they have to leave now, she's willing to keep to the plan since her mom agreed to come in the first place. "I'm so stuffed, I'll just float back like an inner tube," she says.

Chapter 8

When **Mia shuts** the door to her bunk, Lene is standing there with a sly smile.

"What?" Mia says, changing out of the dumb bikini and sliding into bed.

"Bose–Einstein condensates."

Mia groans. Bose–Einstein condensates are a rare state of matter that Einstein and a physicist named Bose identified in 1924. They have nothing to do with Alby.

"Can't we just have a normal conversation about boys?" Mia pleads.

"That's what we're doing," Lene protests. "I was talking about his eyes."

Mia relaxes. She can see it. Alby's gray-blue eyes are kind of like the photos of Lene's lab that show a glowing, blue cloud: the Bose–Einstein condensate. It's something that doesn't exist naturally on Earth, and at first, people thought Einstein was crazy for thinking it was real. To create it, Lene had to supercool a chamber to nearly 460 degrees below zero, making it the coldest place in the universe.

"There's nothing like it," Lene says, entranced. "It's like a portal into another world."

Mia pulls up her bedsheet and remembers Alby's glowing eyes watching her all night long. She smiles when she thinks about the end of the evening, the Australians standing on the back deck of the *Exodus*. Mia had no choice but to pull her clothes off. Maybe she could have swum back in pants and the shirt, but it would have been hard. So she wiggled out of the clothes and, when her head popped out of the T-shirt, she could tell Alby was trying not to look but was also totally looking.

Alby's parents remained deeply confused by these Americans who seemed to prefer to swim everywhere. But the adults were relaxed from the laughter and rum and nobody really cared. Even Izzy was surprisingly okay.

Mia's thoughts shift to Tennessee and she starts to chew on a cuticle.

"You need to know something really important about Bose–Einstein condensates," Lene says, suddenly nervous. "They are very exciting but they only form in completely isolated environments. If they touch the outside world, it's over. Everything vanishes."

"We still talking about his eyes?" Mia says sleepily.

"I'm talking about you," Lene says urgently. "I'm talking about me. Him. Everything."

Mia understands. Lene is worried that if Mia goes to Tennessee, she'll vanish. Lene only showed up once Mia moved onto the boat and had no one to talk to. Who knows how Lene will fit into the real world. She probably won't. Maybe Mia can find someone else, someone real, to help her figure herself out. But Mia doesn't want to worry about that now. She switches the light off, banishing Lene to the dark.

"I'm still here," Lene says, annoyed.

Mia shushes her. She wants to think about Alby lying in his cabin, not so far away. She pictures what's separating them: a short distance of water and a couple of thin layers of fiberglass.

She puts her hand against the *Graceland*'s hull. It's cool to the touch. Outside, a breeze shivers the water between them, swirling the air around the boat.

Chapter 9

She wakes with a start in the murk of the predawn. Her stomach is swirling, and she can't quite remember what she was dreaming about, but it had something to do with Sadie. A dim memory of their sleepovers, staying up late talking. The feeling of closeness they once had. And then God descending and the actual world exploding, like a full-on apocalypse.

It's only 6:04 a.m. and she lies there for a while feeling bad. Not sick, but kind of soul crushed. More than anything, it's like the world is taunting her again, first with Leif, and now with Alby, giving her a glimpse of a better life and then blowing it up.

She shimmies out of bed and wearily shuffles onto deck. It's blaringly bright for such an early hour and she winces, both at the sun and her thoughts. What's the point of trying to get close to Alby if it just ends up hurting like it did with Leif? Her next thought stings more: What happened with Leif was bad, but Sadie's betrayal was even worse. And now the most painful part is that she can't see any way to recover from it. How does she know what the truth is about anything if her best friend lied to her? Her only hope is to build this damn phone, call Sadie and say . . . what, exactly?

The Incident comes rushing back to her. She tries to block it out but there's no avoiding the memory now. She remembers that morning in Duluth, a crisp fall day. It had rained overnight and the pavement in the school parking lot was wet. Mia came across an oil streak on the ground and watched the rainbow colors glisten off the morning sun. It was so beautiful: the light rays bending into shades of green, red, and purple. She took a photo and texted it to Leif, thinking he'd like it. He immediately wrote back, "Wow, cool."

Mia had been texting him photos for weeks now. A close-up of rust flaking off the side of an iron sheet in an abandoned lot. The complex pattern on the sidewalk of sunlight shining through leaves. It was Sadie's idea. "Send photos," she said. "It's better than talking gibberish about things no one understands." Leif always wrote right back, and each response gave Mia more confidence.

So, after he liked her oil slick photo, she decided to take the next step. "Want to get coffee after school?" she wrote back quickly as she stood in the parking lot. It would be her first real date.

She watched with agony as the three dots appeared on her screen. He was writing back. But then the dots went away. *He stopped writing?* Then, they appeared again. *Does he not know what to say?* Finally, the answer appeared: "Sure."

Her heart swelled. "He said yes," she said aloud to no one, in awe as other kids streamed onto campus.

Her next thought was that she needed to talk to Sadie. They were on different schedules this year and Mia didn't get to see her as much so she decided to skip precalc so she could find her during the first lunch period.

Mia buzzed into the cafeteria feeling happy and excited, more so than she had during her entire time in high school. Finally, she was going to be like other kids, with a proper boyfriend. She was going to be normal.

And then, next to the conveyor belt that took dirty trays into the kitchen, she stopped walking.

THE UNCERTAINTY PRINCIPLE

Across the constellation of tables, on the other side of the room, Leif was kissing Sadie.

Mia blinked. Her stomach balled up with a sickening twist. And, before she knew what she was doing, she was grabbing plates of half-eaten food off the conveyor belt and throwing them across the room.

She doesn't even remember screaming.

The sound of a guitar brings her back to the boat. She looks over at the *Exodus* and sees Alby leaning against the mast with his back to her, picking out a song quietly on his guitar. There's no one else on deck on either boat. It's just the two of them separated by a patch of water. She feels better for a moment but then remembers that he's leaving in a day anyway. Everything seems so pointless and depressing. Better to just rely on Lene.

"I have my limitations," Lene says from behind, spooking Mia. She steps back quickly and bonks her head loudly on the ship's boom, sending a low, metallic ring across the water like a church bell.

Alby stops playing and turns to see Mia clutching her head and groaning. It's embarrassing. Hitting your head on the boom is a rookie sailor move. She pretends it doesn't hurt and gives him a small wave. They're too far apart to be heard: They'd have to shout and wake everyone. He doesn't wave back but instead points to the island. She looks over and sees that it is bathed in a caramel-colored wash of morning light. It looks different than it did yesterday, as if they've been transported to some other planet.

Alby flashes the thumbs-up and then the thumbs-down. Does she want to go?

"It's just you two," Lene says. "Sadie can't steal him from you."

"I guess that's true," Mia mumbles, wondering all over again why Sadie did it. Why did she coach her on how to talk to Leif if she was secretly dating him?

Mia looks across the water at Alby and sighs. She flashes him the thumbs-up and then puts both hands up to show ten fingers. Ten minutes.

She climbs quietly back down below deck, hoping not to disturb anyone. If Kaden woke and started making a fuss about going, it would make the outing intolerable. The last thing she wants is to bring her little brother.

In her cabin, she rummages through her clothes and grabs a pair of flip-flops. Since they'll be alone, she wants to send some clear signals, so she pulls on a pair of swim shorts and a skintight, long-sleeve, blue rash guard. The rash guard has three benefits: She doesn't have to put on sunblock, it makes her arms look buff, and it is nearly impossible to take off, like a kind of armor.

Back on deck, she hears her name from the water nearby. She walks to the rail and sees him swimming off the stern. A mesh bag with flip-flops, sunblock, and water bottles floats beside him.

"Hey," he says quietly.

"Hey," she says back, smiling despite herself at the look of him in the water. She likes that he swam to her, and she is also starting to get excited about the idea of swimming away with him. She looks up at the island to gauge the distance. Not too far—a five-minute swim. The sun is still low, cresting over sand dunes and lighting up the water. She isn't often up this early and it's startling, like someone poured pink and blue metallic paint across the surface of the water. A little like that beautiful oil slick in the school parking lot. She feels her heart plunge all over again.

She rubs the sore spot on her head and tries to push the memory away. She shoves the flip-flops into her waistband, grabs the flimsy aluminum ladder hanging off the stern, and glances back at him. He

THE UNCERTAINTY PRINCIPLE

turns away; she caught him looking at her legs. She smiles to herself again and climbs slowly into the water, feeling the shock of the cold.

Getting in the water always feels like entering another world. Even though it's the Caribbean and the water is eighty-four degrees, it still feels chilly at first. She has to will herself down the ladder step by step, the water rising and surrounding her. When she reaches the bottom rung, she lets go, floating silently backward and away from the boat.

The freshness of the water helps clear her head, washing away Duluth, and in a moment, she's beside him.

He isn't touching her, but she can feel the current spinning off his hands as he treads water. It's like the water has extended his fingers and he's running them down her body, surrounding her in small vortices. They're close, their bodies nearly touching below the surface. The bandage is off his forehead. There's a gash above his eyebrow but she's happy to see that he looks good in the daylight. It wasn't just the dim light on the catamaran.

It's not clear what they should do. A high five seems like the only realistic greeting in the water, but Mia decides not to try it and instead starts toward shore.

"Let's go," she says, dropping her head into the water and swimming away from him.

It feels good to move. With each stroke, she stretches farther ahead, putting distance between her and her memories, trying to grab the water just out of reach. She swims with her eyes closed since she doesn't have goggles.

She hears him swimming alongside, his hands splashing in the water, but she keeps her eyes closed. It's nice to just cut through the coolness of the sea and feel it streaming down her body.

She opens her eyes when she hears the sound of small waves breaking on the shore. He's right beside her with his eyes closed too and he swims a few strokes farther before coming to a stop. He drops his feet and stands in the shallow water.

They wade ashore and turn to see their two boats floating offshore. Alby's brother is on the deck of the *Exodus* and waves at them. Alby waves back. The sky is purple and orange and the sunrise streams through the clouds on the eastern horizon, shooting rays across the sea.

"It's beautiful," Alby says.

Normally, she wouldn't admit it. After taking all those beautiful photos for Leif, she doesn't feel like sharing anymore. And if her mom ever said something about how nice it was out here, she'd ignore her. But this feels a little different now. It's just the two of them on the shore of an abandoned island so Mia lets her guard down.

"Yeah, I guess it is," she says, and it feels like a big admission.

Seawater drips down her nose and, as she licks her lips to savor the salt, she notices Alby staring at her.

"What?" she says, suddenly self-conscious. Maybe it's weird that she's licking the water off her nose.

"It's just . . . ," he stammers, clearly flustered by something. "The sea suits you."

Lene walks up behind her, perfectly dry, and whispers in her ear. "He obviously thinks you're hot."

"I'm not sure that's true," she says to both of them and tries to pull down her rash guard, which is tightly hugging her chest.

"When we crossed the Atlantic, we saw this humpback whale cutting through the water right beside us. You're like that in the water."

"You calling me a whale?"

"No, no, not like that," he stammers. "I mean, like, graceful."

Mia smiles at him. "Why don't we head out?"

THE UNCERTAINTY PRINCIPLE

"Sure, yeah," he says, concerned that he offended her.

They trudge through the sand toward a line of low-lying mangroves at the top of the beach.

"When are you heading to Tennessee?" he asks.

"I'm not sure. I just decided to go back yesterday."

He nods. "My first year was really hard too. I fought with my parents a lot."

"And now?"

"We still get on each other's nerves, but I understand why we checked out."

They're at the top of the beach's incline by the mangroves. He's following her and she turns to look at him.

"You're not pissed?"

"I mean, it's a different way of living for sure," he says. "But all those people with regular lives, they're working their asses off so they can afford to come here for five days a year. It's like, what's the point?"

"It's hard to teach religion to no one," Mia says, thinking he hasn't thought this all through.

"Mmmm," Alby says, nodding and acknowledging her point. "But Moses was walking in the desert by himself when God spoke to him. Maybe it's good to be alone sometimes."

"Yeah?" she says slyly. "You want me to leave you alone?"

He smiles back, enjoying this sudden flirtatious flash.

"To be honest, I haven't enjoyed anything as much as this in months," he says simply, and she feels butterflies in her stomach. She's never had anyone besides Sadie say nice things to her.

The thought of Sadie makes the butterflies disappear and she starts to nibble on a finger, searching for a stray piece of skin. Sadie told her how pretty she was, how smart she was, but was she just pretending? They had been friends forever. But then, in high school, things started to get weird. Mia wanted to spend all her time with Sadie but Sadie made other friends. They still hung out, just not as much. And when Mia slept over, Sadie started making her sleep on a futon on the floor instead of in the same bed. She said Mia kicked too much, but Mia missed feeling so close to her.

And now? Her only real friendship was shattered. What's to say she'll do any better in Tennessee? She was never good at socializing and has only gotten worse. Starting over somewhere new sounds terrible. She really just needs to get through to Sadie and actually talk about what happened.

"So what do you do to keep yourself from going crazy?" Alby asks, interrupting her thoughts.

Mia stifles a laugh—she's not feeling very sane. Case in point: Lene trudges in the sand beside her trying to keep up. As always, Lene is wearing the absolute wrong clothes. She's got on a blazer, a pair of slacks, and a fuchsia blouse. The only positive thing Mia can say is that she isn't wearing a turtleneck.

"Who's to say I haven't gone crazy?" Mia points out.

He nods, unsure how to respond. "You don't seem crazy."

"Tell him about the new Grätzel cell you're building," Lene urges. "Then he'll understand what a nut you are."

Mia restrains herself. Back home, when she let herself talk about synthetic valve oil or electromagnetic fields, there was always a point when she looked up and saw the expression of the kid across from her. It was never good. So she took Sadie's advice and learned to say as little as possible.

But she can see Alby stealing looks at her, trying to read her expressions. He's paying attention so she decides to make an effort.

"I take things apart and put them back together again," she says finally.

THE UNCERTAINTY PRINCIPLE

"Like winches or . . ."

"Solar cells right now."

She knows she's making it hard, giving him little to go on. But the alternative seems worse.

"What are you doing with them?" he asks.

"Tell him you hit 25.3 percent solar conversion with those black currants from Nova Scotia," Lene shouts, falling behind.

"I'm not doing much really," Mia says instead.

Alby nods. Mia has clammed up and he doesn't know why. The safe move would be to change the subject. But he's running low on things to talk about so he dives back in.

"Like you're repairing the boat's panel or something?"

Mia looks at him closely. It wasn't just Sadie giving her advice. Her mom always tells her what not to talk about: anything technical ("makes you sound weird"), why she got kicked out of school ("they'll treat you like an outcast"), or why they're so secluded ("makes your family look crazy"). But Izzy never said what she should talk about.

Alby puts a hand up, confused by her intensity. "Hey, no worries, you don't have to say anything."

They walk in an awkward silence for a minute more before coming to a break in the mangroves. A path leads inland.

"This looks promising," he says, coming to a stop.

Lene catches up and sits down in the sand to catch her breath. "Tell him," Lene urges. "He'll realize you're a mess and it's better now than after you start to like him even more."

She looks at Alby and he smiles uneasily.

"Maybe the path—"

"I'm inventing a new type of solar cell," she says, cutting him off.

Alby blinks at her, not sure what to say.

"I'm using fluoride-doped titanium dioxide and coated transparent electrodes with a mix of wild berries from Canada. Basically shingling dye-coated Grätzel cells to break the Shockley–Queisser limit."

It comes out in a rush and she feels better for having said it. At least the truth is out there. Not even her family knows what she's working on because they stopped asking.

Alby nods as if he understands what she said. "Pretzel cells . . ."

"Not pretzel, Grätzel," Mia snaps.

"Sorry, Grätzel."

"You know, the German chemist."

"Uhhh," Alby says. He has no idea what she's talking about.

"He figured out how to mimic the way plants make electricity."

Mia explains that Grätzel cells are pretty easy to make and can crank out decent voltage. They're a lot cheaper than silicon cells since you pretty much just use berries and a smattering of powders. Her plan is to use them to generate more energy than anybody thinks is possible and power a satellite uplink so she can make phone calls.

"You know, because I don't have a functioning cell phone," she says. "I can't talk to anyone back home. I guess I could maybe try calling from the boat but then my mom would listen to everything so . . . yeah."

"You see?" Lene says. "He's looking at you funny."

Mia looks at Alby. She'd been playing with her fingers while she talked and lost track of him. He is, in fact, looking at her strangely.

"What?" Mia demands.

"So you're like really smart," he says.

It's a statement, not a question, so she's not sure how to respond.

"Tell him you're going to be a theoretical physicist like me," Lene urges.

"My mom says I'll probably end up working on engines like a

mechanic or something," Mia says, ignoring Lene. "Which would be cool, I guess. I'd get to take things apart."

"We like to do the same thing then."

She tilts her head, not sure what he means.

"I mean when we read the Torah, we take it apart word by word, sometimes syllable by syllable," he says. "We're trying to get to the bottom of it."

"And do you get there?"

He laughs. "No, never."

"So what's the point?"

"Just because something's impossible doesn't mean you don't try. I mean, you're trying to talk to satellites using strawberries."

"Not strawberries," she says quickly. "That wouldn't work, obviously. You need something with darker anthocyanin."

"Obviously," Alby laughs, but she can tell he's impressed, not mocking her.

She starts walking, silently happy that her first attempt to explain herself didn't totally suck. It also seems like he's still trying to flirt with her. She'd like to talk to Lene about it but doesn't want to talk out loud.

"So who are you going to call when you get it working?" he asks, following behind her.

"I had a friend named Sadie," Mia starts out unsteadily. "We got into a fight and I left so we never really talked again."

"What'd you fight about?"

Mia stops abruptly and he almost walks into her. She looks at him. "She lied to me."

He nods, trying to be understanding, and she heads out again. As they move through the shrubs, it gets warmer. The bushes block the breeze and the sand radiates heat. They round a crop of low-lying mangroves.

"Whoa," Alby says, pointing at two destroyed jeeps. The vehicles are crushed and twisted, as if some kind of monster hurled them here. Pieces are scattered in the sand as if the jeeps exploded.

"I read that Pablo Escobar used to land drug planes here to refuel," he says.

"I guess someone didn't like that too much," she says, pointing to bullet holes in the side of the jeep. Mia imagines a raging gun battle happening. Did the drug dealers get into an argument? Or maybe there was a military raid. People could have died where she's standing. If they did, where did the bodies go?

She leans over the hood of one of the jeeps and starts pulling out wires. It's interesting to see what saltwater corrosion can do over time. The plastic insulation on the car's wiring has turned brittle and when she bends a section, the plastic crumbles off. She jiggles the fan belt and it snaps, so she pulls it out and examines it. "This is a pretty narrow gauge for a car this size," she says. "I wonder where they got it."

She catches Alby smiling at her.

"What?" she says.

"You are an unusual person," he says.

"Me?" she says, standing up with a handful of wires. She looks at him in disbelief. "You're trying to talk to God."

"Oh, I'm pretty sure most people think I'm a total weirdo so I'm not saying you're stranger than me. I meant it as a compliment."

Mia thinks about this for a second. She can tell he's not trying to be mean. He actually does mean it as a compliment, so she decides not to take offense and turns her attention back to the tangle of wires inside the car. A thought occurs to her: If this was where the dealers shipped their drugs, then maybe she and Alby need to be a little more careful.

THE UNCERTAINTY PRINCIPLE

"Do you think they booby-trapped the island?"

"Hope not," he says, swatting away a spiderweb suspended across the path. Mia would like to stay here and scavenge for parts, but Alby heads off. Reluctantly, she drops the wires back onto the engine block and follows after him.

As she pushes through the foliage, she realizes how quiet the place is. The boat is usually noisy, with the wind whistling through the shrouds and the water splashing against the hull. Now there's no breeze, no birds, nothing. The only noises are the sound of their breath and feet.

She imagines what would happen if the place really was booby-trapped. Say she stepped on a bomb. Maybe a soggy kind of bomb that only knocked her down and cut her up a bit. Would he pick her up and carry her back? Would he be able to? He's pretty skinny. She'd probably have a better shot at carrying him.

"What are you thinking about?" he asks as the trail bends toward the left.

"I'm wondering what would happen if we stepped on a bomb."

He nods, taking that in. "Well, if we did, this would be it."

She looks around at the bushes and sand and wonders if this would be an okay place to die.

"What would you do if you only had sixty seconds left?" he asks.

She stops walking. If she only had sixty seconds left, would she wrap her arms around him? She's never kissed anybody. Maybe now's the time?

"Sadie would say definitely kiss him," Lene says. "But your mom would say absolutely not."

In the stillness of the island, the heat has risen, and Mia starts sweating. She's not sure what to do. She can see beads of sweat rolling down Alby's face too. He's framed by the shrubs on either side of the path and looks amazing, like a swashbuckling nerd in the wilderness. Mia is struck by the fact that this is the first time she's been alone with someone other than her family for months. There's no one around to tell her what to do.

"Well, you're a wreck who can't make up your mind about anything," Lene says, marching away disappointed.

Alby withers under Mia's intense, conflicted gaze. She's looking right at him while she thinks about what to say.

"I'd probably kiss you," she says finally and then walks toward him. He stands frozen as she brushes past and walks away down the path, leaving him planted there.

It's the most flirtatious thing she's ever said. It's both thrilling and unnerving because she's not sure what happens next. How does she follow that? What's the next step in the sequence? What will he do now? She's in uncharted territory.

She hears him catch up, but she doesn't look back. She doesn't know what kind of look to give him so she just keeps walking. The ground seems to sway underneath her. It's often like that when she gets off the boat but now it's like the whole island is rolling under her feet.

"Well, as much as I'd hate to die, I wouldn't mind coming across a bomb or two," he says behind her.

"Not seeing any yet, but I'll let you know," she responds. She smiles to herself, pleased that she came up with something witty on her own.

The sun is fully up and the temperature continues to rise. She can feel the sweat rolling down her face now. But it's not just the heat. Her heart is pounding.

Luckily, they've crossed to the other side of the thin island and a breeze returns. Up ahead, the vegetation clears and they can see a stretch of flattened land.

THE UNCERTAINTY PRINCIPLE

"The runway," Alby says.

It's overgrown but she can make out the contours of a dirt airstrip. The far end runs into a beach. If a pilot overshot, they'd end up in the water. Whoever landed here must have been brave.

"Holy shit," Alby says, pointing. She looks over and sees the wreckage of an eight-passenger prop plane. It's on the opposite end of the runway, sitting on its belly without any landing gear or wings. All the windows are blown out and the cargo bay door is gone.

They look at each other. "Let's check it out," she says, a crackle of danger passing between them.

As they walk to the plane, she can see that the fuselage is dented and battered but the white paint still looks pretty good. Alby pokes his head into the cargo hold. It's half filled with sand.

"I wonder if the pilot survived," he says.

The door to the cockpit is missing and Mia can see two yokes, one each for a pilot and copilot. There are clumps of wires everywhere and small sand dunes on the floorboards. Mia decides to climb in.

"Is it safe?" Alby asks nervously.

But she's already in the pilot's seat with her hands on the yoke. It's rusty but still rotates a bit. Through the missing front windows, she can see the length of the runway to her right. It feels like the plane has taxied for takeoff and is now ready at the top of the runway.

"Roger niner niner, this is echo bravo foxtrot," she says, mimicking the way she's seen pilots talk in movies. "My copilot doesn't want to get in the plane with me, over. Should I leave him behind?"

"All right, I'm getting in."

He gingerly lowers himself into the copilot seat. The passenger seats behind them are missing—it's just an empty cabin. "Not sure if we're gonna make it far without wings," he says.

"Details," Mia says, flipping fake switches on the instrument panel and pushing the rusted throttle levers forward. "Don't need 'em where we're headed."

"Right. And where's that?"

"The future."

She pulls the yoke toward her and leans back in the seat, steering the plane through imaginary clouds. She points out the missing side door.

"You see? There you are preaching to a congregation of whales and turtles."

He looks at her sideways. Now she's making fun of him, but he rolls with it.

"And that's you over there, getting the Nobel Prize for Auto Repair."

She laughs. "I don't think they give a Nobel Prize for that."

"For you they will," he says sweetly.

It's nice to think that it could be like that. That people would say nice things about you and give you awards. She's never gotten an award. She didn't play sports and didn't do well in school, mostly because she was bored and didn't hand in assignments.

But now, in Pablo Escobar's destroyed plane, the future feels uncertain in a fun, slightly dangerous, alluring way. She can't believe she ever felt so strongly about Leif. He wasn't half as interesting as Alby. With a pang, she wishes Sadie could see her now, on her own, not following the rules.

She looks over at Alby. They're sitting side by side, just a foot apart, their shoulders almost touching, and he smiles at her. *This is an odd place for a first kiss*, she thinks, but then she leans toward him.

Just as their lips are about to touch, an enormous boom shakes the fuselage and there's a piercing scream. Alby leaps up, slamming his

THE UNCERTAINTY PRINCIPLE

head into the roof. Mia ducks in time to see feet land on the nose of the plane.

Alby crumples, grabbing his head as the screaming turns into an explosion of childish laughter. Another pair of feet land on the nose and Mia sits up enough to see Kaden and Flynn standing on the front of the plane, doubled over with laughter.

"Kissy kissy," Kaden shouts.

"Oh my god," Mia says, trying to catch her breath.

"Kissy kissy kissy," Flynn squeals.

Alby groans beside her.

"Are you okay?" she asks.

"What . . . ," he says, stunned and dabbing his hands to his head, checking for blood.

Mia lunges for her brother through the broken window. The two boys leap off, landing on the sand. She jumps out and they take off into the bushes.

"You are so dead," Mia shouts, disappearing into the bushes after them at breakneck speed.

Inside the plane, Alby glances around. He's sitting by himself.

"What happened?" he says to no one.

Chapter 10

Mia watches from the *Graceland*'s stern as Alby's dad motors away with Alby in their dinghy. Alby waves. She waves back. When Garrett saw Mia pummeling Kaden on the beach, he set off in the boat and pulled her off him.

Now Kaden is sniffling on the hatchway ladder, his shirt flecked with blood and a cold pack on his nose. "It's never okay to punch someone in the face but basically you deserved it," Ethan tells Kaden.

"Ethan," Izzy says sharply from behind him in the cabin.

Ethan glances sympathetically at Mia but she doesn't care anymore. What does it matter? The whole idea of kissing Alby was a mistake. There's no point in getting attached.

"He was cute though," Lene observes, sitting beside Mia in the cockpit and watching Alby climb aboard the *Exodus*. "If you had to choose between him and Tennessee . . ."

Mia knows that Lene doesn't like the idea of Tennessee. Plus, that's not the choice. The choice is between Tennessee and dealing with her mom.

"Okay, I've got everything," Izzy says, coming up from the cabin with a bucket filled with antibacterial sprays and gels. She sits next to Mia in the cockpit, abruptly rousting Lene, who moves away in a huff.

Mia puts her hands out. She knows the drill. Her mom squeezes gel onto her palms and tells her to count to sixty. Mia starts rubbing her

THE UNCERTAINTY PRINCIPLE

hands together. The sting of the alcohol on her raw cuticles brings her back to reality. Nothing will ever change if she stays on this boat.

"This is a disaster," her mom mutters, clearly thrown by the fact that Kaden and Mia didn't swim back and have now brought who knows what kind of germs on board. She doesn't seem to care that Kaden is bleeding or that Mia is simmering. All her mom cares about is disinfecting.

"Don't you want to know what happened?" Mia asks.

"Close your eyes," her mom says, spraying a can of multisurface disinfectant around Mia for thirty seconds. Mia feels her eyes start to sting and finally exhales, waving her hands around to clear the air.

"Mom!" Mia gasps. "That was too much."

"Let me see your hands."

"This is not a big deal," Mia says, letting her mom scrub her hands with a scrub brush even though her cuticles start to bleed.

"You didn't follow the plan," her mom says, splashing the blood away and focusing on the webbing between Mia's fingers. She scrubs ferociously. "You were supposed to swim."

"Ow," Mia says, jerking her hands back. "What's wrong with you?"

"We don't know where that boy has been."

Mia knows that this is only partially about germs. Her mom doesn't like the idea of Mia being out unsupervised with a boy. But Mia doesn't want to get into a fight about it.

"We got drenched on the dinghy ride back to the boat," Mia says, trying to placate her. "It's fine."

Her mom pauses, but it's clear she still wants to wash between Mia's fingers. Mia sees her dad readjust the ice pack on Kaden's nose. He's watching them with a worried look.

"They invited us for dinner again," Mia says.

"That's not happening," Izzy says.

"Why not?"

"You punched your brother, for God's sake!"

"Oh, you noticed? 'Cause you didn't seem to care about him a second ago."

"Hey, you know last night was fun," her dad says diplomatically to avoid a blowup. "But I'm not sure it was worth it."

"Worth it for who?" Mia snaps.

"I just think we're already behind the eight ball for the day," he says, looking anxiously at Izzy.

"Wait, don't change the topic. Worth it for who?"

Her dad scratches his head nervously. "If your mom's not feeling good, you know, it's not good for any of us."

"Yeah, well, it's particularly not good for me," Mia says.

Neither of her parents say anything.

"I meet somebody my own age for once and he's leaving tomorrow and you're telling me I can't hang out with him."

"That's right," her mom says coldly. "You're grounded for punching your brother."

Tears start to roll down Mia's face. "You just don't want me to have a life," Mia snarls, pushing past her mom. She hurries down the hatchway to her bunk and slams the door.

An hour later, she hears the radio chirp, and her dad has an awkward conversation with Garrett, who reiterates the dinner invitation. Her dad says everybody over here is feeling a little under the weather. Mia wants to scream but stays put. Even later, when her dad knocks with a plate of food, she doesn't say anything.

Chapter 11

She wakes before sunrise and climbs quietly on deck. Thankfully, no one is there. It's still dark but the *Exodus*'s anchor light atop the mast casts a dim glow over the boat. Her heart rate picks up when she sees someone reading on deck by headlamp. The beam from the light swivels in her direction. She can't tell who it is.

Slowly, as her eyes adjust, she makes out Alby waving to her. He seems exasperated and she realizes that he's probably been waving this whole time while she just looked at him as if he wasn't there.

She waves back with a dash of extra hand movement to show that she wasn't deliberately ignoring him.

He points to her and then points to his chest. It's hard to figure out what he means. Is this some version of "you will be in my heart forever"? They've only just met. At most, maybe she'll think about him once or twice when she's in Tennessee and chuckle about the spiritual Australian she almost kissed in Pablo Escobar's drug plane.

He keeps gesturing at her and his chest and then twirls his hand over his head like a disco dancer. Lene sits down and watches him closely.

"I think he's trying to tell you he solved a difficult math problem," she says.

"That's not what he's saying," Mia says, but she's baffled. Alby waves his hands around his head, and it gets comical. She has to cover her mouth so he won't see her laughing. But then he starts laughing too because he's waving his arms around like a fool and she's not getting it. She's clearly lost this game of charades.

He stops gesturing and looks at her for a moment. He shrugs and she shrugs.

It seems fitting. She couldn't figure out this coded message just like she can't break the code of how to act in the world. It's all just a messy mystery and she's trapped in it forever.

He disappears and she sits down in the cockpit. The sun is still well below the horizon but she can see more of the sea now. The colors change second by second as the earth rotates, spinning her toward the sun like she's cresting the top of a roller coaster. Tennessee is next and hopefully it'll go better than this did. Maybe it will be simpler there, without her mother or Sadie's interference.

The thought of Sadie gives her a jolt. She *wants* Sadie's interference. She needs it. Without it, she's adrift.

Amid the soft lapping of the water against the boat and the whoosh of the waves breaking on the island, she hears a noise she can't quite place. It's something different, like small fish jumping and splashing down. She looks around and immediately pinpoints the source.

It's Alby paddling his little dinghy toward her with a plastic oar.

"What the heck?" she mutters, standing up. She looks back at the hatchway, making sure her mom isn't awake. There are no lights on below so she tiptoes to the stern. Alby drifts up, winded from the paddling, but smiling roguishly.

"Get in," he whispers.

"And go where?"

"I don't know," he says. "Somewhere."

"In that?"

"Best I can do."

THE UNCERTAINTY PRINCIPLE

She glances back again. It's like a jailbreak. Except her getaway car is a tiny rubber boat.

Still, it's exciting.

She steps into the boat. He offers her his hand, but she frowns at him. He's trying to be chivalrous, but any sailor knows that grabbing onto someone else only throws you off balance. She ignores his hand and he takes it back, chastened.

He passes her a second plastic oar and they start to paddle together. They've got to get farther away before they can start the engine without waking everyone. They paddle in silence, not wanting to risk anything.

Little by little, the *Graceland* and the *Exodus* get smaller behind them. As they paddle, the sun breaks the horizon, bathing the sea in a pink glow. It makes her smile to think she's running away, even if just for the morning. Her mom will make her scrub herself raw but it's already worth it.

After a while, he stops and looks back.

"I think we're good," he says, kneeling in the boat and jerking the engine's starter rope. She watches the muscles in his arm ripple as he pulls a few times before the engine sputters to life.

"There's a restaurant on a little island across the channel," he says, pointing to a thin sliver of white sand about a mile away. "We could sneak over there together."

He looks at her, searching her face for a clue about what he should do next. The boat is so small that their knees are touching. If either of them leaned toward the other, they'd bonk heads.

"About yesterday," he starts awkwardly. "The airplane . . ."

Right, the airplane. It's not like she forgot about it. But the fight with her parents and her decision to leave are so much bigger than the failed kiss. It was a moment, but that was yesterday and the moment is gone. It felt right to kiss him then. Now they're just bobbing uncomfortably in a small boat at sea. It doesn't feel the same.

"Yeah, I'm leaving so . . ."

"Right, absolutely," he says, nodding, his eyes downcast. She's charmed by his bashfulness. It makes her reconsider, but he crunches the engine out of neutral. "It's still early so I'll take the long way?" he mumbles.

"That sounds good," she says, settling herself into the boat as he twists the throttle. *It's better like this*, she thinks, as the dinghy bounces forward through light chop. *Less complicated. Less messy.*

Still, she watches him out of the corner of her eye. He pilots the little boat as if it were an extension of himself. Just a minute ago, he was tongue-tied and confused. Now, he seems like a different person. He veers closer to the island and points ahead at a rock wall that rises out of the sea. The *Graceland* and the *Exodus* disappear around the bend behind them. They're on their own now as the sun rises, pouring light across the face of the rock. There's no way for the younger boys to interrupt them and the boat is so small, there's not even room for Lene.

As he brings them close to the rock wall, she notices that he braided a piece of his hair since she last saw him. It's subtle, a strand buried beneath the top layer, but she finds it captivating. She reaches out and runs her fingers down it. The intimacy of the gesture surprises him and he lets off the throttle.

"You braided your hair."

"Flynn did last night," he says, his breath shallow as her hand lingers beside his face. "His way of apologizing for sneaking up on us, I guess."

She takes her hand back, aware that she's created a physical connection between them. "It looks good," she says.

They glide to a bobbing halt on the water, and it makes the boat feel

THE UNCERTAINTY PRINCIPLE

even smaller, like they're floating together on a postage stamp in the middle of the ocean. He reaches into the pocket of his shorts, pulls out a pocketknife, and deftly slices the braid off.

"Oh jeez," she says, surprised.

"To remember me in Tennessee," he says, handing her the lock of hair. She takes it, simultaneously grossed out and touched. Then she starts laughing, breaking the seriousness of the moment.

"What?"

"You have no idea what my mom would say if she saw this," she says, pinching the braid between her two fingers and waving it back and forth. "She would literally light it on fire and we'd spend two days scrubbing the boat."

"She really doesn't like me, eh?" Alby says.

"No, no," Mia says, putting her hand on his arm to reassure him. "It's not that."

She realizes that she has to say something more, but she has always avoided talking about her mom. One of the few benefits of being at sea these past months has been that she hasn't had to answer any questions. But now, if she doesn't say anything, Alby will think it's about him.

"She's just really into cleanliness," Mia says, using one of her go-to lines.

"Is that why she was spraying you down yesterday with a can of disinfectant?"

She thinks about falling back on her usual answers—can't be too safe, everybody is doing it these days, never know where the next pandemic will start. It's all meant to hide the truth. But why hide now? She'll never see Alby again. It won't complicate their relationship because they don't really have one.

"My mom has issues," she admits. It feels like a big step just to say it.

77

"Is she sick?"

Mia thinks about this for a second. "Yeah, I think she is."

She feels her eyes well up and turns her face away. She doesn't know why she's crying. She doesn't want to cry. But the tears start to roll down her cheeks.

"Hey, it's okay," he says, scooting over and tentatively putting an arm around her.

She hasn't been able to talk to anyone besides Lene since she left. She's kept her feelings pent up for months and now, floating on this tiny dinghy, she can't contain them anymore. She buries her face in his shoulder and lets him hug her. His T-shirt smells like mildew, but after months on a boat, she's used to the smell. She realizes that it feels good to cry.

After a while, the tears stop and she leans back, pulling herself out of the hug. "Thanks," she says, a little embarrassed. "Sorry about that."

"Not at all," he says. "Is it like cancer or something?"

"It's germs. She's scared of germs."

"I guess that's understandable these days."

"Not like normal scared."

Mia can see he's confused. To an outsider, it's hard to understand.

"That's why we swam to dinner," Mia explains. "To clear the germs."

"Is that why you're leaving?"

Mia nods.

"And your parents will just keep sailing?"

"I guess so."

"Your brother's staying?"

"Yeah," she says, feeling the emotion rush back. "He's a pain but he's just a kid."

"How will he hold up?"

THE UNCERTAINTY PRINCIPLE

Mia tries to imagine it. She wants to protect Kaden. But she doesn't think she'd be much help if she's angry all the time. She'll only make it worse.

"I don't know," she says. "My dad says we're here so my mom can get better and that if she's feeling good, it's good for all of us. But you could say the same for me. If I'm not doing good, then it's bad for everyone."

"Yeah, I get that," Alby says with honest sympathy.

"I'm sorry, I didn't mean to turn this into a therapy session," she says, wiping her eyes.

"Hey, no worries. I just want you to know . . ."

His voice breaks and she sees that he's about to cry too. He swallows the tears back and smiles at her. "I just want you to know I am so happy to have met you. Even if just for a day."

She feels a tightness in her chest and realizes that she's forgotten to breathe.

Her default assumption is that people don't really think too much about her. Leif and Sadie didn't seem to care about her at all. Her mom is completely self-absorbed. Kaden and her dad are in their own worlds. Nobody is looking out for her, except maybe Lene, but that doesn't really count. She's basically alone and abandoned.

But now this. It's strange to think that she's had an effect on Alby in such a short time.

Strange but nice.

She's about to reach out to him—maybe to hold his hand or touch his shoulder, she's not sure yet—when he points to the rock wall ahead of them. "Looks like there's an opening," he says.

She looks over and sees a cave at the waterline. It stretches into the rock but there's a glimmer of daylight coming out of it, as if it were a tunnel.

"Take a look?" he says, raising an eyebrow.

"Sure," she says, shelving the idea of reaching out to him. She can tell that he's trying not to pressure her. She said she didn't want to get involved and he's respecting that. But now she's not so sure.

As they get closer to the rock wall, they can see the cave is low to the water but seems to go forever. There's a light source somewhere on the other end. There's only about four feet between the water and the rock ceiling of the tunnel.

"What do you reckon?" Alby asks.

She watches the rise and fall of the swell, judging how close the water gets to the rock ceiling. It's dangerous. If a swell hits them while they're in the tunnel, it will heave them up, smushing them into the rock. But the dinghy is made of rubber tubes like a tire. If it looks like they're going to get slammed, they can lie flat and the tubes should absorb the impact.

"I think we can make it," she says. She's already run away from the *Graceland*. This whole morning feels like a risk.

"Was hoping you'd say that," he says, grinning.

Alby aims them at the tunnel and gooses the engine, pushing them toward the opening. The rock wall rises above; it feels like they are going to crash into it. As they get closer, they bend low and ready themselves to squeeze through the four-foot-tall opening. The tunnel is narrow too; barely the width of the boat. Alby gives the engine a little more gas and they shoot into the opening. They're both lying nearly flat on the bottom of the boat, the rock ceiling gliding just over their heads. Mia reaches up, dragging her hand across the barnacles clinging to the roof. It feels like they're entering a place no one has ever been before.

After twenty feet, they emerge into a circular opening thirty feet tall, with rock rising all around them. At the top, it opens to blue sky.

THE UNCERTAINTY PRINCIPLE

Alby cuts the engine and they float into the space in near silence, the sloshing of the water echoing against the rock walls. Neither of them can believe it. It's a natural amphitheater, a cylinder cut out of the rock that rises thirty feet. Below them, the water is clear and no more than ten feet deep. A school of fish flickers across the stony bottom. They are entirely hidden from the outside world.

"Wow," Alby whispers, shifting so that he lies across the boat looking up at the sky. His head rests on the soft rubber gunwale and his legs flop over the other side, his toes touching the water.

Mia doesn't say anything. It feels like it would disturb the sanctity of the place. She lies with her head by his knees on the opposite gunwale, and the two of them float silently side by side, the boat drifting, bumping gently off the rock walls and bouncing back across the water. Way up above, at the rim, Mia sees Lene poke her head over to check on them but then she goes away. The sunlight reflecting off the water sends waves of blue and white light across the rock walls and Mia knows with 100 percent certainty that there will never be a moment quite as beautiful as this ever again.

She sits up and he watches her move slowly toward him in the boat. He's frozen in place, his eyes wide. Slowly, she places a hand on the gunwale on either side of his head, hovering over him, keeping him locked in place.

Inch by inch, she gets closer, his breath quickening, her lips parted.

She stops, their lips almost touching, her eyes on him.

And then she kisses him.

His lips are warm and soft, his stubble scratchy. It feels perfect and strange and scary and all those things smash into each other. She's not sure what a first kiss is supposed to be like, and she's momentarily confused. *Am I doing it right? Is this even a good idea?* She pulls back and looks searchingly at him.

"What's the matter?" he says quietly.

There's nothing the matter, she realizes, and leans in to kiss him again. His arms surround her, holding her as her chest meets his chest, and she feels herself rise and fall when he breathes, like she's floating on him.

She touches the edge of the jagged cut on his forehead. "Does it hurt?" she asks, thrilled by the intimacy of touching him.

"If you poke it," he says, laughing and pulling her hand away. He pivots, rolling her off of him and catching her in his arms. He holds her gently and runs his hand down her face. She likes the way it feels.

"You know, we were supposed to head north yesterday to the BVI but our electrical went on the fritz so we rerouted," he says. "We weren't supposed to be here."

"Yeah?" she says, distracted by the back of his hand on her cheek.

"This is God's plan," he says, and that gets her attention. If God really has a plan, then should she go to Tennessee or not? How are you supposed to figure out the plan? Alby seems to be saying that God communicates by messing up your boat's electrical system.

"Things break on boats all the time," Mia says.

"You decided to give up on sailing yesterday, right?"

She nods.

"And one of our circuits fries for no reason and we both end up on this island in the middle of nowhere. When was the last time you met someone our age out here? Never, right? I think we were meant to meet."

Mia can hear Lene groan from the lip of the grotto thirty feet up. As a scientist, Lene doesn't believe the universe cares about any of us. It just chugs along according to its laws.

But maybe there is some reason to it all. Maybe this isn't just a random moment. Everything that happened in Duluth with Sadie and Leif,

THE UNCERTAINTY PRINCIPLE

all that pain, maybe it was for a reason? Maybe it was leading her to this? In which case, this moment is more than a boy and a girl floating in a boat. It is something bigger, part of the mysterious logic behind black holes and quantum states. Maybe this was meant to be.

"I don't want you to leave," he says.

Suddenly, she's not sure she wants to leave either. But it's not clear if staying would be any different. "It's not like we'd see each other," she points out.

"My parents don't have any solid plans," he says. "We could go where you go."

Mia tries to imagine it, the *Graceland* and the *Exodus* sailing as a pair. They could have breakfast together, spend the days exploring islands and running solar experiments, and at night, she'd listen to him play guitar and they'd talk about God. It sounds pretty good. It might even make it worth putting up with her mom.

But could she convince her mom to spend so much time with another group of people? Her mother seemed to like them. But seeing them also sent her into a tailspin the next day.

Mia's first reaction is no, there's no way her mom will change. But if it's a choice between Mia leaving or adapting, maybe her mom would budge.

Mia kisses him again.

"Maybe I'll stay," she says, smiling broadly.

Chapter 12

lby runs his dinghy up a two-hundred-foot-wide spit of sand so close to the main island of Anguilla, they could probably swim there in ten minutes. They can see people walking on the beach but this little speck of sand is empty except for a couple thatched huts that make up a low-budget, open-air restaurant. It's early for lunch, but there's already a cook poking at a simple charcoal grill. At some point, their parents will wonder where they went. They both feel like they're running on stolen time.

"I'm glad to be here with you," Alby says sweetly, squeezing her hand as they walk up to the grill. The cook—a tattooed and bearded man in his forties—barely looks up.

"Shrimp or rock lobster?" he says wearily. His eyes are bloodshot and he looks hungover, as if he were marooned here for bad behavior on the mainland. "I might have a fish too."

"How much for a lobster?" Alby asks tentatively.

"Lobster's forty," the guy says automatically.

Alby digs into his pocket and pulls out a twenty-euro note and, after a deep dive into his pocket, a two-euro coin.

"I have basically twenty, uh, twenty-two euros. But I'll spend it all."

"We can just head back," Mia says, trying to get them out of the uncomfortable situation.

"It's embarrassing but that's all the money I have in the world," Alby says, kind of to both of them.

THE UNCERTAINTY PRINCIPLE

Now the moment is even more awkward. The cook looks like he's about to shoo them away.

"I just want to say to this gentleman that we only have so many days to live," Alby says quickly before the cook can tell them to leave. "We will only ever meet so many people. And I've gotten to meet someone so magical, so smart, so stunning that it's hard for me to breathe. I don't want to look back and say I didn't do my best to make the moment as special as she is, in a place this beautiful, with all the money I have in the world. All twenty-two euros of it."

Mia is staring at him, transfixed. She realizes that she's been holding her breath and she looks at the cook, who is also speechless.

"Just wait, um . . . ," the cook says, his voice breaking, before walking abruptly away to a folding table at the back of the hut.

"Alby, jeez," Mia says, catching her breath. "You made him cry."

"I didn't mean to."

"You sound so serious sometimes, it's a little . . ."

"Is it bad?"

"It's just not how people act."

"How would you know?" he says, smiling.

"I'm normal. Normal-ish."

"There's nothing normal about you. That's what I like."

Mia is confused. Sadie spent so much time trying to shape Mia into the expected high school girl, it's drilled into Mia's head. That's the way to be, the way everyone needs to be. As far as Mia could tell, kids in Duluth shunned her for her oddity. All she wanted to do was shed it. But now Alby says it's not only okay but good?

"I don't think he knows what he's talking about," Lene observes as she sits down at a nearby plastic table.

But I like what he's saying, Mia thinks.

The cook is headed back to them carrying a bottle. "He looks upset," Mia whispers to Alby. "I think he's going to kick us out."

"Please, sit," the cook says, pointing to a battered plastic table.

Mia glances at Alby. *What's going on?* But they both sit as the guy lowers himself heavily into a chair next to them. He seems more focused on the old bottle he's holding. He stares at it for a moment. The letters on the peeling label look hand drawn.

"This is a bottle of rum from 1996," he says, inexplicably on the edge of tears again. "Someone very special gave it to me back then. I've had it for decades, just sitting there."

He uncorks it and sniffs the liquid. "She married someone else and I never see her anymore."

Mia glances at Alby with her eyebrows raised. *Wtf?*

The cook wipes his eyes, coughs, and stands up. "I'll cook for you," he announces, looking suddenly serious.

"I really do only have the twenty-two euros," Alby repeats, unsure if the guy heard him earlier.

"First of all, we don't accept euros in Anguilla," the man says. "We use the East Caribbean dollar so your money's no good."

He smiles briefly. "And you were right about special moments. I didn't see mine when it happened."

The cook walks away and they hear the sound of crashing boxes from inside a shack that serves as the pantry. He emerges with pots and pans, and in a few minutes, he has multiple dishes going on the grill. He pours a splash of rum into each pan, sending up explosions of fire.

"Is he okay?" Mia asks.

"Maybe this is therapeutic for him?"

Soon, the cook brings over paper plates of food. There's lobster tail flambé, shrimp scampi drizzled with lime juice and a sprinkling of rum, and sliced plantains sautéed in rum. Mia tries a small bite of the

THE UNCERTAINTY PRINCIPLE

plantains, worried that it's going to be inedible, but the dish is astoundingly good. The alcohol has cooked off, leaving behind a sweetness that lingers.

"Wow," she says to Alby, wide-eyed.

"It's good, right?" the cook says, walking over and sweating from the heat of the grill.

"It's amazing," Mia admits.

The cook mops his face with a rag, the now empty rum bottle dangling in his other hand. "The fire is nice," he says. "It brings out the flavor of the rum."

He takes their empty plates and heads back to the grill. Mia can feel the food fill her with warmth and she takes Alby's hand across the table. "This is the strangest, most beautiful lunch I've ever had," she says quietly.

Alby seems to glow with happiness. "I don't think I'll ever forget this as long as I live," he says, his voice cracking.

Chapter 13

They float lazily away from the island after eating and immediately see the *Exodus* along the coast to the east. It is close in, motoring with sails down, and Alby's mom is scanning the island with binoculars. Mia has a sinking feeling.

"Oh no," Alby says. "They're looking for us."

He revs the throttle and heads after them, waving his hand above his head. It only takes a minute for his mom to spot them and she shouts to Garrett, who quickly turns the *Exodus*.

As Alby brings his dinghy alongside, his mother comes to the railing.

"What the bloody hell were you thinking?" she shouts.

"Flynn, radio the *Graceland* and say we found 'em," Garrett says. Flynn disappears inside.

Mia ties the dinghy off on a stern cleat and they step aboard. Mia doesn't necessarily care about pissing off her parents—they deserve it, as far as she's concerned—but she feels bad to have upset Alby's parents.

"You know you don't go off without telling us," Leah says. "It's past noon. We've been looking for you for hours."

Alby stands shoulder to shoulder with Mia on the back deck. It's like being called into the principal's office.

"Leave a note at least, will ya?" Garrett says. "We thought you'd gone off and drowned."

THE UNCERTAINTY PRINCIPLE

Leah turns to Mia. "Your parents are going around the other side of the island and they're not too happy," she says.

The radio screeches in the main cabin and Mia can hear her dad's voice. "*Exodus, Exodus,* thanks for the good news. We're on our way, over."

Chapter 14

Mia is alone on the bow of the *Graceland*. Behind her, she can hear her mom furiously scrubbing every inch of the boat, but Mia doesn't care. Near the horizon, she can still see the *Exodus*. There's a small figure on the back deck and every now and then it waves. She waves back, trying to control her emotions and not wanting to cry. They'll see each other again. They have to.

The problem is, she doesn't know when. She didn't get to say goodbye. There was no time to plan. In the chaos of the parting, Alby handed her a scrap of paper. But then she stepped across to the *Graceland* and, before Mia could turn around to wave goodbye, she was engulfed in a caustic cloud of disinfectant. She couldn't even open her eyes as the two boats pushed away from each other.

She slowly unfolds the note, trying to pay attention to every detail. Nobody has ever written her a love letter. She savors the still-damp print from his finger. She smooths it out, turns it over, and sees a series of hastily written numbers. She flips it over, looking for more. There's nothing else. Just the numbers: 21461900.

"Looks like someone scribbled down a part number," Lene says, peering over Mia's shoulder. "I think he gave you the wrong piece of paper."

Mia can't believe it. Her first love letter gets mixed up with someone's repair notes. She feels a spike of anger and jams the paper back in her pocket.

THE UNCERTAINTY PRINCIPLE

"You know about Newton's law of gravitational force?" Lene says.

"Not now, Lene."

"Newton figured out that every particle in the universe attracts each other but there is a hitch. The farther apart they get, the less they attract."

"Not helping," Mia mumbles as her dad shuffles toward her at the bow. He kicks the anchor chain a few feet away and squats, pretending to examine the plating around the anchor bay. He was never good at talking about things other than engines.

"Just get it out already," she says at last.

"You shouldn't have done that."

"Fine," she says defiantly.

"I know you think Mom doesn't care but she does. It just comes out differently."

Mia glances at the stern and sees her mom dunking the scrub brush in a bucket of bleach and water. She's got Kaden scrubbing as well. "She should be happy," Mia says.

Her dad looks confused. "Why?"

"I might want to stay now."

"Really?"

"Depends."

He fidgets with the anchor chain. "On what?"

"If we can ever find them again."

"I bet we can," he says, nodding and looking at his feet.

"And if she can calm down and let me have a life."

"That's actually something I talked to her about."

Mia is surprised. He typically doesn't start conversations about anything. Her mom decides what to do and tells him.

"What'd she say?"

He smiles. "She said we could plan a meetup with the Australians as long as you don't run away again."

Chapter 15

She lies in her cabin as the *Graceland* heads due south, the opposite way that Alby went. It's too windy on deck to look at Alby's note and she needs to concentrate. Why does every glimmer of hope have to get so complicated? Things were looking up with Leif until they came crashing down. Now, her mom says she can see Alby again, but she has no way to reach him or plan anything.

Her bunk isn't particularly comfortable, especially with Lene lying beside her. The boat crashes through waves, tossing them into the bulkhead. Periodically, the boat drops into a trough and they free-fall, smacking into the bed.

She stares at the numbers on the note. 21461900. It's so annoying. Why would he give her a bunch of random numbers?

"What do you think?" Mia asks Lene. Maybe Lene's smart enough to figure it out.

"Is there a space in the middle?" Lene asks, squinting at the numbers and pointing to a small gap between 2146 and 1900.

"Could be," Mia says.

"1900 could mean 7:00 p.m. in military time."

"But then what's 2146?" Mia asks.

Mia gets up quickly, an idea forming. She sways through the roll of the boat into the main cabin and plops into the alcove by the ship's electronics rack. She spins the knob on the single sideband, an old-school maritime radio system meant for ship-to-ship communication. In a

THE UNCERTAINTY PRINCIPLE

second, she has 2146 kilohertz dialed in and realizes that his note wasn't a mistake. It was a rushed message that he knew she'd figure out: 7:00 p.m. at frequency 2146.

It might not be a traditional love letter but, for a geek, it's even better.

"I gotta tell you," Lene says. "I think I'm in love."

Chapter 16

Izzy anchors them off the beach of a small desert island called Île Fourchue before sunset. It's bigger than Scrub Island and tall by comparison, with a couple of steep, rocky mountains in the middle. There's no one else there and in the fading orange light, it looks like Mars. Mia isn't paying attention. She's tracking the time.

At 19:00, she dials the single-sideband radio to 2146 kilohertz and rotates the volume.

"You turned it too far," Lene says, hovering anxiously behind her. Mia turns the dial back a smidge. She holds the handset and is debating whether to say something when the receiver squawks. And then Alby's voice breaks through.

"CQ, CQ calling, CQ. This is sailing vessel *Exodus*, over."

She quickly pushes the button on the handset. "SV *Exodus* . . . ," she says, hesitating for a moment as she thinks of a good call sign for herself.

"Choose something flirty," Lene advises.

"*Exodus*, this is Juliet, over," Mia says.

"Hi, Juliet," he says and she can tell he's smiling. "How'd you like my note, over."

Kaden pops his head out of his cabin, drawn by the radio chatter, but before he can say anything, Mia points at him. "I will tear your tongue out and shove it down your throat," she growls in a tone so

THE UNCERTAINTY PRINCIPLE

menacing, he wordlessly slides back into his room and shuts the door. She's thankful Alby can't hear her.

"Juliet, do you copy, over?"

"Yeah, I'm here, sorry. I thought the note was very romantic, over."

"Sorry I didn't have time to explain but I knew you'd figure it out, over."

They talk about little things. How her dad said they could plan to meet up and he tells her about the shock of sailing into the bustle of Marigot Bay on Saint Martin. It's different from talking on the phone because he can't interrupt or chime in. It means there's no way to fill an uncomfortable gap. Until she releases the call button, there's nothing he can do but listen to her. And the same is true when he's talking.

She's struck by how different it is from talking on the phone with Sadie, who would text and scroll through Instagram while they chatted. Here, there are no distractions. Their conversation is slowed down and deliberate and there's an intimacy she's never felt before.

"You know how these radios work, over?" she asks.

There's a pause and then she hears him say, "I love it when you talk techy to me, over."

She laughs before she presses the call button. "Okay, well, right now, my voice is an electromagnetic wave. It's leaving the antenna on the mast and flying up to space, like it wants to get off this planet. And it would if it could but it hits the atmosphere and bounces down to your antenna. Over."

"So you want to leave but can't. And the atmosphere is holding you back. Am I getting that right, over?" he says.

Mia thinks about it for a second. "I guess, yeah, the atmosphere is holding me back. But if it weren't there, my signal would head straight out into space. No one would hear me, besides maybe aliens, over."

"How do you know I'm not an alien, over."

"You kind of are, over."

There's a spurt of static and then a voice cuts in.

"Hola, mamacita. ¿Quieres hablarme sucio? Puedes decirme qué quieres."

Mia waits for the voice to stop talking so she can say something. That's the thing about single-sideband radio: There's no way to break in. Whoever is talking controls the frequency and they can talk for as long as they want. The guy finally stops but before she can press the button, the channel erupts into a riot of mariachi music.

"What the hell," she says, turning the volume down.

She presses the call button and tries to break through but the channel is filled with horns and guitars. There's no stopping the mariachi tunes. She rotates up to 2147 but it's silent. She clicks all the way up to 2155 but there's no sign of Alby. She tunes down to 2140.

"SV *Exodus*, this is Juliet, are you there, over?" she says, increasingly desperate.

Nothing. She's sure he's also hunting for her across the frequencies but it's like trying to find someone in a crowd. Every time she moves, he's probably moving too. It feels equally useless to stay on a single channel and wait for him to show up. With every try, she feels more deflated. Finally, after ten minutes with no response, she gives up.

Chapter 17

The morning dawns but Mia keeps her eyes shut, not wanting to face the day. The boat rolls softly in the light swell and she can hear water sloshing against the hull. She feels around for her phone and cracks an eye to scan her parents' '80s playlist. After a few swipes, she finds what she's looking for: a Dire Straits song. She presses her earbuds in and pulls the pillow over her head as "Brothers in Arms" begins.

The song starts with the sound of thunder rumbling and an old-school synthesizer. And then a weary guitar, as if the musician can't bear to go on. It's about people who are far from home in some kind of war. It's haunting and beautiful and one of the saddest songs she's ever heard.

Lene snuggles up close to Mia in the bunk. "You know what Newton would say?" she whispers.

"About what?"

"About Alby."

Mia thinks for a second. She likes Newton. In addition to inventing calculus and laying the foundation for modern science, he was known to talk aloud to imaginary people and went completely crazy for a while, so Mia feels some kinship with him.

"You know Newton also had a pretty messed-up love life," Lene says.

It's true. Newton claimed to be celibate and never married. He complained that his friends tried to "embroil" him with women and eventually developed a close relationship with a young Swiss guy, whom he sent money to. But then something happened and Newton had a mental breakdown.

"And this helps me how?" Mia asks.

"Because of Newton's second law of motion."

She wishes Lene would just give straightforward advice.

"Newton's second law of motion states that if you know all the forces acting on an object, you can predict the future. So maybe you actually already know what's going to happen."

This gives her pause. Mia would like to know what happens next.

"What is the force acting on Alby? He said he wanted to be with you. And what are the forces acting on you? You know all that too. So Newton says everything is going to happen exactly like you think it will. The future is clear. You and Alby will get married and sail the world and invent new solar cells and have babies and just be so, so happy together."

Mia changes her mind. She likes Lene's relationship advice.

She leaves the music on as she gets out of bed and pulls on her overalls. She's feeling newly energized. With Alby in her life, Sadie's betrayal doesn't sting quite so much and Mia is left wondering why her friend lied. If Newton was right, Mia needs to understand the forces that were acting on Sadie to understand why The Incident happened. Right now, it's a complete mystery and that hurts as much as anything. Mia thought she knew Sadie better than anyone but clearly she was wrong and that makes her feel like nothing is solid. At any moment, everything could fall apart because she doesn't understand the way the world works.

Calling Sadie and figuring out what happened seems like an important next step. Whatever she does, whether she stays on the boat or goes

THE UNCERTAINTY PRINCIPLE

to Tennessee, she's going to have to try to understand her ex-friend, so she readies her handmade satellite phone. It's time to test it out.

She loads the solar cells and radio handset into a backpack along with some water, a can of tuna fish, and a foam pool noodle. When she pops up on deck, her dad is already there even though it's early.

"I'm going ashore," she says as she unstraps the dinghy. "I'll be back before sundown."

"What are you up to?" he says, looking worried.

"I'm going to make a phone call," she says as if it were the most natural thing in the world.

Her dad looks confused. "How?"

"If anybody had been paying attention, you might have picked up on the fact that I built a portable satellite radio."

"You mean it actually works?"

Mia stares at him, hurt that he doesn't believe her. "Yes, it works," she says, though the truth is she's never tested the whole setup together.

"Who are you going to call?" he says, even more worried.

"I can't stay pent up here forever," she says, dodging the question. And then, softening. "I'll be fine, Dad."

"Yeah?" he says, clearly not convinced.

She steps into their dinghy, yanks the starter rope, and twists the throttle, zipping quickly away. She feels better with the wind in her face and the *Graceland* behind her. The little flat-bottomed boat bounces across the water, skimming over the tops of the small waves. She turns side to side, zigzagging, finally free to go where she wants.

She gets close to shore and cuts the engine, coasting silently toward the rocky beach. She pulls the engine up so it won't hit the ground and, when the nose hits the rocks, she jumps ashore and drags the boat out of the water.

The island looks deserted, though there's a weathered picnic table in a patch of trees behind the shore. Somebody was clearly here a long time ago but the place is abandoned now. Mia heads uphill to get a better view. Aside from the trees around the table, there's not much vegetation and the sun is strong on her shoulders.

Lene looks particularly hot in a blazer and turtleneck but she seems chipper. "You know each of these photons has traveled ninety-three million miles to roast you?" Lene says. "Isn't that amazing?"

"You really should take your blazer off."

"I'm fine," Lene says, though she's pouring sweat. "You're the one with a problem. Sadie doesn't want to talk to you. You're a joke to her. That's why she had no problem lying to you. She obviously just didn't care about you at all."

Mia picks a piece of cuticle and feels the sting as the salt in her sweat burrows into the cut. She knew that they were growing apart. Or, at least, Sadie didn't want to hang out as much. She had new friends, girls who dressed well and could talk about things Mia didn't care about. Sadie invited Mia to sit with them at lunch, but Mia never had anything to add to the conversations about rap battles, nail polish, or where to buy a vape pen. Mia would listen without comprehension and steal glances at Sadie, admiring the way she put on gloss to make her lips reflect the light. Mia was captivated by the way her childhood friend was blossoming, becoming so confident and beautiful. Mia just wanted to be close to her.

Mia presses on her cuticle to stanch the trickle of blood. Mia left without ever talking to Sadie. She's not sure exactly how to start again. She's not even sure if her phone will work or what she'll say if it does.

"I think you should ask her about all the fun she's been having since you disappeared," Lene says unhelpfully. "She's probably having a blast without you to slow her down."

"Just be quiet," Mia whispers, already defeated.

Mia clambers to the top of the steep mountain, huffing painfully, with Lene trailing behind her. It's a narrow summit and Mia balances carefully. The north side plummets three hundred feet down a sheer cliff to the sea. She edges around a rock outcropping that blocks the *Graceland* from view. It also blocks the wind, creating a private, quiet place for Mia to lay out her gear.

The sun is strong here, the photons crashing down, driving some pretty good current in the cells. Her multimeter shows nearly fifteen volts, delivering eight amps for about one hundred watts into the radio's depleted battery, enough to keep it powered up and beaming to a satellite in space. She unbundles the foam pool noodle and pokes aluminum wire through it to create an antenna that looks like a sad, skeletal Christmas tree.

The trick is finding a satellite. The last time she had internet access a month ago in the Bahamas, Mia memorized the path that amateur radio satellites trace across the sky from east to west. She plugs the antenna into her handset, aims it at the horizon, and uses the radio keypad to type in the satellite access code she found online.

In order to connect, her miniature uplink station has to lock on to a satellite moving at seventeen thousand miles per hour up in space. At that speed, it takes about four minutes for the satellite to cross the sky. That means that if she finds one, she'll only have four minutes to dial Sadie and talk to her, assuming Sadie even picks up.

Mia arcs the antenna slowly over the sky, hoping to find a satellite. Freshman year in high school, she signed up for the amateur ham radio club and managed to get her radio license before Sadie told her that the club was for "total outcasts" and made her drop it. Still, Mia learned a few tricks. She whistles into the handset, waiting for the sound to get picked up and beamed back to her, the sign of a successful connection.

"I told you to try another substrate," Lene says. "It's never going to work."

Mia checks the multimeter and shakes her head. The cells are kicking out a lot of wattage. The radio is powered up. That's not the problem.

She aims her antenna at the sky and whistles again. On the third pass, she hears her whistling coming out of the speaker—she's connected. She quickly dials the code. In a second, the radio emits an old-school dial tone.

"Ah-ha!" Mia shouts, surging with nervous excitement.

"I always knew it would work," Lene says, changing her tune completely.

Mia quickly dials Sadie's number. She caught the satellite pretty far above the horizon and estimates she only has three minutes before it disappears into the sea behind her. She moves the antenna slowly up, tracking the satellite's movement in her mind even though she can't see it. She needs to stay aimed at it so the signal doesn't drop.

Her excitement disappears when she hears the phone ringing. She tenses and realizes that she is on the verge of reconnecting with Sadie for the first time since The Incident.

"Hello?"

It's Sadie. She sounds guarded, as if this might be a robocall or spam. Mia feels a pit in her stomach. What should she say?

"If you're trying to sell me something, please don't call back," Sadie says impatiently.

"Sadie, don't hang up," Mia says in a rush, pressing the talk button on her transmitter.

"Mia?" Sadie says, astounded.

"I built a satellite phone so I could call you."

"Really?" Sadie says, confused. "Where are you?"

THE UNCERTAINTY PRINCIPLE

Mia looks around at the mountaintop, the blue ocean surrounding her. "It's a little complicated."

"I bet it is," Sadie says, her voice dripping with sarcasm.

Mia takes a deep breath. "I wanted to call you and talk about what happened."

"What happened was that you had a total freak-out, attacked me, and then completely disappeared. Everybody was like, why are you friends with that person?"

Mia feels a tightness in her chest, like she can't breathe. *Is Sadie actually saying this was my fault?*

"You lied to me," Mia manages to say, though it's hard to think straight. Maybe she's wrong, and this *is* all her fault.

"I was trying to help you," Sadie says forcefully. "Leif and I wanted to build up your confidence and get you to talk to people."

"But you knew I had a crush on him."

"I mean sure, but you weren't, like, being serious. You just liked to talk about having a crush. You needed to build some basic talking skills and so I asked Leif to just humor me. I was helping you, and you, like, completely lost your shit."

"Why didn't you just tell me you were dating him?"

"Because I knew you couldn't handle it. And I think I was right."

Mia's heart is pounding. She wants to run but there's nowhere to go.

"Mia, listen to me. We've been friends since we were kids but you're a special person."

The way she says *special* makes Mia flinch. It's like she's saying Mia is broken.

"My mom says your whole family took off on your dad's boat," Sadie goes on. "And, you know, maybe that's the best thing for you. You can just be by yourself with your engines and machine stuff and be happy."

The satellite is nearing the far horizon. The call will drop in less than a minute. A minute to say all the things she's been thinking about for months but already the conversation has exploded. Mia never imagined that Sadie would blame her for what happened and now she feels a wave of guilt for ruining her one friendship.

"Okay, you're right," Mia says, her whole body sagging as if gravity just doubled. "It's my fault. I'm sorry I blew up. You just tell me what I have to do so we can keep talking and I'll do it."

"You need to figure yourself out," Sadie says.

"I'm trying," Mia says pitifully, the tears welling up again.

"And you can't blow up at me when I'm trying to help you."

Mia feels a dose of warmth. At least Sadie was trying to help. *That's good, right?*

"I just want you to know that I really miss you," Mia says, her voice cracking.

Silence and then . . . "If you missed me, you would have called a long time ago."

That hurts. Mia flushes with anger.

"Do you even know what I had to do to call you? I'm literally standing on a deserted island holding an antenna with a phone I made myself and I had to reach the Shockley–Queisser limit to power a satellite uplink and I did it because I wanted to talk to you."

The radio emits some static and Mia realizes the satellite dropped below the horizon. Sadie is gone. The call dropped.

Mia lowers the antenna in defeat and looks around. She's alone on the island. The sea around her is empty and endless. She's holding a ridiculous foam antenna and a tangle of wires.

"I'm not sure Sadie's such a great friend," Lene points out.

Images flash through Mia's mind: swimming with Sadie as kids, building castles in Sadie's room with the couch cushions, going to see

Wicked at the NorShor Theatre freshman year, sitting side by side and leaning into each other. Sadie's her oldest friend and her only friend. She can't let her go.

"Well, here's the good news," Lene says brightly. "The phone worked great."

Mia crumples to the ground.

Chapter 18

Mia slides into the desk below deck on the *Graceland* at a minute before seven. All afternoon, she's been miserable, constantly on the edge of tears, ignoring her parents. The only thing that kept her from a complete breakdown is the fact that she has her call with Alby to look forward to. She dials the single-sideband radio to 2146 kilohertz and the display casts a faint green glow into the dimness of the galley.

Maybe Alby can make her feel better. Maybe he can tell her that everything isn't her fault, though she's pretty sure now that it is. She deserves this punishment, this isolation, because she doesn't deserve to be liked. She's too weird. Too unlikable.

"CQ, CQ calling, CQ," she says softly into the handset. Even her voice sounds weak. "This is Juliet, over."

There's a burst of static but no response. It's exactly seven. The radio is silent.

"This is Juliet calling CQ, over, are you there?"

Still nothing. It's a minute after seven.

She calls again, this time with the *Graceland*'s identification number: "SV *Exodus*, this is KW-ZH-345, over."

He *has to* show up. This is their only connection. He's just a bit late. She has no other way to find him. No email, no phone, no handles. She doesn't even know his last name.

In the silence, waiting for his response, Mia can't help but think of

THE UNCERTAINTY PRINCIPLE

Sadie's accusations. That she didn't know much about Leif. She has to admit it's true. What she liked most about Leif was talking about him with Sadie. It gave their friendship an electricity, a delicious hint of the forbidden. What hurts the most isn't the idea of losing Leif. It is the thought of losing Sadie.

She imagines Sadie with Leif. The way he kissed her. Now that Mia actually knows what a kiss feels like, it's even more painful to picture it. Mia can see Sadie's thin lips clearly, with her shiny gloss. The way she would pout just to make Mia laugh. Her straight, black hair. Her mischievous smile.

The problem now is she doesn't know how to repair things. Sadie says she's got to "figure herself out." How's she supposed to do that if Sadie isn't around to help her? It doesn't even seem like Sadie wants to talk until Mia emerges, fully formed, on the other side of whatever figuring out needs to be done. The only other option Mia can think of is to listen to her mom, which Mia refuses to do.

It would all be okay if Alby showed up. She could talk to him and he could tell her what to do. They could plan their next meeting, and she could confide in him. If Sadie really doesn't want to be friends, at least she has Alby now. They can learn how to deal with life together.

She calls him again on the radio. No response. It's 7:05 now. *Where the hell is he? Hasn't he been looking forward to this all day too?*

"Maybe try again?" Lene prompts from the galley table.

Mia tries for another five minutes and gets no answer.

She puts the handset down and pulls a piece of skin from her index finger in the spot where it hurts the most. A bead of blood appears.

Could he have already forgotten about her? Maybe he feels like Sadie feels: that Mia isn't worth it. Maybe he also met someone and doesn't need to mess around with Mia anymore. He could have met a girl on Saint Martin and he's out with her now. Mia feels her anxiety surging but can't stop the thoughts. She imagines that the other girl is prettier and less awkward. It makes her want to punch him for being nice in the first place.

She knew it was a mistake. It's safer to just keep everyone at a distance. In fact, it's great that she's on this boat, away from people, because it means there's no one around to disappoint her. She's just going to keep sailing forever and never talk to anyone her own age again. She's definitely never going to talk to Alby again.

She looks at the handset and, despite herself, picks it up.

"*Exodus*, this is Juliet, over," she calls with desperation.

"Mamacita, ¿por qué no me dices qué llevas puesto?" the voice from last night crackles over the air and then laughs. "¿Eh? Te estoy escuchando."

She turns the radio off, defeated. It was ridiculous to believe they'd stay in touch, ridiculous to think that a handful of hours together meant anything.

She sees Lene get up to leave, trying to duck out before Mia sees her. "It's your fault," Mia lashes out. "You said we knew what he wanted."

Lene freezes, caught in Mia's glare. She turns stiffly to face Mia. "There's something I didn't tell you," Lene admits.

"What?"

"There's a problem with Newton."

"I thought he was a genius."

"Yeah, I was trying to find the right time to say something about that," Lene says.

Mia stares at Lene, her fury building. She starts picking a new piece of cuticle. "You said we were going to get married and sail together and everything."

"That's the problem. Newton thought everything had one trajectory.

THE UNCERTAINTY PRINCIPLE

It could turn left or right, speed up or slow down, but there was only one continuous path."

"He was wrong?"

Lene does a little shuffle dance and then spreads her hands wide. "Welcome to quantum mechanics, where one thing can go all sorts of ways at once."

Mia sinks her head into her hand. "None of this makes any sense," she moans.

"Bingo!" Lene is upbeat again. She knows Mia is confused, which is perfect because quantum physics makes no sense either. "Newton and Einstein made everyone think the world could be explained but then a bunch of physicists were drinking Carlsberg beer in Copenhagen, which is a great beer, with a fresh, crisp taste—"

"Lene," Mia interrupts. "I know Carlsberg sponsored you."

"I'm just saying it's a good beer."

"I get it," Mia says.

"Anyway, they were drinking beer and thinking about the universe and they realized that we can't actually exactly know everything. That's what quantum mechanics is all about. Sometimes small particles exist in multiple places at once. That was discovered in the 1930s and still no one really knows what it means about the universe."

"I don't know why we're talking about this."

"Because you need to understand that you're getting closer to the truth."

"You just said we're getting further away," Mia shouts, feeling betrayed by the world.

Lene gives her an understanding look. "We don't know why things are the way they are, but we're starting to understand them better."

"Everything okay?" her dad asks, leaning his head into the cabin. Lene uses the distraction to disappear into Mia's berth.

Mia looks up at her dad. "It's fine," she says, her voice cracking and tears starting to run down her face for the umpteenth time today. She wipes them away, ashamed that she's so upset and ashamed that her whole family just heard it because she knows they were all listening to her blabbering. There's no way not to listen. Her dad steps quickly down into the cabin and pulls her into a hug.

"He'll show up tomorrow," he says.

"I'm an idiot."

"You're not an idiot at all." He lets her go and leans against the hatchway ladder. "He was probably away from the boat in town or something."

Mia pulls a piece of skin off her cuticles, imagining all the things Alby was doing besides calling her. A new line of blood appears.

"Sorry, I didn't . . . ," he says, looking at his feet again. "I just, uh . . ."

As usual, he's got something to say but can't say it.

"What do you want?"

"Oh," he says, looking up at her, surprised all over again that he's that easy to read. "Just about tomorrow."

"What about tomorrow?"

"We were going to sail to the nearest island with Wi-Fi and call Uncle Paul."

Damn. She was sure she'd be on the radio with Alby now, making plans to meet up. She wasn't thinking about Tennessee. She was going to tell her parents that she'd stay, at least for a little while longer.

But now everything is different. Sadie is pissed and Alby ghosted her. Her anger at her parents has cooled, replaced by something else, a newfound understanding of what a disaster her life is. Even if Alby had shown up for the call, it would have been a stuttering back-and-forth with everyone in the Western Hemisphere listening. Maybe they could

THE UNCERTAINTY PRINCIPLE

have made a plan to meet again but they'd only see each other a bit more. She'd still be living on the *Graceland*, floating aimlessly. It's not a real life. It's not going anywhere.

Sadie thinks she should stay on the boat, isolated and alone, like quarantine. It's as if Mia is infected with weirdness and has to be separated from the general population, like she's untouchable. *It's true*, Mia thinks. *It's like I've got a rare virus and have to live in lockdown forever.*

But something in her rebels, a small kick of desperation. *Maybe there's more out there*, she thinks. *Maybe this isn't the only solution. Maybe I can crack the code if I go somewhere else.*

"What are you thinking?" her dad asks. "You still want to go?"

He asks it hoping she'll stay.

"I'm leaving," Mia says, uncertain, but feeling like Tennessee can't be worse than her life now.

~~

She wakes up the next morning to the sound of the anchor coming up. She makes her way groggily on deck. Her mom has the helm and her dad is managing the anchor chain on the bow. Kaden isn't on deck so he's probably still asleep, though the mainsail is flapping loudly in the wind.

"Can you pull the mainsheet?" her mom asks gently and Mia cranks the winch, bringing the boom in and tightening up the sail. The lines groan with tension as the sail catches the wind. It's a sound that Mia has come to love because it means the boat is transferring the power of wind into the boat, pushing them forward.

"Coming about," her mom says, spinning the wheel. The boat turns away from shore. Mia automatically cranks in the jib sheet as the boom sweeps over the cockpit and the jib flops over to the starboard tack. They move across the bay and the wind freshens. In a moment, the *Graceland* is rising and falling on five-foot rollers and is headed southeast.

Kaden comes up; the jostling woke him. He sits next to Mia in the cockpit and leans sleepily against her. He's warm and his hair smells like cereal. There are moments like these when her heart swells with love for him, as long as he doesn't talk or do anything. She puts her arm around him and he snuggles closer to her.

Looking around now, it doesn't seem so bad. Her dad sits across the cockpit and smiles at her. It's a blue-sky day and the breeze whips up the salty smell of the ocean. Even her mom is being nice.

But she knows it's temporary. Her mom isn't going to change, nor is the fact that she's the only teenager anywhere around. It'd be easier if she was going back to Minnesota. At least it would be familiar and maybe she could try to fix things with Sadie. Tennessee is a big blank.

She tries to picture her family without her. Kaden will be so lonely, he'll spend even more time reading his copy of *Captain Underpants* over and over. He'll want to talk to her but there will be no way to call. She'll hear from them once every few weeks when they pull into a harbor with an open Wi-Fi signal. She knows they'll miss her, each in their own way. And she'll miss them. They will be a small dot out there on the enormity of the sea, nearly invisible and unreachable.

"You want to take over?" her mom asks, offering Mia the helm.

Normally, Mia would resist any extra work but since this might be one of her last chances to sail the boat, she nods and takes the wheel. Lene sits down beside her and turns her face into the breeze. Her whole family is quiet, enjoying the feeling of the full sails, the wind rushing past, and the boat cutting through the waves.

THE UNCERTAINTY PRINCIPLE

For a moment, Mia feels a sense of control. She's at the helm, in charge of everything.

"Won't get this in Tennessee," Lene points out.

It does seem unlikely that Mia will feel better than this when she gets to Tennessee, at least at first. But she shakes off the feeling. Control is an illusion as long as she's on the boat with her mom. At least by going to Tennessee, she is taking control away from Izzy.

As they round the point of Île Fourchue, Mia spots an island to the southeast. It's long and narrow, with steep mountains rising up out of the water and white and pink houses clinging to the cliffs. She's seen countless islands; this one is prettier than most.

"It's called Saint Barth," her mom says. "It's where the rich people go. It's part of the French West Indies."

Mia aims the boat toward the western side of the island, and they start to see other vessels. Mia feels a stab of anxiety. Could Alby be here? She nervously scans the horizon but the boats are fancy. There's a sleek seventy-foot catamaran that looks like a futuristic flying car. After that, there's a 150-foot megayacht at anchor. It's flying the Kuwaiti flag and is three stories tall. Both boats look like they could eat the *Graceland* and still be hungry.

As they get closer, the small town of Gustavia appears around a point. It's nestled around a small bay and serves as the island's only port. Mia fires up the engine, points the boat into the wind, and they drop the sails quickly before motoring slowly into the bay. The place is densely packed with Caribbean-style bungalows with cute red metal roofs. The bungalows rise up the steep green hills surrounding the rectangular harbor. Little cars and mopeds zip along the waterside main street. It's bustling but it looks like it wouldn't take more than fifteen minutes to walk from one end of town to the other. Everything from the

113

houses to the palm-lined streets seems perfectly placed except for the fact that the harbor is jammed with yachts.

Each yacht is bigger than any building in town and it seems like it'd be impossible to fit them all in the small harbor. But somehow there are nearly a dozen of them lined up side by side. Each one is festooned with fenders so they gently bounce off each other like slow-motion bumper boats. They're backed into the wharf, allowing passengers to simply step off the stern and saunter into town.

"You want me to get us in?" Izzy asks.

Mia eyes a narrow spot on the wharf that isn't taken. It's not much bigger than the *Graceland*. Pulling in will be like parallel parking a forty-foot RV that doesn't want to stop. But Mia wants to show her mom, Sadie, Alby, everyone, that she is a capable human being who can take care of herself.

"I've got it," she says, trying to project confidence.

"You sure?"

"I've got it," Mia insists.

Lene wags her finger. "Don't get a big head and think you can do everything."

Mia aims the boat for the gap and eases back on the throttle. Her dad looks worried. "Coming in a little hot," he says.

"I'm fine."

Mia aims for the gap while her dad hustles to the bow. He grabs a line and gets ready to jump to the wharf.

"Based on my extensive understanding of Newton's laws of motion, I would say you are screwing this up royally," Lene says.

"Hot, hot, hot," her dad shouts from the bow.

"Mia!" her mom shouts as they head straight for the dock.

"Be quiet," Mia orders with such command, her mother freezes.

Mia spins the wheel hard to starboard and throws the boat into full

THE UNCERTAINTY PRINCIPLE

reverse as it glides into the slot between two massive sailboats. The small motor strains against the forward momentum and the boat shudders. Her dad steps over the railing, leaps onto the stone surface of the dock, and quickly ties the boat to a cleat but it's barely necessary: Mia has brought the *Graceland* in perfectly.

"All right," Izzy says, calming down. "That was pretty great."

"Everything moves in a straight line unless it's compelled to change," Mia says defiantly, looking at Lene. "Newton's first law of motion."

Chapter 19

Her dad takes their passports to the small immigration building. They have to stay on the boat until they're officially cleared so she leans against the mast and draws the harbor in her journal, which is filled with equations, calculations, and sketches of plants. In the foreground, she draws Kaden, who is hanging off the bow, throwing small pieces of bread to the enormous carp swimming around the wharf's pilings. The road across the street from the dock is lined with luxury shops: Hermès, Dolce & Gabbana, Cartier. The place seems designed for the ultrawealthy and Mia can already see pedestrians glancing at the *Graceland*, which looks like it just emerged from the 1800s. They clearly don't belong here.

"This is what's wrong with the world," Izzy says, sitting next to Mia and looking around. "You've got people with so much money that they don't even have to think about it, and I made eight dollars an hour. How does that make sense?"

"Maybe because they're actually contributing something to the world."

Izzy glares at her for a second but softens. "You may not believe it, but I worked hard. There was just no way we were going to get ahead. Every time the car broke or we got a parking ticket, it was like falling through a trapdoor and we were broke again. And I know you think I've ruined your life, but I truly am trying my best."

"I think she's being real with you," Lene says, touched. Mia can't

THE UNCERTAINTY PRINCIPLE

decide how to feel. Everybody else in the world somehow makes life work. Why can't her mom?

She sees her dad walking back and stands up to end the conversation. She doesn't want to get emotional right now. Her mom stands up beside her.

"I just want you to know I love you," Izzy says hurriedly, holding back her tears. "And I'll miss you every day."

"Everything okay?" Ethan asks cautiously, looking at his wife sniffing next to his daughter.

"Everything's fine," Izzy says, rubbing Mia's shoulder. Mia notices that Izzy doesn't rush to disinfect Ethan after his visit with the harbormaster. It's the first time she's relaxed the rules a bit and the thought crops up in Mia's mind: *Maybe my mother could change?*

"What'd you figure out?" Izzy asks Ethan.

"Well, we can get Paul on WhatsApp," he says, explaining that he's got his cell phone connected to the harbormaster's Wi-Fi. He looks at Mia for one last confirmation. "Yeah?"

Mia looks at Izzy. The sight of her glistening eyes makes it hard, but she also doesn't want to be blackmailed by her mom's emotions. "Yeah," she says, closing her journal. "Let's call."

"All righty," he says and dials his brother, who picks up quickly. It's been a while since she's seen her dad talk on the phone. She'd forgotten that he's awkward too, even with his brother. "Yeah, we're good. How are you? Good. Good. Great. Super. Great. Good to hear. Yeah. Well, uh . . ."

Ethan glances at Mia nervously. This is it.

"Well, hey, I got a question for you," Ethan goes on, turning his attention to his feet. "It's basically that Mia is kind of wanting to go back to high school. And you know, we were wondering what you'd think about her coming to stay with you in Chattanooga."

Ethan wanders down the wharf. Mia can't hear him and she guesses her dad wants to talk to Paul privately.

She looks down at her hands. There's a rough spot of skin next to her thumbnail. She pulls at it until a tiny ribbon of skin peels off. It hurts but it also helps cut through the confusion she's feeling. A drop of blood pools on her nail.

"You're going to have to figure out how to deal with yourself," Izzy says, looking sad and defeated. "I'm not going to be able to help you anymore."

Mia smiles. "I could do with less help from you," she says with as much love as she can manage.

Izzy laughs darkly. "I wish that were true."

"He wants to talk to you," her dad says, walking back to the boat and raising the phone to Mia.

She jumps onto the wharf and walks away from the boat with the phone even though she knows her mom wants to listen.

"What's going on, kiddo?" Paul says, sounding chipper as always. "I hear you've had enough."

She's always liked her uncle. He's warm and direct and wears khakis and a button-up, even on the weekends. Her mom calls him "strait-laced" and "very boring," but Mia has long dreamed of trading lives. Boring sounds good right now.

Paul was also skeptical of Ethan and Izzy's decision to walk away from the world, so he isn't surprised to hear that Mia wants out. "I don't blame you a bit and if you want to come live with us, we'd be glad to have you."

He says that there's only one issue: The spring term starts in a week. She'd need to leave now to make it in time.

"At the latest, you've got to fly out in a few days maybe," he says. "So you kind of have to decide now. Are you really serious about this?"

THE UNCERTAINTY PRINCIPLE

She looks back down the wharf at the *Graceland*. Her parents are standing in the cockpit talking and looking concerned. After living on the boat for months, some part of her thinks of it as home. And maybe Alby will reappear at some point.

But it's the crumbs of a life. She wants the full meal. She wants what everybody else has. She wants a chance to try again.

"Yeah, I'm serious," she says. "I want to come back."

"Well, then it's decided. Why don't you put your dad back on?"

She walks back, climbs aboard, and her parents stop talking. It all feels surreal. Mia hands the phone to her dad, who takes it to the bow, leaving Mia in the cockpit with her mom.

"Well?" Izzy says in a challenging tone.

"I've got to leave this week to make it back in time for the spring term."

Her mom folds her arms and purses her lips. "So that's it."

"Yeah, I guess so."

Her dad comes back. He's off the phone and back to burying his emotions by focusing on logistics. "So here's the deal. We've got to get to Saint Martin, which is about a day's sail away. Paul is booking a flight for you that will leave from there in three days and go to Charlotte and then Chattanooga."

"Thanks," Mia says, not knowing what else to say. "I'm sure we'll find a way to talk and—"

"I've got a headache," Izzy says, turning away from her. "I'll be down below."

Izzy disappears, leaving Mia, Kaden, and her dad on deck. Kaden has stopped feeding the fish.

"Mom's upset," Ethan explains to Kaden.

"Because Mia's leaving?"

"Yeah."

Kaden gets up and walks over to Mia. He looks angry, but then he wraps his arms around her waist.

"I don't want you to leave," he says, nuzzling his face into her stomach.

"I know." She hugs him and feels a lump in her throat.

Ethan looks anxiously toward the hatchway; they can hear Izzy start scrubbing something below deck. "Why don't the two of you check out the harbor? Spend some time together."

It's a rare treat for them to be let loose in a port so she doesn't ask any questions. Kaden knows something unusual is happening as well and they jump onto the wharf quickly. He grabs her hand, and they head along the waterfront into town.

As they walk along the promenade, Kaden keeps glancing up at her happily. It's been a long time since they held hands. It's something they did when they were younger, when things didn't seem so complicated. He swings her hand and she lets him until he gets carried away and starts swinging her hand wildly back and forth and giggling with boyish glee.

"Okay, enough of that," she says, putting an arm around his shoulder to calm him down.

They follow a road that runs smack into the fenced-in patio of an open-air burger stand. The road forks in three directions, as if the burger stand refused to move and they built the road around it. There aren't any stop signs or stoplights and nobody seems to be in a rush. A hand-painted sign of a burger hangs off an old tree. It says "Le Select—Avoiding Progress Since 1949." An occasional small car or dune buggy lumbers up to the fork and lazily chooses a direction. The whole island moves in slow motion.

"I wish we could get something to eat," Kaden says, knowing they don't have any money. They never do. They are about halfway through a fifty-pound bag of pinto beans and usually mix that with either rice or whatever vegetables they can buy when they dock.

They stand for a moment, looking hungrily at the smattering of people eating at rickety wooden tables. "Come on, let's keep walking," Mia says, not wanting to torture themselves.

They follow one of the forks around the burger place and head down a cobblestoned road. It's lined with a strange mix of decrepit wood buildings and fancy shops selling cigars, woven hats, and hulking wristwatches.

The narrow road winds through the town until it dead-ends at a sandy cove behind the harbor. There's a beachside restaurant and a few sunbathers. A sign made out of painted ceramic tiles identifies the spot as Shell Beach and sure enough, there are thousands of small shells in the sand.

"Look," Kaden says, pointing down the rocky shore to a guy perched on the edge of a cliff. He raises his arms dramatically and leaps off, falling forty feet and making a big splash. After a moment, he pops to the surface. A young woman stands at the top, trying to decide whether to jump.

"Can we try?" Kaden says.

Mia doesn't like heights but she's trying to be nice so she says okay. Kaden pulls off his T-shirt and they leave it under their flip-flops on the sand. They wade into the warm water in their shorts, Mia with a sports bra. One of the perks of living on a boat in the tropics is that you can pretty much wear one outfit for everything: sailing, swimming, exploring.

The cliff is farther than it looks, and it takes about ten minutes to get there. Right as they swim up, the guy hurtles off again, arcing gracefully into the water headfirst.

When he surfaces, he looks back up at the top. The girl peers timidly over the edge. Her skin is light brown like the man's and she's wearing an orange bikini with green polka dots. She's a teenager; probably about the same age as Mia.

"You see?" the man shouts. He has an Indian accent. "It's easy."

He looks over at Mia and Kaden, who are treading water nearby. "She's a chicken," he says. He's in his midforties, and his silver-white hair is cut in a precise crew cut. He seems upset. "I'm not going to wait all day," he shouts at the girl.

"Go back then," the girl shouts back.

"She's been up there for an hour," he says to Mia and Kaden, disgusted.

"It's pretty high," Mia observes diplomatically.

"Mind over matter," he says, tapping his head. "That's all."

He turns away and waves up at the girl. "Nisha, you'll never respect yourself if you don't do this. You'll honestly be so disappointed in yourself."

Kaden glances at Mia, alarmed at the man's intensity.

"Go back," the girl shouts with a combination of anger, frustration, and shame.

"Fine," the man says. He shakes his head, casts a sour look at Mia, and heads toward shore.

Once he's out of earshot, Kaden swims close to Mia. "Is he really leaving her?"

"I guess so," Mia responds, surprised.

"That's not very nice."

"Yeah, I feel bad for her."

Mia looks up and sees the girl leaning over again, trying to steel herself. She is all alone now.

Mia swims to the cliff face. There's a light swell crashing against the rock, threatening to bash them against the wall. She wonders how

THE UNCERTAINTY PRINCIPLE

people get up there and then spots a slimy, knotted rope hanging off the rock. She floats over to it and uses it to steady herself.

"This is not easy," she tells Kaden, her hands slipping.

"I can do it," he says, trying to swim up to her, but a wave surges forward, pushing him toward the rock.

"Stay back," she warns, throwing her feet up out of the water against the rock wall to prevent herself from getting smashed. It works but now she sees that the rock beneath her is dotted with spiny purple dots.

"Sea urchins," she shouts. It's like an underwater minefield. "I don't know if we should do this."

"Let me try."

"No way." She's the big sister. She knows she's abandoning him on the boat and the guilt makes her feel even more protective right now. She puts her feet on the rock, waits for the swell to lift her, and pulls herself up hand over hand onto a narrow ledge above the water. Once she's up, she reaches down and hauls Kaden out of the water like a giant fish, plopping him down on the ledge.

"You didn't have to pull me," he splutters.

"The swell was dangerous."

"No, it wasn't."

Lene climbs up the rope in her blazer, slacks, and turtleneck, water pouring off her. "We should call this off," she says, wiping the water off her face. "It's a bad idea." Mia looks at the cliff. It's straight up and looks even more daunting now that they're at the base of it.

"Okay, let's go back," Mia tells Kaden, but before she can stop him, he's climbed up above her. "Kaden!"

"It's fine," he shouts, scampering up the cliff. He accidentally kicks a rock loose and it cracks down beside Mia and ricochets into the water.

"Kaden!"

"Sorry."

"Come back down."

"What? It's easy." He looks down at her with a mischievous grin. "You'll be safer up here if another rock falls."

"I don't like your options," Lene notes. She's taken off her blazer and wrings out the seawater. "If you stay, you'll probably get hit with a falling rock. But if you climb, you'll probably fall. So basically, you're screwed."

Mia looks up again. Kaden is focusing on the rock, trying not to slip, and is nearly at the top. If she doesn't go after him, he'll be by himself up there with a stranger. "Damn it," she mutters and starts climbing.

The rock is sunbaked and the heat warms her face. As she gets higher off the water, her hands start to sweat, making it even harder to hang on to the rock.

"Rock!"

Mia pushes herself flat against the wall as another rock flies by her head and splashes into the water below.

"You trying to kill me?"

"It just came off."

Mia looks over her shoulder and gauges how far she'd have to push off the wall in order to land in the water if she slips. It's pretty far and it seems like she'd hit the cliff ledge first and go spinning fatally into the sea.

"You have to wait for me," she shouts. She tries to make it sound like she wants to keep an eye on him but really she wants him near to make her less scared.

"You'll be fine," he says, sounding a lot more mature than a ten-year-old. In fact, he sounds more mature than her right now.

"If you drop a rock and a feather in a vacuum, which hits the ground first?" Lene says, standing on a ledge to Mia's right.

THE UNCERTAINTY PRINCIPLE

"Stop it."

"First of all, that was a trick question. They hit the ground at the same time because gravity is the same everywhere. That's amazing, right?"

Mia grabs hold of a rock edge above her but when she pulls, it pops loose. She loses her balance and spins away from the wall. She has to wrench herself back to avoid falling. Lene barely notices.

"The thing about gravity is that it's this mysterious force that no one understands and here you are, really getting into it."

"I don't want to get into it," Mia grumbles. She tries to steady her breathing.

"You might feel like you're falling but really gravity is pulling you toward something. That's what it does. It's about attraction."

Mia ignores her and focuses on finding something else to grab onto. She gets a grip on an outcrop and gingerly pulls herself up.

"You okay?" Kaden shouts from the top.

"I'm going to beat you when I get up there."

She moves deliberately, testing each handhold before she puts any weight on it, and after a few long minutes of intense, nervous attention, she bellies over the top and lies facedown like a beached seal on the blissfully flat top.

"Slowpoke," Kaden says, hurling a rock into the water below.

"Shut up."

He disappears behind some boulders to hunt for more rocks. Mia rolls over onto her back and sees the girl ten feet away. She doesn't seem to be doing well. She's twisting side to side, hugging herself. It looks like she's having a nervous breakdown.

Mia wipes her sweaty hands off on her legs and glances over the edge of the cliff. There's no way they're going to be able to climb back down. She's not even sure how they made it up here. Now she understands why the girl is freaking out. They are *really* high. The only way down is to jump, and the drop looks deadly. They're stuck.

Lene plops down beside her. She's panting and her face is red with exertion. "That was not fun," she wheezes.

"This was your idea."

"I simply pointed out that you were screwed no matter what you did."

"You could have said don't go."

"Are you talking to me?" the girl says.

Mia realizes that the girl is looking at her. Mia wasn't talking loudly and figured the girl wasn't paying attention. But clearly not.

"I was just saying this is messed up," Mia replies, trying to cover for herself.

The girl laughs darkly. "You're telling me. Biggest mistake of my life coming up here."

She looks angry and wounded, with hazel eyes and long black hair that's slightly red in the sun. Her orange-and-green polka-dot bikini must be brand-new—Mia didn't know a piece of fabric could be so orange—and she wears five gold bangles on her left wrist. Her fingernails are painted the same shade of orange as her bikini, which is both astounding and impressive. Up close, she has the high cheekbones, puffy lips, and perfectly plucked eyebrows of the models in clothing catalogs.

But she's also gangly, with long arms that dangle near her knees and knobby shoulders. Her hip bones jut out so that her bikini bottom is stretched taut and floats a fraction of an inch off her stomach. It's not that she's skinny, it's more that she's still growing into her body. Mia can't remember seeing anyone so beautiful in person.

"You should probably say something," Lene says, doing push-ups for no reason. "She's looking at you like you're a psycho."

THE UNCERTAINTY PRINCIPLE

Mia automatically runs through everything Sadie taught her about talking to other girls. But Sadie never gave her any rules for a situation like this. Mia is stuck at the top of a forty-foot cliff with a beautiful stranger in a bikini.

"Ask her if she's a Swiftie," Lene prompts, switching to sit-ups. "That's Sadie's top recommendation."

Mia thinks about it but realizes that it doesn't make any sense to talk about Taylor Swift right now. In fact, Mia decides that Sadie probably wouldn't give her any good advice since Sadie has never been in a situation like this.

"Cowabunga!"

Kaden sprints from behind a boulder and leaps off the cliff, screaming and flailing his arms.

"Kaden!" Mia shouts, rushing to the edge as he hurtles through the air. He free-falls for what seems like forever and impacts the water, sending up a huge splash. After a moment, his head pops up.

"Are you okay?" Mia shouts down.

"I'm fine. It's fun."

"You gave me a heart attack."

"Your brother?" the girl asks.

"Yeah, unfortunately."

Now it's just the two of them and they stand there for a moment looking down. Mia's head spins with vertigo and the palms of her hands start to sweat again.

"Got any advice?" Mia asks, feeling like she needs guidance as usual.

"Me? I'm a total disaster. This is my worst nightmare."

Mia tries hard to think of something to say. "You know if you dropped a feather and a rock in a vacuum, they'd hit the water at the same time."

The girl looks confused. Mia probably shouldn't have said anything. But now that she has, she feels the need to explain, hoping that might help. "Because, you know, gravity is the same throughout the universe."

"That's right," Lene shouts. She's doing jumping jacks now. "Lay some science on her."

"So who's the rock and who's the feather?" the girl asks.

"Oh no, I wasn't comparing—"

"I guess I'm the rock?" She looks down at her stomach.

"No, I wasn't talking about you."

"I've definitely put on some weight," the girl says, patting her bare stomach, which looks remarkably flat. "My dad says I have anyway."

"Then he's a jerk."

The girl is taken aback, and Mia realizes she said too much. "I'm sorry, I don't know anything about him," Mia stammers, trying to backpedal. She's already made multiple blunders and they haven't even been talking for a minute.

But the girl laughs. "You don't need to apologize. He *is* a jerk."

"I shouldn't have said anything," Mia says, picking at her fingers. This is how it always begins. Mia says something dumb and then people walk away.

"No, seriously, nobody calls him on his shit," the girl says, looking at Mia. "You're, like, the first person."

Mia is relieved the girl isn't upset but she's also unnerved by the fact that the conversation is continuing. Mia shifts from foot to foot, unsure what to do next.

"He got me a Peloton for my birthday," the girl says. "You know the one with the screen that swivels so you can do other kinds of workouts? He says he'll get me an Audi TT if I lose ten pounds."

Mia doesn't know what to say. To put the girl at ease, Mia decides to let her know that she's not the only one with problems.

"My parents have basically held me hostage on a boat for six months."

The girl laughs, thinking it's a joke. But then she sees that Mia isn't smiling and she looks sideways at her. "Wait, are you serious?"

"Yeah, pretty much," Mia says, now worried that she overshared again. After all, most parents don't kidnap their kids.

The girl eyes Mia's frayed sports bra, wild, windblown hair, shredded hands, and deep tan. "So how'd you end up here?" she asks, intrigued.

"They let me off the boat for a bit," Mia says, wishing she hadn't said anything.

Mia hears Kaden shout from over the edge of the cliff. She can't see him so she steps carefully to the lip. It gives her butterflies just looking down.

"You coming?" he shouts.

Mia looks back at the girl. She can't leave Kaden there much longer. "You want to jump together?"

The girl hesitates. Mia can see her trying to calculate how crazy Mia is and whether it's a good idea to tie their fates together.

"We can go at the same time," Mia says. She instinctively feels like it's the only way either of them will get down.

"I'm really scared," the girl says.

"Me too," Mia says. It feels good to admit that she's scared, not just about jumping off this cliff, but about almost everything.

They barely know each other but they're on the verge of flinging themselves off a cliff into the abyss. Even though Kaden and the girl's dad already did it, it's different when you're the one jumping. They hold each other's gaze, two strangers a moment ago but now feeling a sudden bond.

The girl nervously rolls her right foot on its side and juts her bony hip out. She wobbles a little, off balance. It makes her seem younger, more vulnerable, and Mia feels a wave of sympathy for this girl whose dad abandoned her.

"Okay," the girl says at last. "Let's try."

"We're either going or not," Mia says, not wanting to fling herself off the cliff with someone who might hesitate at the last moment. "You have to decide."

They look at each other, neither of them smiling now.

"That's, like, the most badass thing anybody has ever said to me."

Time slows down. It's like they're the only two people in the world right now.

"So?" Mia says.

"Okay," the girl responds. "We'll go together."

It feels like they've just signed a suicide pact.

"I'll count to three and we'll run, okay?" Mia says.

"Okay."

"All right, one . . ."

She can hear the girl's shallow breathing.

"Two . . ."

The girl looks at Mia, panic in her eyes.

"Three!"

Mia starts running and the girl follows but she's screaming like someone is attacking her. They reach the edge and, without breaking stride, leap together. Mia didn't think the girl would go through with it but now they're plummeting in a torrent of screams and flailing arms.

They smash into the water and shoot below the surface. Bubbles explode all around them, and then they pop back to the surface, gasping for air.

"Oh my god," the girl says, her face aglow. "We did it."

She reaches over to Mia and they give each other a triumphant high five. Mia feels like she stepped across the threshold from one reality to another and now she's a new, different person, bobbing easily alongside her friend. Somehow, the intensity of the jump erased any feeling she had that she needed to make pointless small talk with this girl. This stranger now feels like someone she's known forever.

The girl looks to shore. There's no sign of her dad and the glow fades from her face.

"You want to hear a crazy idea?" Mia asks, not wanting the moment to end. The girl glances back at her.

"Okay," she replies cautiously.

"Let's do it again."

"Yeah," Kaden chirps, floating nearby.

"You're out of your mind," the girl says, looking wide-eyed at Mia.

"The first time, I was too scared to pay attention."

The girl shakes her head, but she can't stop a small, nervous smile from growing. "I really don't want to," she says.

"I know, but let's do it anyway."

The girl laughs. "I just met you and you're already bossing me around."

Mia smiles, amazed at the idea that she could boss anyone around. She kind of likes the way it feels. "It'll be easier the second time," Mia says. "I promise."

The girl looks at Mia for a second and then dips her face into the water. Mia can hear her yelling underwater. She surfaces and says, "Okay, let's go."

They swim back to the cliff and carefully climb the slimy rope to the first ledge. They let Kaden dart to the top and stand to the side to avoid the rocks he kicks off as he climbs up.

"This is so wrong," the girl says. "I don't even know your name and I let you talk me into this."

"I'm Mia."

"Nisha. Funny way to meet someone, right? On the side of a cliff."

"Jumping for no good reason."

"I don't even have my phone so no one's going to know I did this. It's basically like it didn't happen."

"I'll know you did it," Mia says.

"Mmmm," Nisha says doubtfully, flashing the kind of patronizing smile somebody with a lot of followers bestows on the unloved and unfollowed. Mia notices that her teeth are perfect, like she started wearing braces in kindergarten. Her black hair is pin straight and dripping down her back. Everything about her seems fancy, exactly the kind of person who's an influencer.

"Okay, let's go," Mia says once Kaden crests the cliff. They climb slowly, carefully, and without looking down. Both Mia and Nisha are so focused on the rock, they don't say a word. Just as they make it to the top, Kaden catapults off the edge, squealing with glee.

"Oh my god, your brother is going to kill me," Nisha says as they get their bearings again on the flat top of the cliff.

"I think I got all the fear and he got all the recklessness."

"I don't know, this is pretty reckless right now and it's your idea, but okay, whatever," Nisha chatters nervously, trying to keep the conversation going to distract herself. "You on spring break too? We're just here for a week and then I'm back at school."

"I don't go to school."

"Really," Nisha says, furrowing her brow. "How's that even possible?"

THE UNCERTAINTY PRINCIPLE

"We just took off and nobody chased us."

"No shit," Nisha says, a hint of worry in her voice. "Are you, like, on the run?"

Mia laughs. "You mean, like, did we rob a bank?"

"I didn't, uh . . ." Nisha trails off, worried that she might be in the presence of a real criminal.

It's nice to be taken seriously rather than as an oddball who isn't worth talking to. Mia kind of likes the idea of being a criminal. "I guess we are kind of on the run," she says.

"From what?" Nisha says cautiously, not wanting to pry but clearly curious.

"Yeah, that's the problem. We don't know what we're running from."

Nisha squints at Mia, trying to make sense of her. "I guess I'm confused," she says.

"We're just aimlessly wandering for no reason."

Nisha watches her for a moment, trying to decide whether to keep asking questions. Mia told the truth, but it seems to have created an aura of mystery.

"Well?" Mia says, nodding at the lip of the cliff.

"It's just so far down," Nisha says, shelving her questions and focusing on the jump. Nervousness crackles through her and she hugs herself.

Mia feels a protective urge. She wants to hold Nisha's hand, squeeze it, and tell her it'll be okay. Instead, she just stands there, worried that grabbing her hand is too forward.

They look at each other and Nisha holds out her hand, catching Mia by surprise. Could she read her mind? Mia wordlessly takes her hand; it's cold, drained of heat by the chill of the water and the fear.

"Okay, it's you and me," Nisha says. And without saying anything more, they hurl themselves over the edge again.

Chapter 20

The girls walk out of the water and onto the beach, talking excitedly. They debate how high the cliff was, each coming up with a bigger number until the cliff is a skyscraper. Lene and Kaden trail behind them, ignored.

"The water hit my arms so hard," Nisha says, showing Mia the red undersides of her arms. "Like I got slapped."

French reggae floats out of the cove's restaurant and Mia sees Nisha's dad at a table filled with people. The restaurant rises out of the beach like a chic tree house with multiple levels. The middle level is dotted with bed-like couches. Nisha's dad lies back on one while a waitress in short shorts hands out rum-filled coconuts. Nisha is looking at the cliff so her back is to the restaurant. She seems to have forgotten about her dad for the moment but he notices them and stands up.

It's going to be over fast now, Mia thinks. He will walk up, they'll chat for a moment, then say goodbye and that'll be it. Mia wants to ask Nisha what she's doing tomorrow. She wants to keep swimming and talking about jumping off cliffs. She doesn't want it to end but she doesn't know how to say it. Nisha looks like the type of super-popular girl who has lots of friends and doesn't need another. She reminds her in a way of Sadie. And maybe, like Sadie, Nisha just doesn't need a friend like Mia.

The thought stings and Mia starts to steel herself for a rejection. What would Mia do with a friend now anyway? She's leaving. There's no point. And she just tried to be friends with Alby—or more than

THE UNCERTAINTY PRINCIPLE

friends—and it didn't work out too well. So she just stands there, her smile fading as Nisha's dad approaches.

"You did it!" he shouts, pulling Nisha into a bear hug and swinging her back and forth. "I didn't think you would."

"Mia helped me," Nisha says, smiling with a mix of embarrassment and happiness from inside her dad's smothering embrace.

"Ah, I was wondering," he says, releasing his daughter and looking at Mia. He narrows his eyes, nodding in appreciation. "A tough cookie. You've got that badass look going with the ponytails. Like if Pippi Longstocking was an assassin. You a Pippi Longstocking fan?"

"Uhh . . ."

"Well look, you got her to man up, which isn't easy, so kudos to you."

Nisha stares at the sand, looking horrified.

"Anyway, you gotta come up because everybody wants to congratulate you," he says to Nisha. He points at Mia and gives her a grin. "Nicely done."

He walks away with Nisha under his arm, talking about how he bet five hundred dollars she wouldn't jump but it was worth losing. Nisha looks back and gives Mia a sad wave. Mia watches them walk into the open-air restaurant.

Mia is shocked by the whole encounter. He bet *against* her? And who has that kind of money to throw around?

"Well, let's head back," Mia tells Kaden sadly.

"Who's Pippi Longstocking?" Kaden asks.

"I have no idea," Mia sighs, putting her arm over Kaden's shoulder and turning them back toward the harbor.

"She was a mess," Lene says, walking beside them. "You didn't want to hang out with her anyway."

Mia is pretty sure she *did* want to hang out with her and wonders if she'll see her around the harbor before they leave. She's pissed at

135

herself for not saying anything, for missing the chance, and pissed at life for doing this twice. She doesn't see any teenagers for months and now meets two people in the span of a week?

It makes her think about Alby and the idea that God has a plan. If there is some kind of higher power, then it has a sick sense of humor, constantly dangling the hope of a better future and then jerking it away from her.

"Hey!"

Mia turns and sees Nisha running back through the sand. She's breathless but clearly happy to have caught them before they disappeared.

"Hey," Mia says, a warmth spreading out from her chest to her fingers.

"I'm so sorry about him," Nisha apologizes. "He's just a giant pain in everyone's ass."

Mia laughs. "It's okay," she says. "I can handle it."

"I wanted to ask if you want to come to lunch with us tomorrow?"

Mia smiles. She tries to play it cool and not look too excited.

"Uh, sure." But now she worries that she's playing it too cool. "Yeah, totally."

"Okay, give me your number and we'll coordinate on WhatsApp."

"My phone doesn't really work," Mia says, embarrassed. "I built a satellite phone but I can't receive calls on it so . . ."

"Uh, okay," Nisha says, confused and unsure what to do. "I guess maybe we go old school? Like say noon at Nikki Beach?"

"Oh, yeah, okay," Mia says, pretending she knows what Nikki Beach is. It's bad enough that she doesn't have a working phone; she doesn't want to come across as even more of a dork. "Noon at Nikki Beach. I'll see you there."

Nisha smiles at her. "Perfect," she says.

Chapter 21

The **harbormaster charges** twenty euros a day to tie up to the dock so they motor *Graceland* outside the harbor and drop anchor. There's a collection of battered boats clustered there, some tied to buoys, others anchored. It's a motley collection of vessels. There are a few sailboats with no masts and a handful of once-grand motorboats with boarded-up windows. Most of them appear to be abandoned.

In deeper water a little farther out, there are four gleaming megayachts. Each one looks like a monstrous shiny grand piano. The *Graceland* is wedged between the derelict boats and the hundred-million-dollar ones.

Mia waits for the right time to bring up the lunch. Her dad wants to sail for Saint Martin tomorrow and figure out how to get to the airport. They don't really need to be there three days early but he gets antsy if he doesn't know every step of the itinerary in advance. Her mother doesn't want to spend too much time on an island as populated at Saint Martin so she's arguing they wait a day or two.

"What are you going to say when your mom asks who these people are?" Lene demands while Mia listens to her parents debate. "And where the heck is Nikki Beach?"

They're all good questions and Mia doesn't have answers.

"Mia made another friend," Kaden blurts, interrupting their parents.

He's probably hoping that this development will somehow lead to Mia staying.

"Kaden!" Mia snaps.

Her parents look at Mia, confused.

"Mia is going to have lunch—" Kaden tries to explain.

"Let me tell them," Mia interrupts. "Jeez."

"What's going on?" her dad asks, worried that it'll impact his planning.

"Kaden and I met someone on the beach behind the harbor and the family invited me to lunch tomorrow."

"Who are they?" her mom asks, already concerned.

"I told you so," Lene says.

The question annoys Mia. She doesn't want to admit to her mother that she doesn't know. She also doesn't want to say anything that might endanger lunch. She just wants her mom to say yes and stop asking questions.

"I don't know, they're nice people."

"The dad is a jerk," Kaden says.

"I am going to smack you," Mia hisses. Rather than keep answering questions, she tells the whole story: how they met on the cliff and how Nisha asked her to meet at Nikki Beach.

"Where's that?" Izzy asks.

Mia's anger spikes again. "I don't know," she's forced to say.

Her mom nods with a tight smile and Mia can see it coming before she even starts talking.

"I thought we were going to spend our last few days together," Izzy says, trying to make it sound fun. "I mean, we're not going to see you for a while."

"It's just lunch," Mia says. "I'll be right back."

THE UNCERTAINTY PRINCIPLE

"I think we kind of need to head out of here tomorrow," Ethan says, still focused on logistics.

"We don't need to be in Saint Martin for another three days," Mia says. "We have plenty of time to figure out where the airport is."

That quiets him down, but her mom is stewing. "You really want to get away from us that bad?" she says.

"It's not that," Mia says, deploying her best argument. "If we sail for Saint Martin tomorrow, we're going to spend our last few days in a big harbor on a giant island. This place is a lot nicer so we might as well have family time here."

She knows it's a mix of truth and manipulation, but she doesn't care. Izzy looks at Ethan, somewhat convinced. He throws up his arms.

"Fine, whatever," he says.

"Can I go with her?" Kaden asks hopefully.

Izzy and Mia speak at the same time, overlapping in a rare moment of agreement.

"Absolutely not."

Chapter 22

That night, down in the galley on the *Graceland*, Izzy hands Mia a Romanesco cauliflower and looks like she might cry.

"I got this in town for you," Izzy says. Mia knew her mom had left the boat because her hands are rubbed raw. Instead of watching the sunset, Izzy had been scrubbing and disinfecting the cans of food she bought in town. Mia was surprised Izzy was even thinking about her in the middle of a germ-filled store.

The cauliflower is like a science experiment gone wrong, like someone nuked a piece of broccoli and it turned into a million tiny broccolis glued together. Izzy knew her daughter would like it. Mia is actually touched.

"It's amazing," Mia says, marveling at the thing. It's a fractal pattern: Each little bud rises out of the one below in a swirl. "We can't cut it. It's like art."

"I'm sorry," her mom says.

"No, we can cut it. It's fine."

"I mean, I'm sorry. About this," she says, waving her hand around the boat. "About messing your life up."

Her mom starts to cry, and Mia tries not to react. She's used to this. Her mom acts like a tyrant and has a meltdown when she doesn't get her way. It's emotional blackmail. But what does it matter now? Mia is leaving so she pulls her mom close and gives her a hug.

"It's okay."

It feels good. They haven't hugged in a long time.

Her dad rumbles down the hatchway holding up a local newspaper.

"Look what I found," he says.

The paper is called *Le News* but doesn't look much like a newspaper: It's a bunch of regular printer pages folded together, like something a middle school would put out. The headline news is about the turtle population on the island. An ad highlights a cheese sale at the market and a small section called "International News" contains a sentence or two on what's happening on the rest of the planet as if it weren't that important.

Her dad puts his finger on a full-page ad on page three. It's a festive drawing of two bottles of champagne and says *Nikki Beach–Live Your Best Life.*

"Nikki Beach," Mia marvels. "You found it."

Her dad scans the bottom of the ad and taps the address. "Baie de St Jean is around the other side of the island," he says. "We can sail there in the morning."

"Looks like a nightclub," her mom says and Mia tenses. There's no way her mom would let her go to a nightclub, even if it was for lunch. A club packed with people seems almost synonymous with sicknesses and disease.

But her mom shrugs, seemingly relaxing the rules for this special occasion. "It sounds like a good adventure."

~~

Mia lies in her bunk that night and puts her hand on the hull. At Scrub Island, when Alby's boat was nearby, the sea was sparkling and magical. Now it just feels cold. On the other side of the hull, buoys with algae-covered chains disappear into the murk. It's like being surrounded by slimy aliens.

She picks a piece of skin off her cuticle and feels a sharp pain. If only it was that easy to get rid of her thoughts. She didn't even bother with the radio tonight. Why waste her time if he's not going to show up? And why try calling Sadie again? If she's going to Tennessee, it's kind of pointless.

She rolls over and sees Lene, who leans against the door of the bunk watching her.

"What?"

"Polka dots."

"What about them?"

"Think about it."

Mia remembers how Nisha looked on top of the cliff. The pure gold bangles jangling on her wrist, the green polka dots offset against the orange on her bikini. Orange with green polka dots sounds like an impossible combination but, on Nisha, it actually worked. It felt like another signal that she had entered a parallel universe, a world where unimaginable color combinations suddenly made sense.

"See?" Lene says. "This is what quantum mechanics is all about."

"You think quantum mechanics is about swimwear?"

"That and the fact that the space around us isn't stable."

Mia taps the hull. "Seems solid."

"It's an illusion. Everything around us is vibrating, shaking, trying to break free at the molecular level but we don't see it with our eyes."

"Okay, sure," Mia says, remembering Nisha's smile when they popped out of the water after their first jump. Lene starts babbling about cats and a guy named Schrödinger and the boat rocks gently, lulling Mia to sleep.

Chapter 23

Getting dropped off for lunch in a boat sounds a lot more glamorous than it is, at least when that boat is the *Graceland*. Mia knew from the beginning that it was a junk heap, but she never felt quite so embarrassed as she does now, motoring slowly into Baie de St Jean.

The bay is lined with a beautiful, mile-long crescent beach. On one side, a short, paved runway dead-ends into the beach. The far end of the runway is jammed into a mountain and Mia watches in wonder as a tiny plane accelerates and lifts off just before it runs into the sand.

On the other side of the bay, a rock promontory juts into the turquoise water. Surprisingly, there's a hotel built into the rock, like something the Swiss Family Robinson would build if they were billionaires. There's a wooden walkway snaking across the sheer rock face, a roof peaked like a wizard's hat, and bungalows cascading down to the water. The bungalows have wooden decks with red lounge chairs that match the red metal roofs. It's easily the most enchanting hotel Mia has ever seen.

The *Graceland*, in comparison, looks like the boat the Swiss Family Robinson abandoned as it sank beneath them. Hotel guests sit up and shade their eyes to get a better view as they putter past. Mia's stomach starts to churn as she realizes the mistake she's made. She's going to arrive at lunch with her entire family in the equivalent of a horse-drawn wagon.

"Maybe I'll swim ashore from here and I'll get them to drop me back in Gustavia this afternoon," Mia tells her mom hurriedly.

"You can't swim in your overalls. You'll be soaked."

Izzy has a point. She wasn't planning to swim. After the bikini debacle on the *Exodus*, Mia decided to revert to her comfort zone. She's wearing her brown Carhartts over her favorite shirt: a rust-red V-neck with the NASA logo.

"Plus, we're already here," Izzy adds.

Mia notices her mom smiling and realizes that this was a ploy. Her mom went along with the offer to sail here so she could keep an eye on her daughter. Mia's nervousness and embarrassment add fuel to her sudden anger.

"Turn the boat back," Mia growls. They round the promontory and Mia can hear music and laughter. She grabs the wheel and spins it out of her mom's hands. "Turn it back!"

"Mia!" her mom snaps, using her hip to shove her away and spinning the wheel back.

"You can't do this to me!"

"Will you two stop it?" her dad says, knowing that neither of them will listen to him.

Mia pushes against her mom and jerks the wheel again, veering the boat back off course. To the patrons of the hotel on the rocky ledges above, it's a strange sight, this cobbled-together boat zigzagging while the two women fight over the helm.

The music intensifies into a deep thud-thud-thud. The sound forces Mia and Izzy to look up. What they see dumbfounds them.

There's a beachfront restaurant that spills onto the white sand and it's packed with people, half of whom are dancing in the water, fully clothed. A DJ on a platform in the middle of the tables waves her hand in the air as she holds headphones to one ear. There appears to be a line

THE UNCERTAINTY PRINCIPLE

of beds on the beach filled with writhing bodies while waiters in rabbit costumes serve huge bottles of champagne.

Mia and her mom stop fighting and take it in. Her mom starts shaking her head, clearly changing her mind. "Oh, there's no way you're going there."

Mia hesitates. It's like nothing she's ever seen. She's never loved big gatherings, particularly with people she doesn't know. But she feels ready for an adventure.

"I'll see you later," Mia says, and leaps overboard.

"Mia!"

She knew her mom was going to try to stop her from going; that was enough to make her jump. Izzy throws the engine into neutral, so Mia isn't in the water with the spinning prop.

"You have no idea what's going on there," her mom says in a more pleading tone. She leans over the starboard railing, keeping one hand on the wheel. "There's germs."

"There are germs everywhere," Mia says from the water. "The world is full of germs."

"This is different."

Mia swims backward for a second, looking at her mom, and then rolls into freestyle, swimming away as fast as she can.

Chapter 24

Mia wades ashore into the midst of the party. The pockets of her overalls are full of water and she has to push them in like balloons, draining the water in a puddle around her feet. The thick cotton of the Carhartts sticks to her legs and her shirt feels like it's shrink-wrapped onto her body. If anyone was paying attention, they'd think her boat just sank and she's the only survivor.

But no one is paying attention. The music is blasting, and the adults are behaving oddly: Women in skintight cat outfits are chasing men dressed as babies. There are tables in the sand piled with towers of seafood and buckets of wine. The baby-men are sucking on pacifiers and laughing. It's like she's landed on another planet.

"Now might be a good time to talk about Heisenberg's uncertainty principle," Lene says, standing beside Mia.

Mia knows the basics from Lene. This guy named Heisenberg was drinking Carlsberg beer in Copenhagen in the 1920s, and he discovered a bunch of things about the universe. First, he appreciated the fact that the beer was crisp and refreshing. Second, he proved that the closer you look at something, the less you can say about where it is exactly.

"So I shouldn't even look for her?" Mia asks. She hasn't seen this many people in one place since she left high school. She could easily turn around and swim back.

"The question is, what are we looking for?" Lene says. "Are we looking for Nisha or are we looking for something else?"

THE UNCERTAINTY PRINCIPLE

"What else would we be looking for?"

"The uncertainty principle says that if you start to really look at something, it begins to lose its identity. You don't know what it is anymore."

Mia looks at Lene quizzically. "What are you talking about?"

"I'm just saying, are we trying to find Nisha or are we trying to figure out who you are? Because the harder we look, the more confusing things get."

Mia looks away from Lene. She doesn't like this line of thinking. It's not helping her figure out what to do next. Plus, her overalls are starting to get really uncomfortable as the sun dries them and the saltwater-soaked cotton turns scratchy.

She scans the crowd again and notices two men pointing at her. They're wearing matching red shorts, bright yellow shirts, and blue bow ties and Mia worries that they're security guards. Maybe she wasn't supposed to swim ashore. She glances down the beach where the crowd thins out and it's just white sand. She could walk away quickly but, before she's decided what to do, the men march over and stand shoulder to shoulder in front of her.

They're a strange sight. In addition to the matching shorts, they're wearing matching red suspenders and small red hats topped with plastic spinning propellers. Mia has never seen anyone wear shorts with suspenders, and with the spinning hats and the bow ties, they look like oversize children.

"Are you Alice?" one asks, wide-eyed.

"Uh, no, I'm Mia. I'm just looking for someone."

"Is it a rabbit?"

"Mia!"

She turns and sees Nisha weaving through a pack of dancing adults. She trots up and gives Mia an impulsive hug. Mia returns it, relieved that she's not alone anymore with the man-child twins.

"You made friends?" Nisha asks innocently.

"Are you the rabbit?" one of the men asks Nisha.

Nisha grabs Mia's hand and leads her quickly away. "I think they're on drugs," she says. They duck past a group of bikini-clad women dancing with wineglasses over their heads, spilling it on the floor around them. Nisha is wearing a see-through silk tunic that seems like it floats over her white bikini. She fits perfectly in this crowd wearing clothes that look expensive. Mia is sloshing across the restaurant in a soggy pair of overalls, her hair stuck together in wet clumps.

Nisha doesn't seem to mind and squeezes Mia's hand. "I'm really glad you came," she shouts as they push through a wall of dancers. Suddenly, they're standing in front of a table of twelve people. Nisha's dad sits at one end, smoking a cigar and talking to a young woman.

"There you are," he says, noticing Nisha and Mia, and then goes back to his conversation. Mia is happy he isn't interested in them; she doesn't want to be the focus of his attention.

They slide into two open spots on the cushioned banquette at the end farthest from Nisha's dad, another small blessing. The people at their end are talking about classical music but pause when they scooch in.

"You're the girl who jumped off that cliff with Nisha, right?" says a bald man with a German accent. He's sitting across from her and wears white pants, a white T-shirt, and thick, rectangular black glasses. His accent and stark clothing make him seem like someone out of the pages of a European edition of *GQ*.

"Yeah, that was me," Mia says, feeling the burn of attention.

"Well, that was brave," he says. "We were cheering for you, but you probably couldn't hear us."

"I couldn't hear anything because she was yelling so much," Mia says, pointing at Nisha.

THE UNCERTAINTY PRINCIPLE

She didn't mean it as a joke—it was just a statement of fact—but everyone laughs, including Nisha.

"Yeah, I was super freaked out," Nisha admits.

Mia relaxes a bit. These people seem friendly, and Nisha explains that they are part of a string quartet. There's Helen, an Argentine viola player; Genevieve, the first violinist, whose arms are covered in geometric tattoos; and Hermann, the bald German, who's the second violinist. Nisha says the group has been playing together for years and are one the world's top classical quartets.

They don't look like classical musicians to Mia. To be fair, she's never met a classical musician but on TV they wear tuxedos and are really old. These people seem more like a dirtbag rock band, like the kind she's seen loading drum kits into bars in Duluth.

Helen lights a cigar and blows out a huge plume of smoke. It smells like leather and pepper. Mia has never seen anyone smoke a cigar close-up; certainly not a viola player. She's not even sure what a viola is. Helen is dressed like a punk: She's wearing a tattered T-shirt that says "Morrissey—1991 American Tour." It's hard to imagine her playing in any kind of famous orchestra.

"Where are you from, Mia?" asks Helen, blowing out a cloud of smoke.

"Duluth," Mia says. "In Minnesota."

"Ah," Helen says, disappearing behind another cloud of smoke. "We played in Minneapolis once, you remember?"

"I remember they didn't invite us back because you shot arrows all over the concert hall." Hermann chuckles.

"What were you hunting?" Nisha asks, laughing. Mia feels like they're speaking a different language.

"A man," Hermann says gleefully.

"The timpani player," Helen says wistfully.

"He was very handsome," Hermann points out.

149

"Very handsome," Helen agrees. "He was an archer, I guess. I don't know. He had a bow and arrow in the pit and offered to teach me how to shoot."

"He taught you more than that!" Hermann shouts. Helen throws a piece of bread at him.

"Behave," Helen says, raising an eyebrow. She turns to Mia to change the topic. "And you, my darling. Do you go to the symphony in Minnesota?"

"No, never."

"Well, next time we are there—"

"They're never inviting us back," Hermann interjects.

"Can I ask a question?" Mia asks, struggling to understand everyone's relationship.

"Of course."

"You're a quartet," Mia says. "But there's only three of you."

"Ah, I like her very much," Helen coos. She pats Mia on the shoulder affectionately. "She's so perceptive."

Nisha nods down the table to the Japanese woman sitting next to her father. "That's Jesse," she says. "She's the cellist." Nisha's shoulder presses against Mia and it feels like she's letting her into a secret.

"They're a couple?" Mia guesses.

Nisha flashes a smile that's somewhere between a grin and a grimace. Mia can't decipher it but Nisha keeps leaning against her, and Mia senses she needs a friend as much as Mia does. It's a nice feeling and Mia lets herself relax a bit more. No one seems to have noticed her clothes, or at least they don't care. In fact, in a place where people are dressed as babies and bunnies, maybe it doesn't matter what she's wearing.

"Can I ask another question?"

"You don't have to ask permission," Helen says.

THE UNCERTAINTY PRINCIPLE

"Why is everyone acting so strange here?" She motions around the restaurant.

Nisha and the musicians laugh again and explain that this is a restaurant known for its lunch parties. Today, it happens to be themed *Alice in Wonderland* and things click into place. The man-child duo were Tweedledee and Tweedledum, just like in the Disney movie. Mia spots a guy on the dance floor sporting an enormous hat—the Mad Hatter clearly.

Soon, a team of waiters dressed as playing cards arrive with grilled lobster, ahi tuna sashimi, mozzarella burrata dusted with pink Himalayan sea salt, and razor-thin slices of Italian white truffle delicately laid over angel hair pasta. Mia doesn't actually know what most of it is. She's never had a meal like this, with famous musicians and fancy food. She waits to see how Nisha eats and follows her lead, scooping small portions onto the empty plate in front of her.

"Do you think the paps are after you, Darshan?" Hermann says.

"What?" Nisha's dad asks, glancing around nervously. "Where are they?"

"Out there," Hermann says, pointing outside. "On that boat."

Everybody follows Hermann's eyes and Mia's stomach drops. Hermann is looking at the *Graceland*, which is moored in calm water thirty feet offshore.

"That woman is pretty focused on us," Hermann says.

Izzy is squatting at the bow, eyeing them through binoculars. Mia glances at Nisha in a panic, about to apologize.

"Hey, it's okay," Nisha says, misreading her worry. "My dad and Jesse are kind of tabloid fodder so there's usually some paparazzi chasing them around."

"They're famous?" Mia says, trying to turn everyone's attention away from her mom.

"I mean, Jesse is, like, the best cellist in the world and my dad's a loudmouth venture capitalist who says a lot of ridiculous things so he's kind of made for the internet."

Hermann is still looking at the *Graceland*. "The paparazzi must have hit hard times," Hermann says. "That boat looks like it's about to sink."

The table laughs and Mia flushes, unsure whether to be angry or pretend she doesn't know anything.

"Actually, that's my mom," she says sharply. It just comes out.

Everybody looks at her, confused. Is she joking? Darshan looks worried like he's wondering: *What if she's part of a paparazzi family sent to infiltrate our lunch?*

"That's your mom?" Helen asks. "On that boat spying on us?"

"She's a germophobe," Mia explains, thinking that will clear it up but she gets blank stares from around the table. "She just doesn't want me to bring back your germs. That's why she's watching us."

"You're not joking," Helen says, putting her cigar down.

"That's why we're on the boat," Mia says, surprised that anyone would doubt her. "It keeps us away."

Helen glances at Hermann with evident concern. "When was the last time you were off the boat?" Helen asks.

"Oh, we get off all the time. Just mostly on deserted islands. We don't see a lot of people. Yesterday was special."

Helen nods, trying to wrap her mind around this. "You're like a castaway. Our own little castaway."

"What is your mom going to do about all this when you get back?" Hermann asks, waving his hand around the restaurant.

Mia knows her mom is spying on her partly to track the germ exposure but also because Mia is out with a bunch of strangers. It's a mix of motherly concern and obsessiveness. Mia decides to stay focused on the germs. "Depending on how bad she thinks it is, I'm going to have to scrub myself for anywhere from ten to thirty minutes."

THE UNCERTAINTY PRINCIPLE

Darshan walks to their end of the table holding his cigar and glass of wine. "We have all our vaccinations," he says, standing behind Hermann.

"It's not about vaccines," she says. "I mean, maybe COVID made it worse, but she just thinks the germs are everywhere."

She can see the group reacting. For the first time, Mia feels an urge to defend her mom. "She just thinks we're safer at sea."

"She's probably right," Darshan says, looking over at the *Graceland*. He raises his wineglass to Izzy. "I don't suppose she wants to join us."

"Definitely not," Mia says quickly.

On the *Graceland*, Izzy can tell she's been spotted and drops the binoculars. Darshan waves to her and she waves back uncomfortably. He motions for her to come ashore. Izzy quickly waves goodbye and disappears below deck.

"I guess that's a no," Darshan says, chuckling.

"She wouldn't like it here," Mia explains, happy that her mother is out of sight and the embarrassment can stop.

"Let's shuffle the table," Darshan says authoritatively, shooing everyone down so he can sit opposite Mia. "Jesse, come listen."

Hermann and Genevieve obediently give up their seats for Darshan and Jesse, who settle in across from Mia and Nisha.

"Dad, don't grill her," Nisha warns, and Mia realizes that the embarrassment is only just beginning.

"Grill her? I'm not going to grill her. I'm just curious. These kinds of people have thought very deeply about the world so we can all learn something."

He scoots his chair in and peers at Mia. An interrogation in front of a group of strangers is one of her worst nightmares. Plus, what does he mean by "these kinds of people"? Even Nisha looks worried. Lene has

153

emerged from the crowd and helps herself to a plate piled with lobster from the table. She doesn't seem to care that Mia is being interrogated.

"This looks pretty damn good," she observes.

"Okay, so when did you become a recluse?" Darshan asks Mia point-blank.

"Dad!" Nisha shouts.

"What? They live on a boat and don't see people. They're recluses."

"Tell him that your parents think you're broken," Lene says through a mouthful of lobster. Mia keeps her eyes on Darshan.

"It's okay," Mia says to Nisha, trying to wrest back some control. "We left six months ago."

Darshan pulls a giant bottle of rosé out of a silver ice bucket and refills his glass. Mia feels like she's suddenly the entertainment.

"And school?" he asks.

"School is for people who know how to behave," Lene chimes in.

"She doesn't go to school," Nisha says, trying to help out.

"You know what?" Darshan says. "No one should go to school." He launches into a lecture about how schools were built to churn out assembly-line workers and how the system hasn't adapted to the modern world. He sounds surprisingly like her mom but even though they feel the same way about education, Mia is pretty sure they'd hate each other.

"And nobody likes school," he concludes. "So it's been great, right?"

"I miss school actually," Mia says and smiles, enjoying the opportunity to undercut his theory.

"But you hate school," he says.

"She never said that," Helen interjects protectively from down the table. "You're putting words in her mouth."

"Okay, okay, it doesn't matter," he says. Mia notes how good he is at deflecting any indication that he might be wrong. He just keeps talking. "My question is, what have you been doing with your time?"

"The seafood is excellent," Lene says, her mouth jammed with shrimp as she stands behind Darshan. "So don't start talking about Grätzel cells or satellite uplinks because they'll ask us to leave."

Mia takes the point and decides to just say the simplest part of what she's been working on. "I've mostly just been repairing the solar panel on the boat," she says.

"What brand is it?"

"SolarJuice."

Darshan smiles. "I led their Series A," he brags. He tilts his wineglass toward Nisha. "You see? My daughter thinks all I do is make money, but the truth is, venture capitalists help people."

"The panels are terrible," Mia says, stating what should be obvious.

Darshan stops smiling. "What do you mean?" he says, displeased.

"I mean they don't work."

"Did you read the instructions?"

He's assuming it's her fault and it irks her. "I read them a dozen times. They're basically useless."

"The team came out of the National Lab program," he says, getting defensive. "It's actually a pretty good product."

"Don't do it," Lene warns, her plate piled with clams, crab claws, oysters, scallops, sushi, and an entire fish. "Just play it safe and we can stay."

But they've landed on a subject that Mia is fully comfortable with, and she decides to tell this guy what she really thinks.

"Actually, the panel is garbage. First off, there are manufacturing problems. I've got a list of sixteen issues. But the main problem is they went with polycrystalline, probably for cost reasons, but at sea or in places where you need durability, it doesn't hold up. I basically threw the whole thing out and started over from scratch."

Helen clasps her hand over her mouth in disbelief and then erupts into applause. "Así es, dile cómo son las cosas," she says in rapid-fire Spanish.

Darshan blinks. He wasn't prepared for a takedown from a sixteen-year-old girl.

"Okay, and what would hold up?" Darshan asks slowly.

"I'd use fluoride-doped titanium dioxide."

Darshan rubs his earlobe, a nervous tic. The DJ is building to a drop, the music pumping. At their table though, everyone is focused on Mia. Darshan tries to shake off the three glasses of wine he already drank.

"Okay, that's good. That's interesting but everybody knows Grätzel cells don't hold up either. If the electrolyte leaks, it's game over."

"I'm using photonic crystals," Mia parries, happy to hear someone other than herself say "Grätzel cell." A minute ago, this was one of the worst conversations she'd ever had. Now, she's improbably met someone who actually knows what she's talking about.

"You're doing solid-state?" Darshan asks, dumbfounded.

"That's right."

"On that boat?"

"Yeah."

"And what kind of efficiencies are you getting?"

"25.3 percent is the best reading so far."

"Not possible," he says condescendingly.

"I can show you."

There's a crackling intensity between them. Lene grabs another crab claw from the tower of seafood on her plate.

THE UNCERTAINTY PRINCIPLE

Nisha abruptly stands, breaking the moment. "I didn't invite her so you could talk business," she says.

"What?" he says, looking over at his daughter and blinking, as if he forgot she was there.

"I'm glad you finally have something to say to a friend of mine but you have plenty of people to talk to," Nisha says, on the verge of tears.

"Nisha, come on," he says sternly. "We're just talking."

"Talk to Jesse," she says and storms off.

Mia watches her go with alarm. She doesn't know what to do and looks back and forth between Darshan and Nisha, who disappears in the crowd.

"Whatever," Darshan says. He turns his attention back to Mia. "She's emotional. It doesn't matter. So how in god's name did you get 25.3 percent?"

"Uh, shouldn't I, you know, go—"

"Don't worry about her. She does this all the time."

This is the first real conversation she's had about her solar cells, but Mia doesn't want to mess up another friendship. Mia looks down at her napkin, trying to think.

"I told you it was a bad idea," Lene says. "You should only talk to me about science."

"So start at the beginning," Darshan adds, looking at Mia expectantly. "How'd you learn all this?"

Mia makes a decision and stands up. It's nice to talk about solar cells, but she felt even better with Nisha on top of the rock. She'd rather feel like that again.

"I'm just going to go check on her for a minute," Mia says, and she walks away.

157

Chapter 25

Mia finds Nisha standing on the side of the road outside the restaurant. The area has been turned into an elaborate entrance in the shape of a ten-foot-tall keyhole surrounded by fake grass. The word *Wonderland* is emblazoned across the top of the keyhole in loopy letters. It feels like walking onto a stage.

"Hey," Mia says, walking up to Nisha.

"I'm sorry I uh . . . ," Nisha says, trying to wipe away tears but looking grateful.

They can still hear the thud of the music inside. Mia notices that Nisha has lined her lower eyelids with black kohl, now smudged a bit from crying, and Mia feels an intense urge to touch her face and wipe her tears. She is the most beautiful person Mia has ever seen and it's not only the way she looks. It's something about how her emotions are so on the surface. Mia's always trying to hide her thoughts and feelings and now feels a gravitational pull toward Nisha's tears.

"I'm sorry if I did something wrong," Mia says. "You can just tell me what to do because I generally have no idea how to act and I definitely don't know what to do in a fancy place like this."

Nisha cocks her head, amused and touched. "No, it wasn't you," she says. "It's my dad. I shouldn't have left you there with him."

Mia doesn't say anything because she did in fact like the

THE UNCERTAINTY PRINCIPLE

conversation with Darshan. Nisha picks up on it. "But yeah, you two seemed to hit it off. Sounds like you're really into solar stuff."

"It's what I've been doing, I guess."

"Well, he loves talking about anything techy. You can go back in." It comes out sounding harsh, like Nisha wants her to go away.

Mia doesn't know what to do. Should she go back in? It seems like Nisha is angry now. Mia silently curses herself for screwing up again. It's just like it was with Sadie. She's trying to do what people want her to do but she just can't seem to do it right. Mia feels defective, like an engine with a cracked piston. She just keeps making people mad.

So Mia surprises herself when she steps forward and hugs Nisha.

"Oh," Nisha says, not expecting it.

"I'm sorry," Mia says, and the words come out in a rush. "I'm not good at knowing what to say and when to say it. I'm just so happy you invited me to lunch and I'm really sorry I messed it up."

Now Nisha doesn't know how to respond, both to the hug and the rush of words. But after a moment, she returns the hug.

They stand there holding each other as Nisha's tears drip onto Mia's shoulder. For the first time in a while, everything feels all right. Sad, but all right. Mia doesn't feel strange or out of place even though they're standing on the side of the road in front of this fancy restaurant and the valet guy is looking at them.

"Hey, you want to get out of here?" Nisha says, still hugging her.

"And go where?"

"I don't know. Somewhere else."

"My parents . . ."

Nisha lets her go and smiles. "I got an idea," she says, taking Mia's hand and walking her over to the valet guy, who is dressed in a skin-tight purple-and-pink-striped suit and is wearing cat whiskers. He looks like the male stripper version of the Cheshire Cat. Nisha slips her hand into her bikini top and pulls out some carefully folded cash. She peels off a one-hundred-euro note and hands it to him. "Do you think you could get a note to the boat that's right there?"

"Of course, mademoiselle," he says with a heavy French accent. "Le *Graceland*?"

Nisha looks to Mia for confirmation. Mia can't believe any of this, starting with how cool it is to carry money in your bikini, particularly when it's hundreds of euros.

"Uh, yeah, that's right," Mia manages to say.

The valet hands Mia a pad of paper and a pen. "Tell your parents you'll be back in a couple hours," Nisha says.

"I don't know about this," Lene interrupts while Mia writes a message. "Your mom is going to freak."

Mia glances out at the *Graceland* and bites her lip. Her mom will be pissed but Mia has been following her mom's orders for months now. *Going to explore the island with my friend*, she scribbles. *Be back in a couple hours.*

Nisha plucks the note from Mia's fingers, reads it, and, satisfied, passes it to the valet.

"And we'll take the key as well."

"You have a car?" Mia asks, her mind blown again.

"Something better."

Nisha takes a key from the valet and gets on a shiny orange moped parked on the edge of the fake lawn. "Come on," she says, hiking up her silk tunic and tucking it under her legs so it won't billow. She takes the sunglasses hanging from her collar and puts them on.

Mia doesn't move. It's like Nisha has short-circuited her brain. She looks like a teenage goddess on an orange Vespa.

"Don't be scared. I know what I'm doing. Kind of."

THE UNCERTAINTY PRINCIPLE

"No, I'm just . . ."

"What?"

"I've never been on a moped," Mia says, pretending that's why she's riveted.

"We'll go slow, don't worry."

Mia gets cautiously on the back and puts her hands on Nisha's shoulders.

"You gotta hug me. You won't be able to hold on otherwise."

"Okay."

Mia puts her arms loosely around Nisha's waist and she can feel her body through the thin tunic. It feels like snuggling with Sadie in bed: warm, intimate, thrilling.

"Seriously, you better hold tight," Nisha says and pushes the moped off its brake stand. It bounces forward and she flicks the accelerator. Mia yelps and almost flips off the back.

"See?" Nisha says, laughing and twisting the accelerator so they bounce off the curb and onto the road. "You gotta hold on."

Mia inches closer, her arms wrapped a little tighter around Nisha's stomach. Mia's never held anyone like this, their bodies pressed firmly together. In a flash of memory, she remembers lying in the dinghy with Alby—how close she was to him, their bodies touching—but she pushes that memory away. He ditched her.

A dune buggy hurtles toward them—its honk sounds like a squeak—but Nisha curves left onto a road leading inland. Mia looks back and sees Lene waving goodbye from the curb. It feels strange to leave her behind but there's no room on the moped and she can't run that fast.

The road is empty and Nisha accelerates, the warm, humid air whipping their hair. It feels wildly, thrillingly dangerous to be moving so fast on dry land with no seat belt.

"Don't we need helmets or something?" Mia shouts over the rush of wind.

"This is France. Don't worry."

The road leads through lush jungle and Mia catches glimpses of a lagoon through the tangled vegetation. It smells like rotting fruit, adding to the feeling that she has arrived in a foreign land. She thinks about asking where they're going but decides it doesn't matter. She's happy just like this, her arms around Nisha, swerving left and right as the road twists up a mountain. They angle through hairpin turns and Mia squeezes her legs around Nisha's hips so she doesn't fall off. With each turn, they become more in sync, leaning together.

A tiny dump truck rumbles downhill followed by a cute car with no roof. The road is lined with an endless handmade rock wall, as if a puzzle lover moved here and spent a lifetime fitting stones together.

They arrive at a three-way intersection in a dip between two mountains and Nisha slows to a stop. Two signs say "Gustavia" but point in opposite directions.

"Luckily you can't really get too lost," Nisha says. "There's only one road that just loops around on itself."

"If there's only one road, then how are we at a three-way intersection?"

Nisha twists around and looks at Mia with a smile. "You are smart, aren't you?"

In the past, Mia would have denied it. But now she lets the compliment linger, enjoying the feeling of it.

From up here, they have a view of much of the island. To her left, there's a series of jagged mountain peaks. To her right, Saint-Jean beach is a thin strip of white fringed with cactuses, palm trees, and dense green foliage. Even if they did get lost, there's nowhere really to go.

THE UNCERTAINTY PRINCIPLE

"There's my boat," she says, spotting the *Graceland* rocking slowly at anchor just offshore Nikki Beach.

Nisha hits the accelerator, almost flipping Mia off the back again. "Forget about them," she shouts gleefully. Nisha slaloms around stray rocks on the road, getting dangerously close to the edge, which plummets to their right.

From this height, they can see a new beach on the other side of the island. There's nothing on it. In a second, they're rocketing downhill toward it. After a few minutes zipping alongside a salt flat, the pavement ends and they bounce down a dirt track. The path gets rockier until there's no way to drive farther.

"We walk from here," Nisha says, turning the key in the ignition. The engine cuts off and it's quiet. Birds flit through the trees, chirping and turning their heads, trying to get a better view of the intruders. Now that there's no breeze, the heat hits them and they both start sweating.

Nisha looks at Mia and smiles mischievously.

"What?" Mia asks, glancing down to make sure she didn't spill something on herself at lunch.

"You look amazing," Nisha says and frames Mia in her phone camera. "Like Dora the Explorer grew up."

Mia is immediately stung. She thought Nisha liked her but maybe Mia is just a curiosity. Someone to laugh at.

"I didn't mean it like that," Nisha says, seeing Mia's smile fall.

"It's hot," Mia says, self-consciously patting her salt-water-encrusted overalls and feeling deflated. "I don't know if I'm up for a hike."

"No, no, no," Nisha says, rushing forward and taking Mia's hand. "I blurt out random things sometimes."

"No, it's fine," Mia says coldly.

163

Nisha lets go of Mia's hand and stares down at her feet. "I'm sorry."

"It's probably just better if we head back."

"Yeah, okay," Nisha says, sounding sad. "But I just want you to know that you're the coolest person I've met in a long time."

Lene comes crashing out of the underbrush beneath the squawking birds. "I think you should give her a second chance," she says, picking pieces of vegetation off her blazer.

Mia still isn't willing to forgive Nisha but she also doesn't start walking back to the moped.

"We can go back if you want," Nisha says.

"I'm just trying to decide if you're mean or not," Mia says, matter-of-fact.

"Oh jeez," Nisha says. "You're really honest, aren't you?"

Mia shifts her weight but doesn't answer the question, which seems to have unsettled Nisha.

"Some people probably think I'm a bitch," Nisha says finally. "I guess it depends who you ask. I get in trouble a lot."

"What kind of trouble?"

Nisha laughs. "All kinds. Expelled. Suspended. Yelled at. I haven't been arrested, so that's something to look forward to."

"What'd you do?"

"Which time?"

"I don't know, any time."

"Well, my last suspension was because I threw a book at a teacher."

"Why'd you do that?"

"She said I was acting like a privileged brat."

"Seems like something a privileged brat would do."

Nisha glowers at her and they stand in silence for a moment. If Nisha can call her Dora the Explorer, then Mia is fine telling it like it is.

THE UNCERTAINTY PRINCIPLE

"Well, you're a weirdo and I'm a privileged brat," Nisha says. "At least we've got it all out in the open."

Mia likes the honesty, as long as they are both admitting something. It actually feels freeing. Maybe they're more alike than they thought. Even if they come from completely different backgrounds, they have similar reactions to difficult situations. They act impulsively.

"I kind of got kicked out of school for throwing stuff too," Mia admits.

"Oh yeah?" Nisha says, surprised. "What'd you throw?"

"Food."

"Mmmm," Nisha says, closing her eyes and imagining it. "That's good. That's satisfying."

Mia remembers the moment, the pain she felt, the humiliation. But she also remembers the sound of the yogurt splatting on the floor, the thwack of a hamburger patty slapping onto a table. For the first time, Mia realizes that throwing all that food helped somehow. It let out some of the pain. She hadn't thought about it that way until now and she looks at Nisha appreciatively.

"I think I'd actually like to see this beach after all," Mia says.

Nisha's seriousness switches to a smile. "You are unpredictable," she says. "And I mean that in the best possible way," she adds quickly.

Mia hides her own smile and sets off toward the beach. "So what's the deal with Jesse?" she asks.

Nisha snorts. "It's kind of messed up," she says. "Some duke in Scotland invited my parents to an ayahuasca ceremony at his castle and my dad was sitting next to Jesse, and by the end of the weekend, he realized he wasn't interested in my mom anymore and got together with Jesse."

Mia has so many questions, she isn't sure where to begin. How do you get invited to a duke's castle? How do you fall out of love in a weekend? How do you fall *in* love in one weekend? She decides to start with some basics.

"What's an ayahuasca ceremony?"

"Yeah, I don't know if that's a thing in Minnesota," Nisha says, and explains that ayahuasca is a South American drug that people drink. It makes you throw up a lot and then sometimes you hallucinate.

"It sounds terrible."

"Old people love it," Nisha says. "It's a midlife crisis thing."

Nisha seems to know a lot about it. Mia wonders if she's taken it but decides to stay focused on the split.

"How's your mom?"

"She's pregnant."

Mia is taken aback. She tries to imagine what it'd be like to have a baby sibling while your parents are getting divorced. "What's your dad say?" she asks as they pick their way through the boulders leading to the beach.

"It's not his. She got a new boyfriend."

"Whoa. So who do you live with?"

"I go back and forth. They don't really care."

"How are you doing with it all?" Mia asks.

Nisha stops and turns to her. She's balancing on a rock and leans down to put her hands on Mia's shoulders, bringing her face close.

"You know what?" she says, and there's something about the closeness that gives Mia butterflies. "I think you're the first person to ask me that besides my therapist."

"What's your therapist say?"

"She says I'll be fine in the long run."

"Will you?"

"Probably not," she says with a wry smile and continues up the hill.

THE UNCERTAINTY PRINCIPLE

Mia watches her walk away, fascinated by her I-don't-care attitude and the way her hips sway through the see-through tunic.

"Are you checking her out?" Lene says, catching up with her.

"What? No."

"Because it looked like you were checking her out."

"I wasn't," Mia says.

"The same way you didn't used to try to steal looks at Sadie when she was in the shower?" Lene taunts.

"I never did that," Mia protests, a little too loudly.

"What's that?" Nisha says, stopping farther up the path.

"Nothing," Mia says, hurrying to catch up.

They emerge from the boulder-strewn path onto a beach that spreads out to their left and right. It's so gorgeous, it looks fake. It's a perfect half-moon beach with shallow turquoise water. To the right, a woman sunbathes topless on a towel. Otherwise, the beach is empty.

"It's a nudist beach?" Mia asks.

"The topless woman?"

"Yeah."

"That's because this island is part of France. It's not naked for them. And seriously, why should it be? Guys can go topless but we can't? It's sexist."

Mia sees the logic but can't imagine herself topless in public.

They walk toward the water and sit in the sand just above the rush of the waves. With Sadie, she was constantly trying to behave the right way. She felt like an actor playing a part and doing a bad job. And Sadie always made sure she knew she was doing a bad job.

With Alby, she briefly glimpsed another way of being. There didn't seem to be any rules to follow so she just did what came naturally. She could talk about what she was really thinking and he seemed genuinely interested. He felt steady, dependable, honest . . . until he wasn't.

Now, with Nisha, she's in uncharted territory again. Nisha is the opposite of Alby: She's wild, erratic, and fiery. But Mia feels a deep physical pull, a desire to touch her that she can't explain.

Lene sits down beside them and Mia can't help smiling at the fact that she is fully clothed in her usual attire: beige trousers, white button-up, and yam-colored blazer. She's completely out of place on the beach but it's nice to have her here anyway.

"I like the way the sunlight turns her hair slightly red," Lene says. "Wouldn't it be amazing to be a photon and burrow into a strand of hair like that?"

"So what's up with your mom?" Nisha asks.

"What?" Mia says, distracted by Lene's idea of diving into Nisha's hair.

"Is she getting help?"

Mia focuses on the question and realizes that she's not sure what help would look like. But she knows that whatever it is, they can't afford it. "We don't have health insurance so that's kind of why we're on the boat."

"For real?" Nisha says, surprised. "How does that work?"

"I guess there's just less to obsess about when you're super isolated."

"Shit," Nisha says, taking it in. "I'm sorry. That's rough."

It's just a few words. But it's the first time anyone has acknowledged that this is tough for Mia.

Her family thinks they're doing her a favor, Lene is Lene, and Alby apparently got what he wanted from her and sailed away.

But Nisha seems to get it and the empathy is nice. Really nice.

"The hardest part is that I wonder if I'm losing it too," Mia says.

"You seem like you're doing okay."

Mia wonders how honest she should be. For months, she's

THE UNCERTAINTY PRINCIPLE

deliberately kept almost everything to herself so that she'd have something of her own, a private life when nothing was private. Also, she didn't want to give her mom any more ammunition by telling her the truth. So what would it be like to actually talk to someone?

Lene waves her finger in warning. "I know what you're thinking and it's a bad idea."

But Mia sees Nisha looking at her with kind eyes, her own sadness on the surface. She decides to risk it.

"I have an imaginary friend," she says warily. It's the first time she's told anyone.

Lene slaps her forehead. "You've ruined everything."

Nisha tilts her head. "Like someone online?"

"No, she's sitting right next to you," Mia says, pointing to where Lene is sitting with a panicked look.

Nisha looks to her side, bewildered. There's no one there.

"Her name is Lene," Mia says. "She's a physicist at Harvard."

Nisha looks back and forth between Mia and the empty space where Lene is supposed to be.

"Can she see me?"

"Oh yeah," Mia assures her.

"And what does she think of me?" Nisha says, breaking into a sly smile.

"I don't trust her," Lene says, still fuming.

"She likes you," Mia says carefully. "But she's a little worried."

"I didn't say that!" Lene protests.

"What is she worried about?" Nisha asks.

"Maybe that I've got a new friend and she's jealous."

"I'm not jealous," Lene lies.

Nisha's smile grows and she laughs. "You know, this is one of the nicest and weirdest conversations I've ever had."

"It's not weird," Mia says defensively.

"It's you, me, and your imaginary physicist friend having a talk. That's pretty weird."

"See?" Lene says. "She doesn't understand."

"You know, I don't really talk about anything with friends at school," Nisha says. "We just post silly shit that makes everything seem great and kind of avoid everything else."

"At least you have friends," Mia says. Lene raises her hand in protest. "I mean, like, nonimaginary friends."

"Well, I'm your friend now," Nisha says.

Nisha looks at Mia and they're face-to-face, only a few inches apart. It's hot in the sun and Nisha's cheeks are damp from the sweat, her eyeliner smudged even more. It seems like Nisha is about to say something but then changes her mind. She looks away and stretches her back by arching her chest up. It looks like a yoga thing.

"So tell me about Lene," Nisha asks. "What's she like?"

"Tell her how great I am," Lene says.

"Well, she's going to be the sixth woman to win a Nobel Prize in Physics," Mia says, and then explains how Lene made a beam of light stand still, takes showers with her clothes on, and was sponsored by a beer company. "She's basically the coolest person on the planet."

"So she's, like, a real person?"

"Yeah."

"And you've met her?"

Lene jabs Mia in the side again. Nisha sees the pained look on Mia's face and corrects herself. "I mean, I know she's here," Nisha says, not sure how to talk about an imaginary friend.

"It's like . . . ," Mia says, fumbling to explain. "I just started reading about her experiments and then one day, she was just standing next to me."

THE UNCERTAINTY PRINCIPLE

"I know this girl in high school who has an anime lover," Nisha says. "It gets pretty steamy actually."

"I am not your anime lover," Lene snaps indignantly. "You need to explain that we have a purely professional, scientific relationship."

While Lene is ranting about the nature of their relationship, Nisha stands up. "Damn, it's hot," she says, taking off her silk tunic so that she's just wearing her bikini. She piles her sandals on the tunic to keep it from blowing away. "Take a dip?"

"I didn't bring a swimsuit."

"You swam to lunch, didn't you?"

"That was an emergency."

"Go naked," Nisha jokes as she walks toward the water. She looks back over her shoulder. "You're sweating like someone who takes PE class too seriously."

Mia watches her dive in and it feels like the surreal vividness of a dream. The water is so clear, Mia can see Nisha arc under the waves, skimming along the sand.

Mia glances left and right. There's no one there besides the topless woman, who appears to be asleep. If anybody was watching her, they'd probably be laughing. Mia is sitting fully clothed on a shimmering tropical beach.

Lene takes her blazer off and lays it on the sand. It's the first time Mia has seen her with her jacket off. She's still got her white button-up though. "What?" Lene says. "It's hot."

Nisha pops her head out of the water and laughs again. "Come on," she says, pulling her bikini top off underwater and waving it over her head. "You'll be fine."

"Look, normally I think it's great that you're overdressed like me," Lene continues. "But we're sitting in a burning plasma cloud here and you're wearing overalls, so I think you need to get the hell in the water."

"Oh my god," Mia mutters to herself, her heart rate picking up. She can see Nisha's bare shoulders poking above the water but her body is blurred below the surface so she only sees the outline of her chest.

Mia unclips her overalls so she's just in her NASA T-shirt and underwear. The only time she ever undressed in front of someone else was with Sadie. Sadie often had her try on a series of outfits, almost as if Mia were her dress-up doll. Mia felt at ease then, partly because they had been changing in front of each other since they were kids but also because she kind of liked it when Sadie examined her body, trying to find an outfit that might possibly work.

But now, Mia is standing exposed on the beach. She quickly tosses the overalls into the sand and hustles into the water, looking nervously from side to side. But as soon as she's in the water she's glad she got in. It's cool and, as promised, refreshing.

She swims past the waves but it's so shallow, she can stand. Nisha walks toward her, the chest-high water slowing her down so that everything moves in dream time, a sort of deliberate half speed. Nisha float-walks closer, her hair swept back and beads of water running down her face.

"It's really pretty here," Mia says nervously.

Nisha smiles and floats past Mia, moving slowly around her. "Have you been here before?" Mia asks, trying to fill the silence as Nisha circles her like a shark. Mia feels Nisha's arms wrap around her from behind, hugging her, her bare chest pressing against Mia's back.

Nisha rests her head on Mia's shoulder and they float there, nearly weightless in the water. At first, Mia feels trapped and a surge of panic hits her. Should she step away? Is there something more happening here?

The waves rock them together like they're dancing. They're bound together, in sync with everything around them: the water, the waves, the wind, each other.

Mia turns to Nisha, who keeps her in a tight embrace. They're inches apart, neither looking away.

"I'm not sure—"

Before Mia can finish the sentence, Nisha kisses her and Mia inhales sharply. It feels like her lips are touching a nine-volt battery, like a current is suddenly running between them. The taste of salt water and Nisha's cantaloupe lip gloss mixes and when Nisha pushes her stomach forward, Mia pushes back, pressing their bodies even closer together. Their hair floats on the surface, twisting together as the water rises, and Mia's mind melts. This is only her second kiss ever and it feels different. With Alby, it was slow, quiet, gentle, and beautiful. Now, wrapped around Nisha in the water, it's explosive, like a bomb is going off inside her.

A wave rolls over them, dunking them underwater. They surface, still kissing, barely aware. Nisha wraps both legs around Mia's waist, suddenly above Mia now. Mia holds her, standing on her tiptoes and tilting her head back as she kisses upward blindly, the sun in her eyes. Another wave washes over her and she comes up laughing and choking and gasping for air.

"Oh my god, did I drown you?" Nisha asks.

Mia spits out salt water. "Yeah," she splutters. She's still holding Nisha and, with the sea rushing around her, she falls back and Nisha shrieks. They crash underwater and Nisha clings onto her, finding her lips again.

They jolt to the surface, both coughing up water. It turns out that kissing underwater only works in the movies. Nisha retches salt water. Mia tries to lift her up, imagining that she'll carry her out of the water like a hero but only makes it two steps and falls down on top of her, plunging them underwater again.

Nisha erupts out of the water, gasping, and staggers onto the beach.

Mia stumbles out of the water and collapses beside her on the hot sand, giggling and hacking up seawater. "I tried to save you."

"You tried to save me," Nisha wheezes, laughing until she snorts.

"You snorted."

"No, I didn't," Nisha protests, snorting again.

Each time they look at each other, Nisha involuntarily snorts, triggering more laughter. In a second, they're both laughing so hard, tears stream from their eyes.

"Stop, you're going to make me pee," Mia warns.

Nisha rolls on top of her, trapping her between her legs, and pokes Mia's sides. "Don't pee!" she taunts, bare-chested and looming over Mia. Mia manages to roll away and sprint back into the water to pee before it's too late.

"You're terrible," she shouts from the water. Nisha flops back on the sand with her arms above her head, her chest heaving from the laughter.

Mia doesn't rush back to shore but instead floats on her back for a moment to try to process everything that just happened. The last week feels like complete madness, from the decision to leave for Tennessee, to Alby, and now this. Instead of figuring herself out, it feels like things are just getting more complicated.

The sight of Nisha's body glistening in the sun on shore does in fact remind Mia of those glimpses she stole of Sadie in the shower.

"And you tried to deny it," Lene says, floating on her back next to Mia. She's put her blazer on for some strange reason.

"Okay fine, I was looking," Mia admits uncomfortably.

"There's a lot of prejudice out there," Lene warns. "If you want to try to fit in, this will make it harder. You should call this off. You just say, 'this isn't going to work,' and go back to the boat as fast as you can."

"Mmmm," Mia says, distracted by Nisha beckoning her out of the

THE UNCERTAINTY PRINCIPLE

water. Mia feels the pull of her gaze, and as Mia wades ashore to her, she can't help but kiss her again. It just feels right, no matter what Lene says. Mia is amazed by Nisha, by her beauty, her sparkling emotions, and how ridiculously comfortable she is without a bikini top on.

"Are you like this at school?" Mia asks, their lips hovering apart.

"Like what?"

Mia runs a hand down Nisha's half-naked body. "Like this."

"You think I prance around topless?" Nisha says, laughing. "We wear uniforms."

"No way."

"It's true."

"What else?" Mia says, hungry for more. "What do you do when you're not throwing books at the teachers?"

Nisha smiles at her. "I'm on the badminton team. I'm number three in Northern California."

"Badminton's not even a sport."

"It's totally a sport."

"It's just something people do at picnics."

"No, it's really serious."

It seems like a normal conversation, but for Mia, every second is on fire. She can barely pay attention to what Nisha is saying. All she sees are her lips, her breasts, her hazel eyes.

"You going to say something or just stare at me?" Nisha asks, smiling.

If someone had told her six months ago in Duluth that she'd be on a beach in the Caribbean with a half-naked badminton champion, she would have laughed. It sounds ludicrous.

"I think I'm just going to stare at you," Mia decides.

Nisha pulls her down onto the sand in an avalanche of kisses until the two of them are lying side by side in the sand.

Mia notices the sunbathing woman on the dune packing up. Lene has waded out of the water and is doing burpees, getting her daily exercise. The poor lady: Her beach got taken over by two teens and an imaginary physicist. The lady hooks her bikini top and heads out, unimpressed.

"Maybe Lene scared her away," Nisha says.

"I think she did."

"I'm liking her more and more," Nisha says, pulling Mia back and kissing her. "Let's talk about everything we're going to do tomorrow." She kisses her again. "And the day after that." Another kiss. "And the day after that."

Mia feels ice water flooding through her veins. She stiffens.

"What?" Nisha says, immediately aware that something is wrong.

Mia knows she was fooling herself, ignoring everything that was already set in motion. It felt too good. But now the reckoning is here.

"I'm leaving tomorrow," Mia says quietly.

"Like for the next island?"

"No, I'm moving to Tennessee."

"Ten-ah-fucking-see?" Nisha shouts. "Are you kidding me? They hate gay people there."

"Tell her you're not gay," Lene advises. "You need to be clear with everyone about that."

Mia ignores Lene, not wanting to get into that. Instead, she fires back at Nisha. "You're going back to California soon too, right?" she says, not wanting to be the only one to blame.

"Yeah, but not for a week. I thought we'd have more time."

They sit in silence for a moment, processing the fact that their connection seems doomed from the start.

"Everything has been awful these past few months by myself," Mia says quietly. "And then this week, everything is suddenly topsy-turvy."

THE UNCERTAINTY PRINCIPLE

"Because of me?"

"Yeah, basically." There's no need to complicate things by mentioning Alby.

Nisha kisses her but now Mia doesn't feel the same way she did seconds ago. Nisha sits back, looking at Mia closely. Mia feels like she's being scrutinized and it doesn't feel great so she says that she needs to go back to a normal high school and that living on a boat with her parents has been too much.

Nisha pulls her top out of her bikini bottoms and puts it back on, taking a moment to think. She turns her back to Mia. "Tie me?"

Mia slides close and ties a nice bow. It's hard to imagine landing in Tennessee in a few days. This will probably all still seem like a dream. A really good dream.

"I guess we were both going to leave eventually," Nisha says. The intense happiness they both felt a moment ago is gone, replaced by the reality of their situation. Floating in the water together, it was like nothing else existed. "Does it really have to be tomorrow?"

"We've got to sail to Saint Martin and find the airport."

"What about the airport here?"

"Can you fly to Tennessee from here?"

Nisha laughs. "Of course not. You're like from another century or something. You take a prop plane to Saint Martin and pick up a jet."

Pick up a jet. Just the way Nisha talks about it sounds expensive. Mia's never been in a prop plane. She's pretty sure her parents won't go for it.

"We'll probably sail . . ."

"It's a ten-minute flight," Nisha says. "It literally costs nothing. Like a hundred euros."

"A hundred euros is a lot."

"When's your flight to Tennessee?"

"Friday."

"Are you kidding me? Let me buy you a ticket to Saint Martin from here. That'd give us two more whole days."

Mia tries to restrain a burst of excitement. She knows her parents won't let her accept money. And they are already upset about not spending time with her today, not to mention whatever feelings Kaden might have. "I don't know, I don't think my parents will go for it," she says. But the idea of never seeing Nisha again hurts.

"You've spent months with your parents, right?"

"Yeah," Mia says cautiously, not wanting to get cornered.

"So now it's you time. You get to make your own decisions. And one of them is to move to Tennessee, which I get and makes sense. And maybe"—she smiles—"spend two days with me."

Mia is fascinated by the idea that she could make her own decision without consulting anybody. Back at school, her mother chose her classes and pretty much made every big life decision for her. Sadie determined everything about her social life from what she wore to how she was supposed to talk. But now, maybe it could be different? What if she simply came back and said this is the way it's going to be? It feels so grown up.

"Maybe," Mia says, holding back a smile.

"Maybe?"

"I can try."

Nisha leaps up and does a dance in the sand, waving her hands over her head. She hauls Mia to her feet and spins her around. "We're going dancing!"

"This girl is trouble," Lene says, but she's dancing a very awkward dance in her soaked blazer.

"We're definitely not going dancing," Mia says, though she can't help but laugh at the sight of Lene dancing.

THE UNCERTAINTY PRINCIPLE

"You don't want to dance with me?" Nisha asks, pouting while she dances in a slow circle. Mia has never in her life wanted to dance but, right now, she realizes she'd do just about anything with Nisha.

"Okay, maybe I'll dance," Mia says.

It's the wildest thing she's ever said to anybody.

Chapter 26

Everything feels different for so many reasons. The most immediate: She's hugging Nisha, their bodies pressed together as they speed toward the mountains on the moped. Before, she held her lightly. Now, she envelops her.

The other thing: Nisha pilots the moped in her bikini, sunglasses, and sandals. She jammed the tunic under the Vespa's seat and now somehow looks even cooler wearing just her white bikini as they fly along the salt flats. The edges of the flats are dotted with twisted stumps bleached white from the sun. It's like being in the desert and the jungle at the same time.

They buzz up the curves on the mountain and, as they drop back into the jungle on the other side, Mia tries to think. Back in Duluth, she recognized when people were pretty or handsome. But she never really processed the fact that she noticed both boys and girls. Maybe that was because she had always been more attracted to how someone made her feel.

Like Sadie.

Sadie paid attention to her in a way that other people didn't. Even if Sadie was always telling her how to act and what to say, it was better than being ignored. It showed that Sadie cared about her and that felt good, even if Mia had to learn to censor herself.

But now, having met Alby and Nisha, Mia feels different. They seem genuinely interested in what Mia has to say about everything. They aren't asking her to change or be someone different.

It strikes Mia that maybe the reason she did whatever Sadie told her to do was that she had a crush on her. Was she willing to sacrifice herself because she wanted Sadie to like her, to love her? It seems true. If Sadie needed Mia to be someone else, someone different or better, then Mia was willing to be that person. At least until she couldn't anymore.

And now? Mia has spent so much time trying to fit into Sadie's mold, she's not sure who she's supposed to be when there's no one to tell her. Like right now, there's no one to tell her why she's attracted to both Alby and Nisha. They're so different. What does it say about Mia that she likes them both? It seems worrisome, just another sign of Mia's confusion and inability to know herself.

Nisha twists the throttle coming out of a curve and Mia has to hug her tighter. It's confusing, yes, but it's also thrilling. She is giddy with the idea of just looking at Nisha for the next two days. The thought of touching her, talking to her. She only half listens as Nisha describes all the things they're going to do: Jet Ski, snorkel, and have lunch by the pool at this great hotel. At night, they'll dance on the beach.

But as Nisha excitedly maps out the options, Mia starts to feel a nagging worry. She knows she won't fit in at all these fancy places. Why can't they just be together by themselves? She doesn't need to hang out with a bunch of people or go to parties.

Nisha finally notices that Mia isn't saying anything and abruptly stops the moped in the middle of the road.

"What?" she says, twisting to look back at her.

"You're stopped in the middle of the road," Mia says, half amused, half worried about getting run over.

"Then you better tell me what's wrong fast."

Mia thinks about how to say it and decides to start with something fundamental. "I don't have the kinds of clothes for all that. I just have my overalls."

Nisha smiles mischievously. "Oh, I like that problem," she says.

Before Mia can respond, Nisha revs the throttle and they shoot up and over the mountain, descending into the town of Gustavia. Nisha navigates the cobblestoned roads past crumbling blue and green bungalows, open-air bars, and harbor-side restaurants before parking in front of the Dolce & Gabbana shop. The window display is dominated by surfboards painted with celestial patterns and starfish. It looks extravagant, sophisticated, and strange, all at the same time.

"I don't know what you're thinking but—"

"Just stop talking," Nisha orders, taking her hand and leading her inside. Mia relaxes a little; this is what it was like with Sadie. It's easier to have someone tell you what to do.

"Except Sadie lied to you," Lene points out as she walks into the store beside Mia.

The boutique is all polished stone with tables made of jagged rock. As far as Mia can tell, there are only three small racks of clothes. It doesn't look like they actually sell much. But it is deeply air-conditioned, which feels great after the heat of the beach. And it's nice to follow Nisha's lead.

A middle-aged French woman with a deep tan smiles as they walk in.

"Bonjour," Nisha says in perfectly accented French. "Nous avons besoin de quelque chose pour mon ami."

Nisha and the woman start chatting and Mia has no idea what they're saying. Finally, the lady walks up to Mia, taking in her overalls, and says something. She waits, looking at Mia expectantly.

"She wants to know your favorite colors," Nisha says.

THE UNCERTAINTY PRINCIPLE

"Or is there a theme for the party tonight?" the woman asks, switching to English.

"What party?"

"Don't worry about that," Nisha says.

"I'm not going to a—"

"She looks good in blue and green," Nisha says, cutting Mia off.

"I think you're right," the saleswoman says. "Can I offer a glass of champagne perhaps?"

"No, thanks," Mia says reflexively.

"Yes, absolutely," Nisha corrects. "Two glasses."

"This is ridiculous," Mia whispers while the woman walks to the back of the boutique. "I can't buy any of this stuff."

"You're not going to."

The saleswoman returns with two long-stemmed glasses of bubbling pink champagne and hands one to Mia, who takes it gingerly. She's never held such a delicate glass. The stem is so thin, she worries she might snap it between her fingers.

"Here's to us," Nisha says, clinking glasses. Mia worries that they'll break but nothing happens and Nisha drinks half the glass in one sip. Mia tries a small sip and the bubbles erupt in her mouth. The sweet fizziness reminds her of sitting with Alby at the small island restaurant and she's racked by the confusion of his disappearance all over again. But the kindness and innocence of that lunch are gone. Nisha is all energy and confidence and her in-the-moment intensity paves over the memories.

"So blue and green," the saleswoman says to Mia, smiling helpfully as Mia wipes her mouth with the back of her hand. "A skirt and top maybe? Or perhaps a culotte?"

Nisha gives Mia a severe look, warning her to take this seriously. "I don't know much about clothes," Mia says, trying to be honest without shutting everyone down. She is accustomed to digging through bargain bins and mostly focuses on functionality rather than looks. As far as she's concerned, you can't beat Carhartts so why waste time?

"She's nailed the overalls look so let's see what else she can rock," Nisha says.

The saleswoman holds up a wild, floral-print sundress and watches Mia's reaction. There is nothing about it that makes Mia want to wear it. The saleswoman picks up on it.

"I see," she says, nodding wisely. "Come."

She leads them up the curving marble staircase and through a bunch of brightly colored men's clothes that look like they came from a circus act. The lady opens a door onto a covered veranda and then takes out a set of keys.

"This is our special collection," she says with a wink and unlocks a glass door at the end of the veranda.

Inside, it's like a museum curated by a deranged child. On a pedestal, under a glass dome, there's a necklace made of cookies and little blue seahorses. The shelves are lined with heart-shaped sunglasses and a pair of shoes with six-inch-tall cheetah figurines serving as heels. The smell of rosewater swirls through the room.

"Whoa," Mia mutters.

"I'm thinking these are for me," Lene says, trying on the heart-shaped sunglasses.

"Don't touch anything," Mia says quietly.

"You can touch anything you want," Nisha says seductively. "Including me."

The saleswoman pulls a sleeveless pink dress off a rack and holds it in front of Mia. "This is beautiful on you," she says, ushering Mia into a dressing room that is bigger than her cabin on the *Graceland*. The lady pulls the curtain shut, giving Mia a shred of privacy.

The first thing that grabs Mia's attention is the full-length mirror in the changing room. She has a palm-sized mirror on the *Graceland*. It's only big enough to see her face, and not even all of it. She hasn't gotten a good look at herself in months and her body looks different. It's like when she sees her cousins after a year and they're four inches taller. Her torso is thicker, more muscled, and her breasts fill out the top of her Carhartts. She's not used to the person looking back at her.

Mia examines the outfit. Why would anybody think that pink is her thing?

"I don't know—" Mia starts to say.

"Put it on," Nisha says from outside. She uses the commanding tone parents employ with young children.

Reluctantly, Mia changes and can immediately see the dress's faults. She's been wearing a short-sleeved rash guard for months and has an intense farmer tan around her neck and biceps. The dress puts her arms on full display; it's like someone painted a line across her upper arms. Everything above a certain point is white.

Lene appears next to her wearing a floral-print dress and bright red lipstick. It's the first time Mia has ever seen her wear something other than a blazer and slacks.

"Maybe if I win the Nobel Prize, I'll wear this."

"I think they'd take the prize back."

"We're waiting," Nisha says.

Mia walks out feeling completely ridiculous.

"Oh shit, you look like a skunk with those white stripes on your arms," Nisha says, drinking another glass of champagne.

Lene stands beside Nisha and laughs. "That is exactly what you look like."

"I told you I don't wear this kind of stuff," Mia says miserably.

Even the saleswoman holds back a smile. "This is not perfect," she admits.

Mia proceeds to try a series of awful skirts, dresses, tops, and wraps, all of which make her feel like an impostor. She's not like Nisha or these French women who have no tan lines and perfect skin. She's got black grease under her fingernails and cuts all over. The saleswoman gets increasingly flustered. Nisha takes the champagne bottle and refills her own glass.

When Mia tried on clothes for Sadie it was never about finding something that fit Mia's personality. It was about getting Mia to fit into something conventional, something that might make her look like the other girls at school. It was actually easier to slide into those clothes than to try to think about what kind of clothes might actually match her personality.

But she always felt that it was also kind of limiting to just wear the same thing every day, as if her personality was one-dimensional. She kept trying new things with Sadie but it never felt right and eventually she just gave up. Maybe she was simply an overalls kind of person. Now, standing in the dressing room waiting for the next horrible outfit, she pulls a piece of skin from her pinkie.

"Ah-ha!" the saleswoman says triumphantly, digging something out of a wooden trunk under one of the racks. She guides Mia back to the changing room and hands her a new outfit.

Behind the curtain, Mia shakes the fabric out. It's olive green. At the least, Mia likes the color. The style is also different. It's a romper, like a pair of shorts connected to a slightly militaristic, lapelled jacket. She sluffs off the hideous red floral explosion she's wearing and steps into this new outfit. It slides on easily, not too tight anywhere, but snug around her stomach and shoulders.

It gives her an unusual feeling. She's never worn anything that fit

THE UNCERTAINTY PRINCIPLE

like it. Her overalls are more like a tube that she inhabits. They are comfortable because they're a defense against the world, like the walls of a fort. This romper shows off her legs, which are uniformly tan, though cut and bruised from working the boat. And the sleeves come to her elbows, covering the night-to-day transition on her upper arms. The jacket creates a V over her chest but not too deep. It has a belt that she ties around her waist and she walks out.

"Oh shit," Nisha says, smiling broadly.

The saleswoman starts clapping. "This is good," she says, retying the belt so that it is slightly askew.

Lene wobbles in a pair of high heels and agrees. "You look great."

Nisha walks in a circle around her. "It's like Barbie banged a Soviet tank commander."

"That doesn't sound good," Mia says, confused.

"It's fucking amazing."

Nisha pulls her phone out, snaps a picture, and starts typing.

No one has ever complimented Mia on her clothes or sense of style. But it feels nice to wear this. It has the look of something functional, without being functional at all. It's like a sexy mechanic Halloween costume. It's refreshing that someone could see her, and just based on how she looks, have a positive reaction. It's shallow, she knows, but it's still nice.

"Everyone loves the outfit," Nisha says holding up her phone as the likes pour in.

"Who's everyone?" Mia asks, worried.

"You know, the internet."

"Uh okay," Mia says, not really sure how to feel about it. It's nice to hear that people like how she looks, but Nisha didn't ask her. Plus, it felt good to have all of Nisha's attention. Now she's busy responding to comments.

"How much is it?" Mia asks the saleswoman, hoping to get some information while Nisha is distracted.

"It's on sale for 3,900 euros," the woman says helpfully.

"Get outta here," Mia blurts. It's more than four thousand dollars. For one small piece of cloth that isn't at all useful.

"We'll take it," Nisha says decisively, looking up from her phone and handing the woman her credit card. She points at a pair of five-hundred-dollar sandals. "And she'll take those cute cork wedges too."

~~~

The island is so small, it only takes fifteen minutes to get back to Nikki Beach on the Vespa. The handsome valet nods approvingly at Mia. Nisha insisted that Mia wear her new outfit and, to force the point, had the saleswoman wrap her overalls in a glossy D&G bag.

"You look different," the valet says, glancing between Mia in her romper and Nisha's tunic. "Did you swap clothes?"

"We swapped more than that," Nisha says, glancing at him over her shoulder with a naughty look.

The valet clicks his tongue and says something in French.

Mia is mortified. She's not ready to walk into a bustling restaurant in this outfit.

The valet guy is looking at her now in a way that feels a little icky. "Don't worry, you look good," he says with his French accent. "Your mother, she seems to have made some new friends too."

"She came ashore?" Mia says, suddenly on high alert.

"No, don't worry," he says. "She has just been sending a lot of notes."

"To who?"

THE UNCERTAINTY PRINCIPLE

"To your table."

"Let's go," Lene says anxiously, stumbling forward awkwardly in the high heels. Mia follows her quickly and tries to pull the romper down. Her legs feel exposed but the romper has no stretch. She wonders what her mom will think of it. Izzy is always trying to get Mia to dress like a normal girl so maybe she'll like it?

Inside, the intensity of the party has only increased. The giant wine bottles have been replaced by shots of homemade vanilla rum, distributed by waiters dressed as the ace of spades. Mia weaves her way through the crowd and keeps her gaze down, trying not to make eye contact. She is thankful that everybody is so drunk, they barely notice her.

"You do look amazing in that."

She was so focused on the ground, she didn't see Nisha behind her. Nisha takes her hand as they come to the table and Darshan twists in his chair.

"You finally out of the bathroom?" he says, tipsy and seemingly not aware that they've been gone for over two hours. "I've got to pee too."

He stands up and pats Mia on the shoulder. "And don't worry, I got it all worked out with your mom."

"What?" Mia says, confused.

"You started it," he laughs, digging into his pocket and pulling out a handful of notes with her mother's handwriting. "You sent a note and she sent one back. Actually quite a few. It's like I'm in high school all over again."

"I'm really sorry," Mia says, guessing that her mother spent the past two hours yelling at Nisha's dad. "Is she upset?"

"Not anymore. We're all having dinner together."

Mia looks back and forth between Nisha and her dad, not comprehending. "She's not mad?"

"Oh, she's mad," he says, laughing. "But she can't fit everybody on her boat so I offered to host."

"She wants to have dinner? With you?"

"Me? God no. I don't think she likes me very much. But she said it was your last night and she thought you'd want to be with your friends."

"You mean you?"

"Yeah, us and your other friends," he says, pointing out to the bay.

Mia looks out at the water and sees the *Graceland* floating right where it was before but now there's another boat anchored alongside.

A catamaran.

It takes her a second to realize what it is. The patched hull. The bicycles and surfboards tied to the railings.

"Ooh, you're screwed now," Lene says, losing her balance on the heels and collapsing.

It's the *Exodus*.

Chapter 27

"How could you do this to me?" Mia whisper-hisses at her mom, who looks baffled.

They're standing in the cockpit of the *Graceland*—a waiter piloted her back in the Nikki Beach skiff—and now the *Exodus* is close, only fifty feet away. So far, Mia has kept her back to it so she hasn't seen Alby yet.

"They said they'd been sailing around looking for us since they left Saint Martin," Izzy says. "They came over on the dinghy an hour ago to say how happy they were to find us. Alby in particular."

Izzy glances at Ethan, looking for support.

"We thought you'd want this," he says, confused.

"Are you kidding me?"

"He's waving at you," Ethan says and waves back at the *Exodus*. "At least I think he is. I don't think he's waving at me."

"What am I supposed to do?" Mia says, hyperventilating.

"Just wave," her dad says. "It's not that complicated."

"It's really complicated," Mia snarls.

Ethan and Izzy look at each other again, not sure what to do. Mia feels trapped. She's got no choice but to face him.

"What are you wearing, by the way?" Izzy says. "Where are your clothes?"

"This is a disaster," Mia says and turns around to face the catamaran.

Alby is standing on the back deck of the *Exodus* looking like he did when she last saw him, long hair spread out across his shoulders, tattered board shorts, and a tank top. He's got an anxious smile and waves again.

She waves back, not because she wants to but because she doesn't know what else to do. He points at his chest, then at her, and motions back and forth. He's asking if he can come over. It's just like before with the hand signals but everything is different now.

She immediately shakes her finger no.

He puts his hands up and shrugs. *Why not?* She's got to come up with a fast answer so she puts her two hands together and lays her head down. *Nap time.* Ridiculous, she knows, but it's the best she can come up with on the spot.

"I've basically never seen better proof of the uncertainty principle," Lene says approvingly as she steps carefully into the cockpit. She looks completely out of place in heels and a slinky dress. "There's just no way you can be sure of where anything is."

Alby puts his hand out flat, picks imaginary food, and gives her the thumbs-up. It's a question: *I'll see you at dinner?*

She gives him the thumbs-up and hurries down the hatchway.

She sits at the dining table and tries to steady herself. Her mom and dad climb down and lean against the kitchen counter. The galley of the *Graceland* is claustrophobic in the best of circumstances and with her parents staring at her, it's worse. But there's nowhere to go. If she goes back on deck, she might have to look at Alby or Nisha, who's still onshore at the restaurant. As it is, Nisha was confused when Mia suddenly left the table at Nikki Beach. She's bound to have questions that Mia can't answer.

"What's going on?" Izzy asks.

"I can't breathe," Mia says, swaying back and forth.

Her mom quickly slips beside her and pats her back like she did when Mia was a little girl. "Hey, it's okay," she says soothingly. "You're okay. You're here with us. Everything's okay."

THE UNCERTAINTY PRINCIPLE

"No, it's not okay." Mia knows her mom is trying to be nice. For one, she hasn't sprayed Mia down with disinfectant. But Mia has bigger problems now.

"We talked to them," Ethan says, nodding in the direction of Alby's boat. "They rewired the electrical system in Saint Martin. That's why he couldn't call you."

Mia's mind is exploding.

"He is really excited to see you," her mom says.

"That's not helpful," Mia snaps.

"I guess I don't understand," Izzy says. "It's your last night. Your friend's dad offered to have everyone for dinner on his boat and we certainly can't fit everyone here."

"You know this is a big deal for your mom, monkey," Ethan says. "She's trying. She's really trying for you, so you can have a special last night before you go."

"You think this is a big deal for Mom?" Mia shouts. "What about me?"

"We were supposed to have a family dinner tonight," he says, flustered. "But we want you to have the best time so we agreed to this."

Mia stares daggers at him. "Do you have any idea what is even going on here?"

He tries a smile and realizes that's not the right look so he frowns and that's not right either. He looks to Izzy for help.

"No, you don't," Mia says. "Neither of you have any idea what's happening in my life."

Her parents stare at her, surprised by the outburst of emotion. Tears start to drip down Mia's cheeks.

"We've been on a boat with you for months, baby," her mother says, confused. "We know everything that's going on with you."

"Oh really?" Mia taunts. "So you know I have an imaginary friend named Lene who's a Harvard physicist and that I've set a new international record for solar efficiency?"

"But that's just make-believe stuff," Izzy says. She was trying to be nice but is starting to get exasperated.

"You literally know nothing about me," Mia says, feeling the anger start to burn.

"Because you don't tell us anything," Izzy snaps, her voice rising. "If you wanted to talk—"

"Hey, hey, let's bring it down a bit," Ethan says, putting a hand on Mia's shoulder. She shakes it off.

"I don't talk to you because you hate me."

"That is completely wrong," Izzy says, shaking her head. "We love you."

"You're always trying to change me," Mia erupts. "But every messed-up part of me I got from you so stop blaming me for your crap."

Izzy is shocked into silence. She's never seen Mia so angry.

Mia storms to her bunk. It is even more claustrophobic in her cabin but it's the only place she can hide. She wiggles into the darkness, burying her face in her pillow. She listens for the vibration of an engine somewhere and picks up a low drone, probably a generator from the fancy hotel, and moans along with it. She wanted to hurt her mom, but now that she's done it, it doesn't feel very good.

"Monkey, do you want to cancel dinner?" her dad asks through the cabin door. She can hear him shifting anxiously on the creaking wooden floorboards of the galley. "Just tell me what you want to do."

Mia knows he's deliberately ignoring everything she just said and hoping simple logistics will paper over the problems. In his mind, if they can just decide where to go next, everything should be fine.

It doesn't matter though. He has a point.

What the hell is she going to do?

Chapter 28

She hears her dad raise the sails and haul in the anchor. They're headed back to the anchorage in Gustavia but Mia stays hidden in her room. She doesn't want to see anyone, particularly not her mom.

"You know what? This is better than a soap opera," Lene says, laughing while sitting on the edge of the bunk. "In Duluth, you were in a love triangle and you didn't even know it. Now, you're in a love triangle and you have no idea what to do. It's like the universe is testing you."

"You're not helping," Mia moans.

"I think you should call Sadie again," Lene suggests. "She'll tell you what to do."

Mia pulls out her satellite radio and puts it on the bed. Despite the pain of Sadie's betrayal, Mia *does* want to call her. Sadie would know what to do. And maybe Mia could explain herself better this time. Maybe she could say that she thinks Sadie is beautiful, that her crush on Leif was a placeholder for something else. What Mia liked most about Leif was talking to Sadie about her feelings for him. It wasn't about getting closer to Leif, it was about getting closer with *Sadie.*

"But hold on a second," Lene says. "If Sadie knows so much, why didn't she know that you had a crush on her?"

This gives Mia pause. Despite Sadie's know-it-all attitude, she didn't seem to understand Mia very well. Maybe she wasn't the best person to rely on for advice.

"You should be more like Galileo," Lene says.

Here we go again, Mia thinks.

"Most people thought the earth was the center of the universe until he came along and said, 'Nope, that's not what I see in my telescope,'" Lene says. "He told the truth."

"And how'd that go for him?"

"He spent the rest of his life locked up in his home, but he was free in his mind," she concludes triumphantly.

"You want me to end up under house arrest for the rest of my life?" Mia says, glancing around the cell-like confines of her cramped cabin.

"The point is that you've got to be honest with yourself and everyone else," Lene says.

Mia clenches her jaw, angry at her inability to decipher her own feelings. "Okay, so what's the truth? What am I?" she asks.

"Start at the beginning," Lene prompts. "What did you like about Sadie?"

Mia thinks about it for a second. Sadie is very confident and self-assured ("Sexy," Lene observes). But she is also kind of mean ("not sexy"). She didn't seem to like who Mia was and was constantly trying to change her ("Definitely not good," Lene points out). But maybe Mia wanted to be changed because Mia didn't like who she was either.

"Pretending is a kind of prison," Lene says. "Galileo might have been locked up, but he was true to himself."

Mia feels a lump in her throat. "He had a telescope," she says. "I don't have anything."

"You have me," Lene says softly.

"I'm pretending I have you," Mia whispers.

"And you have an awesome satellite phone."

"It barely works and I have no one to call," Mia says and falls over on her bunk, overwhelmed by the disaster of her life.

THE UNCERTAINTY PRINCIPLE

A knock disturbs the conversation. Izzy opens the door without waiting for an answer and steps inside, forcing Lene out of the room. Mia is expecting some kind of punishment. Instead, Izzy sits down. Mia doesn't budge, not wanting to acknowledge her mom.

"Can I sit?" she asks, even though she already has. Izzy notices the satellite radio and picks it up.

"Don't mess with that," Mia snaps, sitting up and taking the radio away. There's not much room at the end of the bunk so they're shoulder to shoulder. The boat has a way of forcing closeness whether Mia is ready for it or not.

"I've been thinking . . ." Izzy trails off, looking sad.

"What?" Mia demands.

"Maybe you're right. Maybe I'm making my problems your problems."

Mia is about to wholeheartedly agree, but Izzy keeps going. "I knew this whole boat thing was a roll of the dice, but it felt like the only move I had left. I was scared for you. I was scared for myself. I was just trying to hold everything together and hold myself together and it was so freaking hard. And so you're right. I wasn't asking enough questions about you. I wasn't paying enough attention and I'm sorry."

Izzy starts to cry and Mia doesn't know what to do. She doesn't feel like she should have to comfort her mother. It should be the other way around but eventually she puts a hand on Izzy's back.

"It's okay," Mia says softly.

Izzy wipes her nose and shakes her head. "No, it's not okay, but all we can do is keep trying," she says, looking at the radio in Mia's hands. "So okay, I want to know more. What is it?"

"It's basically a satellite phone," Mia says cautiously.

"Okay," Izzy says, taking what she can get. "And does it work?"

"Of course it works," Mia says testily.

197

Izzy smiles sadly, noting Mia's flash of anger, and then gently puts her hand on Mia's arm. "Look, I don't really know what I'm doing half the time. I'm honestly just trying to figure things out and survive."

Mia nods, her anger cooling. She looks down at the satellite system in her lap. Maybe she should try explaining?

"Well, the solar cells power the whole thing because the radio battery won't hold a charge," Mia says, opening up a bit. She describes the uplink process but there's no sun in the cabin so the system won't work. Her mom seems interested anyway.

"I called Sadie with it," Mia admits.

"And how was that?"

"Terrible."

Izzy nods. "Do you know why you got so angry at her back home?"

Mia scans her mother's face and nervously fiddles with the wires running out of the phone. Izzy has never asked for details about The Incident. Everything she knows, she got from the school counselor, and Izzy has only ever punished Mia for what happened. But Mia senses that her mom is really trying so she decides to tell the truth. "Sadie basically lied to me. Or at least hid something from me."

"And was that the only thing?"

"What do you mean?" Mia says cautiously.

"What I mean is, sometimes what pulls two people apart is complicated," Izzy says.

Mia thinks about it for a second. Sadie never seemed to understand her and yet Mia stood by her without hesitation. She didn't even know why until she kissed Nisha. "I might have been hiding something from Sadie too," Mia admits.

Her mom nods, but, uncharacteristically, doesn't say anything, giving Mia room to keep talking. "We were so close when we were little.

THE UNCERTAINTY PRINCIPLE

Our friendship used to be so simple. But I think I wished it could've been a little more . . . complicated." Mia uses her mom's word.

"Your feelings for her grew into something else, but hers stayed the same?" Izzy asks.

Mia nods, realizing that maybe her mom understands her more deeply than she thought. The fact that Mia had stronger feelings for Sadie than Sadie did for her is almost as surprising as the idea that her mom can see it, too.

Mia didn't have the words for her feelings back in Duluth. She didn't even have the words for it yesterday. Maybe that's why she just ended up yelling in the cafeteria, why she couldn't explain herself to Sadie, or anyone really.

To Izzy's surprise, Mia hugs her, suddenly overwhelmed by the idea of leaving her mom, of being a motherless kid in Tennessee. Her mom rubs her back and they hold each other until Mia catches the acrid whiff of smoke.

"What's that?" Izzy asks, sniffing.

Mia spins and sees a line of smoke rising from her bedding. The wires running into the radio's aging battery have crossed and, before she can move, the radio bursts into flames.

Chapter 29

Nisha's speedboat arrives to pick them up for dinner as the sun is setting. The rays cast an amber hue over the anchorage, making the approach of the angular boat feel like the beginning of a Bond film. The vessel has an almost entirely open stern, as if it's daring the sea to wash on board. The thing barely even looks like a boat: It's shaped more like a fifty-five-foot paring knife.

"Wait, that's for us?" Kaden asks in awe.

"Oh my god, I forgot," Izzy says, her clothes sprayed white from the fire extinguisher. Mia managed to hit the radio with enough foam to snuff out the fire but she also drenched her mom. They've spent the past two hours cleaning up and assessing the damage. Nobody was thinking about dinner.

"Should we say we can't go?" Ethan asks.

Izzy looks at Mia. "What do you want to do?"

Mia is confused. Her mom never asks her opinion.

"I don't know," Mia says honestly. It's not like it will be easy dealing with Alby and Nisha together. But, after the talk with her mom, she also feels more sure of herself, more confident. And she can't bear the idea of never seeing them again.

The speedboat pulls up alongside the *Graceland*, making their sailboat look like a floating junk heap. The captain raises his hand in greeting. He's dressed in a black uniform with a strip of colorful, military-style awards and arched epaulets that mimic the angles of the

THE UNCERTAINTY PRINCIPLE

boat. The outfit looks like it was designed by someone who'd never been to sea.

"I think I want to go," Mia says.

"Okay then," Izzy says decisively. "We've got to eat and nobody is going to cook in our galley tonight."

Izzy disappears into her cabin and emerges with a fresh pair of shorts and a clean tank top. The deckhand on the speedboat offers her a hand and she pointedly refuses, not wanting to touch him. Mia follows and Ethan and Kaden hop on board behind her.

"Welcome," the captain says with an unplaceable accent. "Our voyage will be about fifteen minutes."

Izzy looks at Ethan with raised eyebrows and mouths the word *voyage*. A woman in an angular, tight-fitting black dress emerges from the boat's hatchway. Her outfit is like the captain's—clearly designed to match the boat. She sports as many fake military awards as the captain and carries a jagged silver tray bearing four champagne flutes. She presents the tray to Izzy.

"You want me to hold that?" Izzy says, surprised.

"No, madame," the woman says, confused. "I am offering you a glass."

"What is it?" Izzy says suspiciously.

"For madame tonight, we have Ruinart Blanc de Blancs from 2010." She hands a glass to Izzy, who takes it hesitantly. The woman hands Ethan and Mia each a glass as well.

"You're not drinking that," Izzy says, taking the glass from Mia.

"And for le petit we have a spritz of ananas," the woman says, handing Kaden a flute of yellow liquid.

"It's alcoholic?" Izzy asks defensively. She'd take the glass from Kaden but she doesn't have any hands left.

"It is the essence of pineapple with sparkling water."

"Oh," Izzy says, dialing her alert level down from red to orange. "You can try it."

"Please be comfortable," the captain says, motioning them to the lounging beds.

"Are we supposed to lie down?" Izzy asks, perching uncomfortably on the edge of one of the beds.

"As you please," the captain says, accelerating slowly away from the *Graceland*. The boat makes almost no noise, as if nothing is actually happening, but somehow the *Graceland* gets farther away.

Her dad leans over to Mia and says something.

"What?" she says in a daze.

"This is a VanDutch," he repeats.

"What's that?"

"It's got nine hundred horsepower."

Mia's never heard of a boat with nine hundred horsepower but she doesn't really care. Her dad waits for a reaction but she looks away.

"It's a million-dollar boat," he adds softly. "And it's their dinghy."

"Wait a second, are we underdressed?" Izzy asks. She points to Ethan's stained pants. It's the same thing he wore to dinner on Alby's catamaran. A pocket on Izzy's shorts is ripped and her once-red tank top has faded to a rust color. They look like deadbeat sailors. "And you've got that thing on," she says, waving at Mia's romper. "What are we getting into here?"

Mia doesn't answer. She honestly has no idea what they're getting into, or even how she's going to handle what's about to happen. It occurs to her that she's in a raw state and there's no telling how she'll respond. After everything from The Incident to now, she's not sure she entirely trusts herself, particularly when it comes to sides of herself she doesn't fully understand. She glances over at her mom, wondering if

THE UNCERTAINTY PRINCIPLE

she should confide in her, but Izzy downs a glass of champagne and takes another. Mia realizes she's trying to calm her own nerves.

"Hey, I've got a question," Izzy says to the captain. It sounds like the champagne has hit her and she doesn't give a damn anymore. "What's the deal with these people? They rich? Must be rich, right?"

"Izzy, you can't ask that," Ethan says.

The captain smiles and points ahead. They round a peninsula and see a small bay with a perfect white-sand beach. Anchored in the middle is a boat so big, it makes the bay look small. It is four stories high, with multiple lounging decks, umbrella-covered seating areas, a hot tub near the top, and a huge swimming pool dominating the back deck. It's like a floating wedding cake: three gleaming white upper decks atop a sleek, shiny black platter of a hull. It even has a helicopter landing pad on the bow. In comparison, the *Graceland* looks like a bread crumb. Mia has never seen anything like it.

"The *Alfa Nero*," the captain says with pride. "Two hundred and sixty-nine feet, designed by Nuvolari and Lenard with over four thousand square feet of living space and a range of six thousand six hundred and thirty miles. It is one of the largest private yachts in the world."

"It's got a pool," Ethan says in disbelief.

"And umbrellas," Kaden says, for some reason thinking umbrellas are more impressive than a pool.

"That's where we're having dinner?" Mia's mom asks.

"Yes, madame," the captain responds.

"It's frickin awesome," Kaden says.

"Watch your language."

"I just said frickin."

"Enough," her mom says, raising her eyebrows at Kaden. "There are people sleeping on the street and these folks are living like that?"

As they cross the mouth of the bay, the other side of the *Alfa Nero* comes into view and they see a three-story detachable water slide off the side of the ship. The slide plummets nearly forty feet and curves at the bottom into the bay.

"Seriously?" her mom says.

"I'm going to tell everybody I ever meet about this," Kaden says in awe.

Lene emerges from the VanDutch cabin wearing the same angular outfit as the crew. "I should probably tell you something about black holes," Lene says, the dark hulk of the yacht approaching steadily.

Mia jerks a piece of cuticle skin off and covers her nail with her other hand so no one will see the blood.

"Their gravity is so strong that nothing can escape once you cross a certain point," Lene continues. "And anything that falls into the hole is basically destroyed. Or at least, we never hear from them again."

A chunk of the sidewall of the ship has been hydraulically popped out and laid down on the water to create a dock, leaving a hangar-sized opening in the hull. A team of four crew in uniform stand on the dock with more champagne.

Nisha walks out onto the floating dock and waves. She's wearing a red, sleeveless dress and heels, which seems both sophisticated and ridiculous on a boat.

"That's your friend?" Ethan asks, surprised by the fact that Nisha looks like a fashion model.

"Yeah, that's her," Mia says, anxious but also suddenly excited to see her again.

"We are definitely underdressed," Ethan says, looking down at his pants.

Deckhands on the dock grab bow and stern lines and pull the boat

THE UNCERTAINTY PRINCIPLE

in. "Please have a wonderful dinner," the captain says, bowing slightly to them.

"Okay, yeah," Ethan says, bowing back.

"You don't have to bow," Izzy hisses.

"I didn't bow," Ethan protests.

They step onto the deck arguing about whether he bowed and Mia is now convinced that the evening is going to be a disaster. Nisha puts her arms out in greeting.

"Hello, wonderful people," she chirps, and gives Mia a hug. With heels she's taller than Mia and she's wearing makeup, all of which makes her seem much older. Mia doesn't like it: She seems like someone different, someone fake.

"This is my mom and my dad, and you remember my brother," Mia says miserably, doing a bad job of even pretending she's okay. Nisha doesn't seem to notice and radiates happiness, shaking Izzy's hand enthusiastically. She even covers Izzy's hand with her other hand, trapping Izzy in a cocoon of good cheer and germs.

"It's so nice to meet you," Nisha coos.

Izzy pulls her hand back, takes out sanitizer, and coats herself up past her wrists. Nisha ignores it and shakes Ethan's hand. Izzy immediately squirts a dose of disinfectant into his hands.

"Well, come on up," Nisha says, unfazed. She loops her arm through Mia's and leads them into the yacht.

"I'm going to need that," Izzy says, grabbing another glass of champagne from one of the deckhands.

The inside of the boat is like a museum. The wooden floors shine as if they've been lacquered and there are framed works of art. The hallways are wide and the doors are full size. It's the fanciest house she's ever been in and it's not even a house. Nisha leads them up a circular staircase that wraps around a glass elevator.

205

Kaden tugs urgently on Ethan's shirt. "An elevator," he whispers.

"Don't touch anything," Izzy warns him.

They arrive in a living room crowded with people. There are couches, vases overflowing with lilies, and a white grand piano painted with black squiggles. Off to one side, Alby and his family are talking to Helen and Hermann. Alby turns, sees her, and smiles.

Mia stops, not wanting to go any farther. Nisha stays with her but Kaden and her parents head in, distracted by the splendor of the room and not registering Mia's nervousness. Mia can't help but wonder what would have happened if she had left for Tennessee a week ago. There'd be no Nisha, no Alby, no gut-wrenching dinner on a megayacht. How is she supposed to behave here?

Lene steps up beside her with a man dressed in Italian Renaissance garb, like he just walked out of a Shakespeare play. "I brought a friend," Lene says.

Mia sighs. "Galileo?" she asks. The pressure of the situation seems to have further splintered Mia's mind.

Galileo doffs his puffy hat. "These people better not be flat-earthers," he says. "I will literally start screaming."

Mia sees Alby walking toward her. *Please don't hug me, please don't hug me*, she thinks over and over.

He hugs her.

"I'm so sorry," he says and she's instantly taken back to the cove, the smell of his coconut sunblock surrounding her. He's wearing green khakis cut off at the knee and a white button-up shirt with the sleeves ripped off. His hair is tied into a clump and the wound on his head has faded into a jagged red line. He looks like a character from *Mad Max* dressed up for a ball. She stands frozen inside his embrace.

"I didn't know they were going to mess with our radio. We sailed

THE UNCERTAINTY PRINCIPLE

around looking for you. Thank God you hadn't left or I never would have found you."

He lets go and steps back to look at her and she can tell he's about to say something nice.

"Snacks!" Mia announces and marches over to a waiter holding a tray of appetizers.

"Seared ahi on a crispy risotto chip," the waiter says and Mia shovels three into her mouth. Nisha and Alby trail after her, exchanging concerned looks.

"I guess you two met already?" Mia says with her mouth full.

"Yeah, just now," Alby says. "I'm pinching myself. This is the most amazing boat I've ever been on."

Mia looks back and forth between Alby and Nisha. Nisha is perfectly put together, her hair radiant, her eyebrows shaped, her skin glowing. Alby's clothes are threadbare and patched and he's got a few days of scruffy stubble.

"So what's going on?" Alby asks, nervously glancing at Nisha since he doesn't know how much she knows about them. "What's the latest with Tennessee?"

"I convinced her to stay another couple days," Nisha chirps. "My dad is stoked, by the way. He's got a million questions for you."

"So you're leaving?" Alby says, disappointed. "I thought you were going to stay."

"No, I'm leaving," Mia says definitively, trying to stop any conversation about her plans.

"What'd your parents say when you told them you were going to stay for two more days?" Nisha asks.

"I haven't talked to them yet. All I did was light part of the boat on fire."

"Wait, what?" Alby says.

"There she is, the lady of the hour," Darshan says, walking into the room and saving her. "My little solar genius. And where is this germophobic family of yours?"

Normally, Mia would recoil from someone asking to meet her *germophobic family* but she doesn't waste a second now. "Over here," she says, walking away from Alby and Nisha. Alby and Nisha glance at each other, registering the fact that Mia didn't give either of them a clear answer about her plans.

"Mom, this is Nisha's dad," Mia says, abruptly interrupting Izzy's conversation with Alby's family.

"Izzy, Izzy, Izzy, my pen pal, my note passer, you make me feel sixteen all over again," Darshan says, his arms wide like he's about to hug her. Mia sees a look of horror sweep across her mom's face. Mia is not the only one struggling here. She's in it together now with her mom.

"Don't worry about me," Darshan says, as Izzy takes a step backward. "I don't like touching people either. Unless they're naked and look like Jesse. In which case—"

"Dad!" Nisha snaps as she joins them with Alby.

"What? What'd I say?"

Now that Izzy knows Darshan isn't going to hug her, she recovers enough to be polite. "Thanks again for being so kind to Mia and all of us really."

"I liked it better when you were calling me names and accusing me of holding your daughter hostage."

Izzy laughs nervously, unsure how to handle this guy. "I was just, you know, worried because you wrote that she disappeared into the bathroom for hours."

"I thought it was weird too," he says, turning to Mia and losing his smile. "What were you doing?"

THE UNCERTAINTY PRINCIPLE

Mia freezes again as everybody looks at her.

"I'm just kidding, I don't really care." He laughs, breaking the tension. "What I do care about is dinner."

Darshan ushers everyone into a gigantic dining room. There are upholstered seats with the same squiggle design that was on the piano. The gleaming black table is strangely dotted with colored polka dots. It looks expensive and ugly at the same time. Mia tries to move away from Nisha and Alby—she doesn't want to sit next to either of them—but Darshan says that she's the guest of honor and seats her in the middle of the table with Alby and Nisha on either side.

Waiters emerge from a side door and pour glasses of wine for everybody except Kaden and Flynn, who look ridiculously small in the big, plush chairs. Mia decides that there's no reason not to drink at this point and takes a big gulp of wine before anyone can stop her. Lene and Galileo stand in the corner and watch her closely.

"Careful," Lene warns.

"Somebody's ready to get this party started," Darshan says, standing. "I like that."

Mia notices that she's the only one holding her glass. The others were waiting for the waiters to finish pouring. Even her mom picked up on the social cues and didn't reach for her wine. Mia coughs—the wine burns the back of her throat—and Nisha pats her on the back. "You okay?"

"I'm fine," Mia croaks, racked with embarrassment but feeling the warmth of the wine spreading through her.

"This is a special dinner for all of us," Darshan says, picking up his glass. Everybody follows his lead and lifts their glasses so now Mia isn't the only one. "Usually Nisha's friends are a bunch of vapid, shallow dimwits—"

"Dad!"

"I'm joking, they're great people. Not really but fine, whatever. But at last we meet someone who is actually interesting, who can hold a conversation—"

"Don't embarrass her," Nisha warns, taking Mia's hand under the table in a hidden show of support.

"And now we get to meet more interesting people," Darshan says, turning to Garrett and Leah. "All you guys are so amazing. It's like being on the set of *Pirates of the Caribbean*."

Mia can feel Nisha's hand tighten as Garrett and Leah shift uncomfortably. Mia's sympathy for both Alby and Nisha returns a little as Darshan's speech veers deeper into cringe territory.

"That isn't a costume, right?" he asks Garrett. "It's actually what you wear?"

"Yeah, uh, this is just how we dress."

"Cheers to that," Nisha shouts, interrupting her father's toast to clink glasses with Mia and Alby. Everybody toasts as the waiters bring in plates of salad. Darshan sits down, much to everyone's relief. He's at the far end of the table, sitting next to Izzy, and Mia hopes his attention won't return to her.

But now she's wedged in between Alby and Nisha and there's no escape. "I'm so glad we're together again," Alby says, sliding his hand over hers and her face starts to burn. She's now holding *both* of their hands under the table.

Her heart is beating so fast, she can't think. It was the same way in the cafeteria when she saw Sadie kiss Leif. It's too much. She doesn't know what to do. She wants to stand up, scream, and leave.

"It's time for another incident," Lene whispers in Mia's ear. She's standing behind Mia with Galileo.

"You could start throwing things," Galileo suggests helpfully. "See how gravity acts on that plate."

THE UNCERTAINTY PRINCIPLE

"You know what Newton would say?" Lene says, pointing to the left where Sir Isaac Newton now leans against the wall in a burgundy robe.

"When objects collide, they push away in opposite directions," Newton says, his shoulder-length gray hair shimmering like he's in a shampoo commercial. "You bounced into these people and now you're going to bounce away."

"But then there's Heisenberg," Lene says, pointing to the right, where Werner Heisenberg stands in a three-piece suit and bouffant brown hair. Mia groans. Another one.

"The better we know your position, the less we know about where you're headed," he says, sipping a mug of beer. "The only thing we can say for certain is that Carlsberg beer has a clean, crisp taste—"

"Stop!" Mia shouts, jerking her hands away from Nisha and Alby and lurching to her feet.

Everyone at the table suddenly looks at her. She can see the sudden concern in her mom's and dad's eyes. She's holding her plate as if it were a Frisbee, her salad strewn on the table in front of her.

Mia feels the room's attention. She wants to throw the plate and run away.

"Breathe," Lene counsels.

Mia takes a deep breath. This doesn't have to be like before in the cafeteria. Yes, she's overwhelmed, but maybe there's another way to deal with it.

"You know, Galileo was completely wrong about the tides," she announces to the room, looking pointedly at the Italian scientist. "He thought the earth was slowing down and speeding up all the time, making the water slosh around."

"It seemed right at the time," Galileo says, miffed.

"And Newton couldn't actually explain what gravity was," Mia says, turning her attention to the man with the beautiful hair. "He didn't realize it was the curving of space and time."

"I figured out a lot of other things," Newton sniffs.

"And Heisenberg led the Nazi atomic bomb program, so that sucks," Mia says, glaring at Heisenberg.

"They were all completely wrong about big things," Mia says. "So it's fine if I don't always know what to say or do, okay?"

The three scientists slink out of the room grumbling to themselves.

"I think you hurt their feelings," Lene says, but she's smiling.

The room is silent. It's just Mia standing with the salad plate and everyone looking worried. Izzy glances at Ethan with a look that says, *Should we take her and go?*

But then Darshan starts clapping. "I don't know what is happening, but I love it," he says. "You are absolutely amazing. So tell us how you became a genius."

"I'm not a genius," Mia stammers, looking around for Lene, who is nowhere to be seen. She desperately wants someone to tell her what to do now.

"Well, I can tell you that I've never met a sixteen-year-old who can talk about photonic crystals."

"It's just my hobby," Mia says, still standing and feeling like she's being interrogated for everything that she's ever done wrong.

"Why did you move away from Grätzel cells?" he says, pushing her to talk. Everyone around the table shifts in their seats.

Mia looks around and wonders if they're really going to talk about this in front of everybody. But the group is looking at her.

"I didn't move away from Grätzel cells," she sighs and sits back down. "I combined them with photonic crystals."

Darshan furrows his brow. "Why would you do that?"

THE UNCERTAINTY PRINCIPLE

Mia glances at her mom, who looks more confused than anyone. She doesn't know about Mia's conversation with Darshan at Nikki Beach and, even if she did, she's never heard Mia talk about her experiments. She never asked, at least not until earlier today when she wanted to know about Mia's radio.

And even that is embarrassing since the radio caught fire. Mia feels a flush of anger. Yes, it caught fire but it basically worked. Just because she constantly messes up doesn't mean she didn't accomplish something. She looks at Darshan, peeved that he doesn't seem to understand what is obvious.

"I wanted to use the slow photon effect to localize the light in the cell and increase absorption," she says, feeling vulnerable and proud at the same time.

Darshan nods, impressed but not fully comprehending. "How do you combine them?"

"I've been using a nanoporous gradient-index filter functionalized with titanium dioxide and then I'm downshifting the bandgap."

The table is absolutely silent.

"I've got the chills," Darshan says, looking at the hair on his arm standing on end. "I know everyone in this field and no one has ever thought to try that."

Everyone has forgotten about the dead scientists. It's clear that Mia knows what she's talking about. She sees her mother looking at her with a smile and she feels a wave of confidence.

"So, uh," Darshan says, uncharacteristically trying to gather his thoughts. "What does the filter do for you?"

"I'm going to break the Shockley–Queisser limit."

"That can't be done," Darshan says reflexively.

"Wait, what limit?" Izzy asks, suddenly worried. Breaking a limit sounds bad.

213

"It's the maximum efficiency for a single-junction solar cell," Darshan explains. "It's 33.7 percent and it is impossible to break."

"It's not impossible," Mia says, feeling annoyed again.

"If someone could break the SQ limit, it would fundamentally change the modern world," Darshan says, looking dead serious.

"Well, I'm pretty sure I know how to do it," Mia says confidently. She's not sure that this conversation is useful: Darshan says it's not possible, she thinks it is. He seems to think it's a big deal.

For Mia, the big deal is the fact that the clock is ticking on her time with Nisha and Alby. She realizes that, despite her panic, what she really wants is to spend time with these two people.

"Anyway, I'm going to step out now," Mia says. "And I'd like it if Nisha and Alby came with me since I don't have much time with them. The rest of you should just keep having a good time."

And Mia walks out, leaving them all dumbfounded.

She walks down a glossy hallway and waits by a door leading to the starboard deck. In less than a minute, Alby turns the corner and she's alone with him for the first time since they left the cove.

"You really blew people away in there," he says.

"It's just normal stuff," she says.

"Yeah, I don't think so," he says, smiling and taking both her hands. "I just need you to know that I convinced my parents to sail wherever the *Graceland* goes. We could be together just like we talked about. I know you're still thinking about Tennessee but I've got everything sorted now."

A few days ago, Alby's words would have made her wildly happy. Now it's like two waves that are so out of phase, they cancel each other out, leaving her feeling blank. She wonders if she can turn back the clock on her feelings. If he had told her this on the radio that night, she wouldn't have decided to leave. And then she wouldn't have gone on

THE UNCERTAINTY PRINCIPLE

that walk with Kaden and met Nisha. Even if she had, she wouldn't have kissed Nisha, that's for sure. They'd be friends and all of this would be a lot simpler.

It occurs to her with a flash that maybe *she's* the one complicating things. She could just make a decision. She could choose Alby, try to be friends with Nisha, and have a great time sailing the Caribbean with a boyfriend. And maybe she and her mom could learn how to get along at last. It could be great.

But if she has to choose, would she choose Alby? Does she want his calm kindness or does she want Nisha's intensity?

"We hung out for two days," she says, trying to explain her feelings. "I just—"

"But what did it mean to you?" he says, holding her hands tighter. "It meant a lot to me."

"It meant a lot to me too," she admits, though she knows that's not the right question. The right question is what does it mean now? "It's more complicated now," she says.

As she says it, Nisha turns the corner carrying a glass of orange juice. "Found you," she sings, bubbling with energy. Mia drops Alby's hands, but not before Nisha eyes her suspiciously.

"Here, have a sip," Nisha says, handing Mia the glass.

"What is it?" Mia asks cautiously. It smells like orange juice and something else.

"It's what made the pirates brave," Nisha says. "Rum and orange juice."

"I don't think pirates had orange juice," Mia points out.

"Whatever, try it."

Mia takes a little sip and recoils, her mouth on fire. "Not much orange juice," she says, handing it back to Nisha, who takes a gulp. Nisha offers it to Alby.

"I don't drink," he says.

"But you're the most pirate-like," Nisha says, pouting. "But okay, more for us. Let's get out of this hallway."

She leads them up a set of stairs. Alby looks back at Mia, wanting to continue their conversation, but there's no way with Nisha there.

"By the way, my dad wants to give you a lot of money," Nisha says. "He says you need a proper lab and a staff and, wait, what do you want to do right now?"

Nisha spins to face Mia on the stairs. Alby is looking up at her. What *does* she want to do?

Mia thinks about it. Lene is still nowhere to be seen. Nor are any of the dead scientists. It's just Mia. She feels like she needs to say something profound, something that will solve everyone's problems, including her own.

"I think we should go down that giant slide sticking off the side of the boat," Mia says, unable to come up with anything profound.

"Oh you know I won't go down that," Nisha says. "That's for my dad."

"Not anymore," Mia says, starting to feel a strange kind of confidence. She squeezes Nisha's shoulder affectionately. "You're a cliff diver now."

"I'd go sliding for sure," Alby says.

Nisha wrinkles her nose and then points at Mia's romper. "You can't go down the slide in that."

"Oh, right," Mia says, looking down at her outfit.

"We can grab something from my room," Nisha decides, pulling Mia down a long hallway and turning into an opulent bedroom while Alby trails behind. The cabin is lined with bookshelves, a king-size bed, and a television. There's even a sitting area with a couch and a coffee table with oversize art books on it.

"This is your room?" Alby says, amazed.

"Yeah," Nisha replies distractedly, digging through a drawer of clothes. "Give us girls a moment to change, okay?"

THE UNCERTAINTY PRINCIPLE

"Ah right, yeah," Alby says, backing out of the room awkwardly and shutting the door.

As soon as the door is shut, Nisha spins around and holds up a skimpy bikini. "How's this?"

"Eww, no."

Nisha laughs. "I know, you want shorts and a sports bra, right?" Nisha says as she grabs Mia's hand. She smiles flirtatiously, inching closer until they are chest to chest.

Part of Mia's brain is ringing alarm bells, all of them clanging together. *Don't complicate this, don't complicate this*, Mia thinks. The noise in her head gives the other part of her brain—the simpler part—an opening. Mia feels Nisha's breath across her lips, the sweet smell of rum mixing with her vanilla perfume and she wants to lean forward and close the gap.

Nisha catches Mia's feral look and runs a finger across her mouth, pulling her lower lip down. "Maybe I'll come to Tennessee with you," Nisha says, tilting her head sideways.

"And do what?"

"Rock the badminton court," she says.

Being with Nisha is like living in a fantasy world. Anything seems possible. She pictures arriving on Uncle Paul's doorstep in a limousine with a rich girlfriend holding a badminton racket. The thought makes her smile.

"What?" Nisha says.

"I don't think they play badminton in Chattanooga."

"I'll start my own team."

"I bet you would."

"You don't want me to come?"

"I just think, ah . . ."

Nisha slowly slides her dress straps off her shoulders until it falls to the ground. She unclasps her bra and shimmies out of her underwear, never breaking eye contact. Now she's standing completely naked in front of Mia, who is rendered speechless, caught in the tractor beam of Nisha's striptease.

"Never seen anyone naked before?"

"Not like this."

"And?" Nisha says, putting her arms up and twirling slowly. Mia feels like her insides are filling with helium, lifting her up and tickling her from within.

"I think I'm dreaming again."

Nisha smiles seductively and slowly pulls on her bikini bottom. "You can keep dreaming."

She rummages through her drawer, pulls out shorts and a sports bra, and hands them to Mia. "Your turn," she says.

Mia is the opposite of Nisha: She gets embarrassed if she catches a glimpse of herself naked in a mirror when she's alone. She's never been fully comfortable with her body. She grips the clothes and stands there lamely.

"You want me to turn around?"

"Yes," Mia says immediately, but as Nisha starts to turn, Mia feels a swell of disappointment and she realizes that she wants Nisha to watch. It's even more than that. She's excited by the idea, the power to command attention and attraction. It's a power she never had when she changed in front of Sadie.

"Actually, it's okay."

Nisha stops turning, a small smile on her face. "All right," she says, turning back to face Mia.

Mia unties the wide belt on the romper and nervously unbuttons the front. The fabric parts slightly, revealing the space between her breasts,

THE UNCERTAINTY PRINCIPLE

and Mia hesitates. Normally, she'd pull it together. Instead, she slips her shoulders out and the fabric slides down her body like electricity, every inch of her skin alive. Nisha watches, smiling. Mia takes her clothes off every day but it never feels like this.

The only problem: She forgot to take off her shoes. She leans down to get the romper off her feet and loses her balance. Before she can catch herself, she topples sideways, falling in a heap on the ground.

"Oh my god, are you okay?" Nisha says, trying not to laugh but laughing anyway.

"I'm fine," Mia says, stumbling back to her feet and trying to pretend that she doesn't feel like a clown. She hurries out of her underwear and slips the shorts on. She wiggles into the sports bra, which is like wrestling an octopus, and finally pops upright, clothed again, her face flushed from the exertion.

"That was amazing," Nisha says playfully, one eyebrow raised.

"Don't make fun of me," Mia says, defeated. She nervously picks at a piece of cuticle skin.

Nisha takes Mia's hands and turns her tortured cuticles to the light. "What's going on with you?" she asks. "You pick at your fingers a lot. I've seen them bleed."

"It's nothing," Mia says, trying to hide her hands in the shorts' shallow pockets.

"What does Lene think?" Nisha asks, looking around.

Mia glances at Lene, who has reappeared and is now sitting on the bed. Mia gives her a look that warns her not to say anything but Lene shrugs. "It's a problem," Lene admits.

Nisha scans Mia's face and can see the effect of Lene's answer. Mia wasn't prepared for this. She's been caught off guard: She thought Nisha just wanted to play around.

"Look, my parents think I'm super messed up so I've done enough therapy for like five people," Nisha says. "And I know you were saying that therapy wasn't really in the cards."

"So you want to be my therapist?" Mia laughs darkly.

"No, eww." Nisha laughs, digging through her makeup bag. "But I can tell you what I learned."

She pulls a cotton ball out and hands it to Mia.

"Therapy taught you about cotton balls?"

"It did," Nisha says, pulling out another cotton ball and slowly picking a piece off it. "Try it."

"You want me to dissect a cotton ball."

"I do," Nisha says, looking right at her.

"This is taking a weird turn," Lene notes, scooting to the edge of the bed to get a better view.

Mia looks down at the ball of white fluff. It's just a cotton ball but Nisha is watching her so she pinches a piece and pulls. It doesn't come off easily. She has to wiggle it a little and get a better grip. But then a little tuft comes off and Mia looks up with a small inhale of satisfaction.

"Mmmm."

"Right?"

They look at each other and Mia feels a swell in her chest. It's the first time someone has given her a practical piece of advice about her fingers and it takes a lot of restraint not to immediately kiss Nisha.

"It doesn't solve everything obviously," Nisha adds quickly, seeing the glow in Mia's face. "It's just a cotton ball."

There's a knock outside. "Everything okay?" Alby says, muffled on the other side of the door.

"Be right there," Mia shouts anxiously and her first thought is to pick at her cuticle. But now she pulls at a chunk of cotton.

THE UNCERTAINTY PRINCIPLE

Nisha leans against her bureau and looks at Mia carefully. "Does he know about us?"

"I haven't had a second to tell him anything."

"But he knows you're gay, right?"

"Uhhh . . ."

Nisha looks at her more critically. "You are gay, aren't you?"

Mia shrugs and looks at the now shredded cotton ball in her hand. There's nothing left to pull apart. "I guess I just like who I like?" she mumbles. "And I like you. And maybe him too."

"Hmmm," Nisha says uncertainly, trying to adjust to this. "So you and him, were you together?"

"A little bit," Mia admits, trying to smush the pieces of cotton back together. "But he disappeared."

Nisha nods slowly. "I should be jealous, I guess," she says.

"No," Mia says too quickly. She says it again to try to make it sound better, but it comes out sounding even less true.

"I see," Nisha says, picking up on Mia's unease. "I have a rival."

"It's not like that."

Nisha pulls her shoulders back and stretches her neck side to side like a boxer. "I can handle it," she replies, the rum fueling her bravado. "I'll challenge him to a duel."

"No—"

"It's what a pirate would do."

"Don't."

But Nisha has already marched to the door and flung it open. Alby is leaning against a wall in the hallway but jerks up, surprised by the door banging open.

"All right," Nisha says, standing tall in her bikini and staring at him with blazing intensity. "Let's do this."

"Yeah, great," Alby says innocently. "I'm ready."

221

Chapter 30

"**You go first,**" Nisha says to Mia.

They're standing at the top of the *Alfa Nero*'s vertiginous slide, which plunges forty feet into the sea below. The sky overhead is dark now, with a crescent moon hovering over the outline of the island. The water around the vessel's black hull is aglow with underwater lights, creating a shimmering ring. A school of fish darts left and right, drawn by the light.

"Why do I have to go first?" Mia asks, looking down into the half-lit water swarming with sea creatures.

"Because you're the bravest," Nisha says, her fear of heights adding a nervous edge to her tipsy bluster.

"You barely even know Alby," Mia says, deploying logic against rum. "He's probably braver than me."

"That's what I want to find out," Nisha says, patting Alby on the back a little too hard. "Him and I need to have a little chat. Get to know each other. See how brave he wants to be."

Alby looks back and forth between Mia and Nisha, confused.

"Aw jeez," Mia says, her head spinning. For years, neither boys nor girls paid any attention to her. Now, for reasons she still can't understand, a boy and a girl are fighting over her on a megayacht.

Maybe, if Nisha and Alby are into her, she's doing something right? Maybe she's not so off-putting? It seems like Nisha and Alby like her for who she is, which is kind of mind-blowing. And so maybe she should just try to have fun for a change?

THE UNCERTAINTY PRINCIPLE

"Fine," Mia says. "You two can deal with yourselves."

She climbs up the four-foot ladder to the top of the slide, and without looking back or pausing, flings herself into the darkness below.

Her body rapidly accelerates and bounces down the inflated rubber until she's spit out into the sea, tumbling forward so that her face hits the water first, driving a stream of salt water up her nose.

She splutters to the surface, coughing, but nobody seems to notice, at least as far as she can tell. The boat is so huge, the top of it disappears into darkness, and she can't see Alby or Nisha.

"What am I supposed to do?" she says as she treads water. It's a little scary to be out there, floating beside a massive ship.

"You know what would be amazing?" Lene says, swimming alongside her in her blazer. "If you got eaten by a shark while the two of them were busy arguing over who got to spend time with you."

"I'm not going to wait for that to happen," Mia says. She starts to swim toward the stern when she hears a swoosh and a sudden explosion of water at the end of the slide. In a second, Alby pops to the surface.

"Well, that was something," he says, looking around. He spots Mia and paddles over, floating up close like he did that first morning off Scrub Island. For a second, she feels the thrill of being near him in the water, the current swirling from his hands to her body, his long hair floating on the surface. The underwater light refracts to make his blue eyes glint.

"What'd you two talk about?" Mia asks, trying to hide her anxiety.

"She said that you two are together," he says, a sad, puppy-dog look on his face. "So I get what you mean by more complicated."

A wave of compassion washes over her and is followed immediately by a corresponding flood of shame that she's put him through this. But then the shame turns to anger.

"You shouldn't have gone radio silent," she snaps.

"I honestly didn't know the repair shop was going to mess with our

223

comms. I would literally do anything to make it up to you. Just tell me what I can do."

They hear a scream and turn to see Nisha rocket into the water in a tsunami of limbs and flailing arms. She bobs to the surface. "That was horrific," she says, swimming over. She looks at Alby, trying to read him. "Well, did you tell her?"

"I was waiting for you."

"Tell me what?"

"We have a plan."

"More of a proposal really," Alby clarifies.

"Sure, whatever," Nisha says, sounding like her dad. "Basically, it's your last night, so you get to choose."

"Choose what?" Mia asks, confused.

"Who you want to hang out with tonight," Nisha says, as if it were obvious.

Mia feels her chest tighten. Suddenly, she can feel the weight of all the water in the sea pressing against her, making it harder to breathe.

"Nisha's basically saying it's not fair to you that both of us are here," Alby says, sounding achingly reasonable. "If you really are leaving tomorrow and not staying the extra days, we don't want to mess up your last night. So one of us should leave and it's totally up to you."

Mia can't even respond. There is no answer. She can't choose because she has feelings for both of them. She wants to feel the emotional explosion of being with Nisha and she also wants the poignant depths with Alby. She wants Nisha to take her amazing places and she wants to talk about the Bible with Alby. She can't resolve it inside of herself— her own conflicting desires for exploration and stability and impulsiveness and thoughtfulness—and the crosscurrents are suffocating.

Lene paddles over and whispers in Mia's ear. "When things get hard, the best thing to do is run away."

THE UNCERTAINTY PRINCIPLE

Without saying anything to Alby or Nisha, Mia starts swimming toward the boarding platform near the stern of the ship. She swims as fast as she can and reaches the ship's swim ladder well ahead of Alby and Nisha.

When she crawls out, nearly hyperventilating, a crew member is waiting with a red-and-black *Alfa Nero* towel.

"Everything okay?" he asks.

"No," she says, flopping onto one of the lounge chairs.

"Are you hurt?" he asks, alarmed.

"Emotionally, yes."

"Oh," he stumbles, unsure what to say.

Alby reaches the ladder and climbs up, Nisha trailing behind him. In a moment, they're both standing in front of her dripping wet. The crewman hands each a towel but only Nisha wraps herself in one. Alby just stands there as if he might not stay long enough to dry off.

"I know this is tough," he says. "But once you say a name, it'll be a lot easier."

Mia slumps her head into her hands and moans. "What if we're all just friends and hang out together?"

"Nope," Nisha says. "We agreed. We need a clean decision. We'll do whatever you say."

Mia feels her anger rising at both of them. They've put her in a lose-lose situation and there's no way out. It feels like they're asking her to choose between different sides of herself.

Mia lurches up. "You know what? If that's the way it is, then forget it. I'm leaving. I can't take it."

She storms into the ship, beelining upstairs for the dining room, unconcerned that she's leaving a trail of water through the fancy hallways. She hears Nisha shout her name but doesn't look back.

As she gets closer, she follows the sound of a cello into the lounge just in time to see Jesse's string quartet launch into a version of Billie

Eilish's "bad guy." Ethan stands behind Izzy with his arms around her and they're swaying back and forth. Darshan smokes a cigar on the couch and Leah sits across from him, tapping her knee as the song swells with nervous energy.

It's a strange sight. Jesse's cello is stripped of everything but the fingerboard—it's some kind of modern version of a cello that makes it look like she's playing a skeleton. She writhes with each bow stroke while Helen, Hermann, and Genevieve pluck away in support. It sounds like the original song but somehow even more menacing.

"Mom, we've got to go," Mia says softly, kneeling beside her and dripping on the floor.

"Baby, there's no rush," Izzy says. She's clearly changed her mind about these rich people.

"No, we really have to go. I have to go."

"I know. And your dad and I talked about it. We all talked about it actually. And Darshan offered to make the arrangements."

"What arrangements?" Mia says, her voice rising with alarm.

Mia can hear her mom talking but it feels like her brain has stopped working, like it's been overloaded and can't take in more information. There's something about the plan Mia made with Nisha, and how the adults are getting along so well. Ethan says there's a storm coming so they can't sail to Saint Martin anyway.

"What . . . ," Mia interrupts. "What are you talking about?"

"It's good news, baby. We're going to stay a couple more days."

Everything goes silent. Mia's impulse is to scream. It's easier than trying to put everything into words. But she realizes that she doesn't need to explain herself. It's just messy and overwhelming and she can't handle it and that's fine.

So she turns away from her parents and walks out the doorway between Alby and Nisha, not looking at either of them.

Chapter 31

Mia sits in the cockpit of the *Graceland* as it rocks slowly back and forth. Or maybe she's rocking back and forth. She can't really tell. Her parents hustled Kaden to bed and now sit on either side of her as she stares straight ahead like a soldier who survived heavy shelling.

"I just . . . I can't . . ."

She's trying but she can't even form a sentence.

As she walked out of the *Alfa Nero*'s lounge earlier, Mia remembers seeing Alby and Nisha standing side by side in the lounge's wide entry. They both had a guilty look, knowing they had created the pressure cooker crushing Mia.

"You gotta tell us what's going on with you, monkey," her dad says. "We don't understand."

What's she going to say? They probably can't understand what's happening because they can't imagine that she'd be into both Alby and Nisha.

Which is exactly the problem. She can't even explain it to herself. How is it possible to be attracted to two utterly different people at the same time? Maybe that's why she's so messed up. She was born broken, with competing impulses that are bound to destroy her.

She realizes that her parents are looking at her.

"We seem to keep making the wrong decisions so you've got to tell us what to do," her mom says with uncharacteristic softness.

The idea of talking to her parents about this is too much. She sits up a little straighter and pretends to be feeling better just to get them off her case.

"It's okay. I'm fine. I'm just going to go to bed."

She forces herself to stand, steps down the hatchway ladder, and crawls into her berth, which smells of burnt plastic and smoke from the fire. She wiggles into the cave-like space as if it were a straitjacket and groans into her pillow.

~

ere I am again on this mean old boat
And you're so far away from me.

Mia is dreaming, transported back to the night she first met Alby. He's singing Dire Straits though he's not on the *Exodus*. He's flying through space like a photon, his hair blown back, the sun behind him a glowing circle, and the Milky Way stretched across everything. It's like a music video made by a geek with a big budget.

She can feel herself waking up—daylight is peeking through her porthole and actual photons are lighting up her bunk. She wills herself back to sleep. She likes the dream. She likes looking at him. She doesn't want to go back to reality.

But then she opens her eyes, blinking groggily. The song still echoes in her head. It feels like it's all around her, permeating the boat. She blinks some more and shakes her head to wake up but the song is still there. It's like she's still in the dream.

She stands and the sound of the music resolves itself. The song isn't in her head anymore. It's coming from somewhere outside. She snaps fully awake and is certain: Someone is singing. Right now.

THE UNCERTAINTY PRINCIPLE

She looks at her watch. It's 6:50 in the morning. It doesn't make any sense.

She opens her door and climbs into the cockpit, the music all around her. To the east, the sun breaks over a mountain, sending slanting light across the deck and into the blue water. She turns away from the sun and that's when she sees him.

At first, she can't quite believe it's real. Alby is standing in his small dinghy ten feet off the starboard stern. He stops midsong when he sees her, and for a moment, they are just looking at each other in the quiet of the early morning. Flynn holds the dinghy's tiny oars and paddles gently to keep his brother facing her. The dinghy is so small, it looks like he's standing on the water and her first thought is that he's going to fall in with the slightest swell. It seems unhinged and deeply, wildly charming.

"What the hell, Alby?" she says, smiling.

"Eh, Flynn," Alby says, ignoring her. "Get the thing."

Flynn drops the oars, rocking the boat and Alby nearly goes overboard. He throws his arms out to regain his balance and Mia covers her mouth, both for fear that he'll tumble into the water with his guitar and because she's laughing. Nobody should be standing up in a boat that small.

"Careful!" Alby barks at his brother.

Alby steadies the boat with his feet and takes up his guitar again, which he's got on a strap over his shoulder.

"I just want to say sorry and play you this song," he says. Flynn has pulled a small rainbow-colored kid's xylophone out of a backpack and sits ready with a wooden mallet.

Alby clears his throat and starts strumming, expertly playing both the bass line and the melody of the song.

I've waited hours for this

I've made myself so sick

Flynn starts up on the xylophone, hitting five notes.

"What in God's name is going on?" Izzy says, emerging groggily from below deck with Ethan behind her.

"Oh wow," Ethan says, a smile growing on his face when he sees Alby floating off their railing. "He's playing the Cure."

Mia shushes them and turns back to Alby, who is singing with all his heart while Flynn struggles to keep up on the xylophone.

I never thought you could ever be this close to me.

Thirty feet away, a couple emerges from the cabin of a sailboat moored near the *Graceland*. They look at Mia and then Alby, bewildered. Mia notices people on two other boats nearby pop up to find out what's going on. Alby has an audience now but he stares straight at Mia, singing just for her.

When he comes to the horn solo, he starts buzzing his lips, doing a surprisingly passable version of a trumpet. It's ludicrous and impressive at the same time.

"He's really good," Kaden says, surprising Mia. She's been so focused on Alby, she didn't even see him next to her.

Alby strains for the high trumpet notes and then gasps, out of breath, as he strums the last chord of the song. He finishes with a flourish, and the people on the other boats burst into applause. Even her parents and Kaden clap for him.

Alby nods at his audience but his eyes are still on Mia. "Would you go out with me today?" he asks. "I can come back and get you."

The magic of the moment suddenly disappears. She wasn't expecting him to put her on the spot. The people on the other boats start clapping again and she glances at them nervously.

"Dis oui," someone shouts in French.

THE UNCERTAINTY PRINCIPLE

"If you don't go, I'll go," an older woman shouts from another boat, prompting a round of laughter.

It's bad enough to be the focus of everyone's attention. It's worse to have strangers weighing in on what she should do with her life. "Maybe," Mia says cautiously.

Alby breaks into a huge, hopeful grin.

"I won't disappoint you this time," he says.

Chapter 32

She spends the morning trying to repair her satellite radio in the cockpit and thinking about what she wants. There are the immediate questions. Is she really going out with Alby? What is she going to say to him? And what about Nisha?

Her parents bustle around the boat but steer clear of her and don't ask questions. They seem to have decided that asking Mia anything at this point is useless because she doesn't have the answers. In a sign of their newfound understanding of each other, Izzy is just letting Mia be.

"I don't think you're going to be able to fix it," Lene says, pointing at the fried wiring of the satellite radio.

"You don't know that," Mia snaps.

"You overloaded the whole thing so it's now just a pointless tangle of copper and fritzed-out circuits," Lene says.

"Leave me alone!" Mia shouts and her parents look up with concern from the bow of the boat.

"I'm fine, it's okay," Mia says, trying to sound calm. She doesn't want her parents to butt in.

"Here's the thing," Lene says. "You can try to reattach a wire here or there but you're not solving the underlying problem."

"What underlying problem?" Mia asks, annoyed.

"You tell me?" Lene says, taunting her.

Mia looks at the mess of wires in her lap. The system is a wreck but maybe that's not the underlying problem. The question that keeps bugging her is whether she should call Sadie again. That was the whole point of hacking a phone together in the first place. And if she does call again, what would she say? What does she actually want from Sadie? Does she care what Sadie thinks of Nisha or Alby?

Sadie would probably be impressed that someone like Nisha wants to be friends with Mia. She wouldn't like Alby—he's too weird.

But then Mia catches herself. *I don't need Sadie's approval anymore. If I like these people, then Sadie should too if she's a good friend.*

"Being a good scientist means saying what you see," Lene says. "Maybe you have to lay it all out there."

Mia turns at the sound of an approaching motor and sees Alby zipping toward the *Graceland*. It's nearly noon. She puts her head in her hand and groans.

"Hey," Alby shouts brightly, pulling up alongside. He's got Flynn with him but no musical instruments this time.

"Where's the xylophone?" Mia asks. It's the only thing she can think to say.

"I had to pay him ten euros for that," Alby says. "He's a bloodsucking little leech."

"I did it, didn't I?" Flynn shoots back.

"Wasn't out of the kindness of your heart."

Flynn jumps onto the *Graceland* and ties the dinghy off while Alby cuts the engine. Kaden pops out from below deck and her parents walk aft. Izzy is already tense at the presence of someone on the boat.

"I was wondering if I could play with Kaden today," Flynn says.

"Sure, just not here," Izzy says quickly.

"We can take both dinghies," Kaden offers, trying to get ahead of his mother's concerns. "That way the teenagers can do whatever they want and we can come back when you want us."

"Fine by me," Alby says.

"Storm's coming this afternoon so I need everyone back by two," Ethan says.

Everyone looks at Mia. The plan has taken shape without any input from her.

"I was going to work on my electronics," Mia says, buying time to think.

"Hey, I'd be chuffed if you showed me what you're up to," Alby says with such utter sincerity that she can't help but feel a blip of tenderness. "We can take it to shore. Shake the old legs. There's a beach I want to show you."

Izzy and Ethan are staring at Mia.

"Fine," she says as much to get away from the attention as anything.

Chapter 33

Ten minutes later, Mia runs her dinghy ashore near Alby's little boat. Alby and Flynn are already on the sand and Alby grabs ahold of Mia's boat. Kaden immediately leaps overboard and runs after Flynn in an impromptu game of tag.

"How about a hand here!" Mia shouts at her brother. The boat is only nosed onto the sand. The back is still afloat and getting hit by small waves.

"You're all right, I can pull you up," Alby says, straining to pull the dinghy forward. Mia cuts the engine, pulls the prop up so it won't hit the ground, and jumps over to pull alongside him. They're now shoulder to shoulder, their hands touching, hauling together in the heat. There's a sudden intimacy to it that's unnerving but she's got to get the boat above the waterline or it will float away.

They pull the boat into soft, dry sand and pause, breathing heavily. She notices Alby looking at her, enraptured.

"What?"

He flushes and looks away. "Nothing," he mumbles.

Lene stumbles out of the water in a turtleneck, slacks, and high heels. The water streams down her face and clothes. Mia realizes that Lene is starting to show signs of strain as well. Nobody should go swimming in high heels.

"He's ogling you," Lene says, plopping down on the beach and getting herself covered in sand.

Mia chooses to ignore her and glances around, taking in the industrial beach they've landed on. A cargo ship is docked a few hundred feet away and a small power plant behind the beach emits a thin spew of gray smoke. "This the beach you wanted to show me?" she asks, surprised.

"It's where the everyday people go," he says, nodding at the families set up on the beach with umbrellas. "We came here last year and I saw all the fancy stuff but this was the beach that seemed most real to me."

Nearby, a local family roasts fish on a portable barbecue while their kids play in the sand. An old man does slow, lazy laps ten feet off the beach. A redheaded sailor rows a dinghy toward a fuel dock next to the cargo ships. It feels completely different from Nikki Beach.

"I want to show you something else," Alby says. "If I had anything going for me, I'd have a car or something but all I have are my feet. So I could give you a piggyback ride. A fancy piggyback ride."

"That's how we're traveling?" Mia says, laughing despite herself. "By piggyback?"

"Or we could just walk."

Mia thinks about it for a second.

"How far are we going?"

"Just there," he says, pointing to the end of the beach. It's not that far.

"Okay, I'll take the fancy piggyback ride," Mia says, deciding that a piggyback ride is safe enough.

"My lady, your chariot awaits," Alby says, kneeling down and spreading his arms out to welcome her aboard. She hops on his back and he stumbles onto his feet. She's wearing her backpack, which tilts them both back.

"Don't fall!" Mia shouts.

THE UNCERTAINTY PRINCIPLE

He regains his balance, leans forward a bit, and starts trudging through the sand.

"I'll begin this luxury tour of the island with a stunning view of a power plant."

"Charming," Mia says, paying more attention to the feel of his muscles under his T-shirt. She starts to slip and he grabs her legs, taking a little hop to hoist her back up.

"And to the right we have the Saint Barth Yacht Club, which is not fancy at all," he says, pointing to a shack with an old red sail over the veranda. It's got a line of small yellow sailboats sitting in the sand and a gaggle of kids rigging the boats. The kids have thick blue sunblock smeared across their cheeks like linebackers in the NFL.

"They look serious," Mia says, smiling at the little ones.

The beach ends at a narrow road that runs alongside a cemetery. From her vantage on Alby's back, Mia can see over the cemetery wall to the aboveground crypts, which are festooned with a riot of bright red, yellow, and pink fabric flowers.

"And here we are," he says, coming up to the cemetery wall.

"You wanted to take me to a cemetery?" Mia says, surprised.

"It's beautiful, right?"

Mia is, in fact, struck by the beauty. Each crypt has a fresh coat of crisp white paint, which makes the colorful bursts of fake flowers stand out even more.

"You think they parked that there on purpose?" Alby asks, pointing to an aging boat on a trailer on the other side of the cemetery. The boat is called *Last Chance* and it looms over the graves.

"Not sure any of them are going to get another chance, actually," she points out.

Alby leans forward into the wall, still holding her, and the increased angle presses her into his back.

237

"Do you know how Moses died?"

"No, but I bet you can tell me," Mia says, slipping back into the unusual intimacy of a conversation with him.

"If you read a standard English version of the Torah, it'll just say that he died in Moab at the 'command' of God. But if you read the original Hebrew, it's more beautiful."

It's an unexpected conversation but Mia likes it. There's something about standing next to a cemetery that now seems fitting.

"It says Moses died 'al pi Adonai.' 'Pi' means mouth so it means he died by the mouth of God."

He lets go of her legs and she slides down his back to the ground. As she does, he turns, holding her around the waist. Now, she's no longer pressing into his back; she's up against his chest. The sudden change worries her.

"You see what I'm saying?"

"I have no idea what you're saying."

He smiles and she smiles back. They're obviously not talking about Moses. At least, she doesn't think they are. As far as she can tell, this is some kind of flirtation that involves the Torah.

"I'm saying Moses died by the mouth of God," Alby says. "God kissed him."

"That's a pretty bad outcome for a kiss."

"In the beginning, we were exhaled by God," Alby says, pulling a strand of hair away from her face. "It was also a kiss. And now, when God brings you back, it's a kiss again. The world starts and ends with a kiss."

The world starts and ends with a kiss.

Mia can feel herself falling for him again and she doesn't know what to do. Being with Alby is like plugging into the soul of the universe. Even ordinary places are transformed. They're on the side of a

THE UNCERTAINTY PRINCIPLE

crumbling seaside road wedged between the beach, a power plant, and a cemetery. The tropics surround her with a warmth that makes it feel like they're snuggling. She wants to kiss him again.

But Mia's not ready for that. "Come on, I'll show you my satellite radio," she says, deliberately changing the subject. She smiles, grabs his hand, and leads him back to the dinghies.

Chapter 34

Storm clouds are visible to the southeast when they get to the dinghies. They should probably get back to their boats to ride out the storm at anchor. It wouldn't be good to get caught out there in a dinghy when the weather sweeps through.

But they linger by their boats, neither of them wanting it to be over. Mia shows him her radio, the tangle of wires, and explains how it has been her lifeline, her only hope of connection, as her family wandered aimlessly.

"Moses wandered aimlessly like us too," Alby says. At this moment, all she wants is to listen to his Moses stories, the warm sand between her toes, the gentle rush of the waves. She wants to live in this moment forever, before reality rushes back in.

Without thinking, and before he can say anything more about Moses, she wraps her arms around Alby's shoulders and kisses him. He's startled but hugs her tight, pulling her into him. Her heart is racing but it feels right and reassuringly familiar. She runs the back of her hand down his scruffy face and breathes in his coconut sunblock. She feels so alive, like someone turned up her frequency. There's a roaring in her ears—the blood pulsing through her—but then she realizes it isn't just her blood pressure. She turns toward the roar and sees someone fast approaching on a Jet Ski. It's a weird sight because the person is fully dressed in pants and a T-shirt and is racing straight at them.

"Oh no," Mia whispers.

Her heart comes to a screeching halt: It's Nisha.

THE UNCERTAINTY PRINCIPLE

Alby tenses. "Is she . . ."

Before he can finish the sentence, Nisha slams the Jet Ski onto the beach and flies into the sand. The engine revs loudly and then cuts out. Mia runs to her and helps her up.

"Are you okay?"

"No, I'm not okay," Nisha shouts, stumbling to her feet and wiping the sand from her clothes.

"We were just walking on the beach," Mia says lamely.

"Oh really? Is that all? Because it looked like something else was going on."

Nisha is yelling now. Mia glances at Alby, unsure what to say. He's frozen in place.

"You know what?" Nisha says. "You told me the hardest thing that ever happened to you was seeing your friend sneak around behind your back and hook up with someone without telling you. And guess what? That's exactly what you're doing."

"Nisha, it's not like that. We were just . . ."

"Stop lying to yourself," Nisha shouts. "You're the person you hate."

Mia feels like someone punched her in the stomach as the truth of it hits her. Nisha is right. This is exactly what Sadie did.

"You're a hypocrite," Nisha says coldly and then marches over to the Jet Ski.

"Nisha, come on, give me a second."

The roaring in Mia's head hasn't gone away. In fact, it's only gotten louder.

"If you care about me, come get me," Nisha says, dragging the Jet Ski back into the water and firing it up.

"What? Come get you where?"

"Out there," Nisha says and accelerates toward the dark horizon.

"There's a storm!" Mia shouts but Nisha is already flying away.

241

"Oh my god," Mia says, panic mixing with shame. "I've got to stop her."

"Whoa, whoa," Alby says, catching her hand. "She's trying to manipulate you. She'll turn around."

Mia looks out at the water. Nisha is going full speed away from them. "I don't think she will," Mia says.

"Then let's call the coast guard or something," he says.

Mia looks at him, and then out to sea, calculating the time it would take to call someone and convince them to go after her versus just heading out there herself and making Nisha come back. "It'll be faster if I just go after her," Mia says decisively, and she shoves her dinghy into the water.

As the boat slides into the sea, Mia sees Kaden and Flynn down the beach stop wrestling and look at her, wondering if she's leaving without them.

"Let me go with you then," Alby says. "We'll leave a boat for the boys."

"If she sees you, she won't turn around," she says, jumping into her boat and hurriedly closing the ziplock on her electronics. She shoves them all in her backpack and ties it down, so it won't bounce out. "Can you take Kaden back for me?"

She pulls the starter rope and throws the engine into reverse without waiting for his answer. She takes one look back at him onshore. He looks like he's going to cry but she spins the boat and accelerates into Nisha's still-bubbling wake.

～

The problem starts when she comes out of the lee of the island and loses the wind screen. Suddenly, the wind goes from twenty knots to forty, and the mild howl turns into a full shriek. Nisha is still a quarter mile ahead but disappears into the mist streaking across the water.

THE UNCERTAINTY PRINCIPLE

Mia glances back and, with a shock, sees Alby round a point, chasing after her in his dinghy. He's alone; he must have left the boys on the beach.

"Go back!" she shouts, but it's useless. The wind is too loud and he's too far away.

Ahead, she sees Nisha slow down and look back, making sure that Mia is following.

"Stop!" Mia shouts.

But Nisha smiles. She likes being chased and doesn't seem to understand the danger. She vaults forward into the wind, her head thrown back, her hair streaming behind her magnificently like some kind of deranged mermaid.

The swell and chop make Nisha flash in and out of Mia's view. By now, even the smallest of the waves is double Mia's height as she sits in the dinghy. Cresting the top of one, she barely catches a glimpse of Nisha's red Jet Ski in the midst of the stormy dark blue water. But then Mia speeds down the back of the wave and is surrounded by walls of water.

"This is insane," Mia mutters. The wind is whipping her in the face with blasts of spray. She knows she should turn around but if something happened to Nisha, she couldn't live with herself. She already lost so much: her home in Duluth, her best friend, any pretense of normalcy. She can't bear to lose anything more. Heading into the storm seems like the right choice.

At least until the wave appears.

At fifteen feet tall, it's at least double the height of all the other waves. And it's starting to break as it races toward her. There's no way around it, no way to hide anymore. The best she can do is to angle for the side, away from the white foaming top about to collapse on her.

The dinghy's engine strains as the boat rises up the base of the wave. If she can just eke out even a little more torque, she'll hit the shoulder of the wave and ride safely down the back instead of getting caught as it breaks. She's so close but the boat slows as it tilts higher and higher up the slope.

This wave is really starting to piss her off. All she's trying to do is help someone she cares about. She's trying to do the right thing. She just wants to be normal, have normal friends, have a normal life, be a normal person. And instead, she's now trapped in a life-and-death battle with a fifteen-foot wave in the middle of a tropical storm somewhere off the French West Indies. It's so not normal, it's disgusting. It's infuriating.

As the wave rises above her like a monster trying to eat her alive, she lurches to her feet in the dinghy and roars. It's a mix of everything inside her: fury, pain, self-loathing, strength, and power. She lets all the anger and fear boil out. She stands defiantly, facing the wave, and rages against everything, a primal, wild war cry—a warning to the wave, to the sea, to the world—that she's not giving up.

And then the wave hits her.

Chapter 35

The wave sweeps her into an underwater avalanche. She can't tell which way is up or down. She's rolled like she's in a washing machine and tries to cover her head to protect against getting smashed by her own engine, wherever it is. But after thirty seconds underwater, her lungs start to burn and she realizes she's going to drown.

Just when she thinks she's going to pass out, a current sweeps her up and spits her back on the frothing, angry surface. Her dinghy is partly deflated and folded on itself, but she manages to haul herself on board. The motor was ripped off by the wave and is gone, sunk to the bottom of the sea. The backpack is still tied in but there's nothing in it besides her fried satellite radio.

Now she's at the mercy of the elements. There's nothing she can do for anyone anymore. Maybe Nisha or Alby will save her, if they're able to stay afloat.

Mia can't help but laugh at the dark humor of it. In movies, when people get shipwrecked, the actor splutters awake on a white-sand beach. In reality, it's a minute-by-minute fight to stay alive for hours on end. Every time a wave hits, Mia fights to keep the boat from flipping. Or, if the wave is too big, she dives under and then swims after her twisted dinghy once the wave has swept over her.

By nightfall, she's shivering but the worst of the storm seems to have passed and a full moon breaks through the clouds. The mist starts to clear and she spots a rocky island ahead. Maybe, if she can kick hard enough using the dinghy as flotation, she can get to land.

~~~

lso not like the movies: swimming ashore on a rocky desert island and sleeping facedown on a pile of rocks. But she was so tired, the rocks didn't matter. What mattered was the minefield of sea urchins she crawled over to get ashore. When the sun rises, she can see the broken purple needles embedded in her hands. The sea urchin pinpricks start to sting.

The island is bigger than she thought. From the rocky shore, it angles away so she can't see the whole thing, but it's pretty bleak. A few cactuses break through the rocks. Nothing else is visible offshore. No boats. No help.

The good news is that she managed to make it with the remains of the dinghy and even her backpack. She'd trade the backpack in a second for some water but she's still happy to have it. She pulls the radio and solar array out of the ziplock and is glad to see that it stayed dry. It's useless but it's also kind of her comfort blanket. The pool-noodle antenna is even still in there.

She drapes the backpack over a shoulder and stands, her body aching from the pummeling she took at sea. There's a small hill in the center of the island. Maybe if she can get to a high point, she'll see a boat or plane. At this point, her parents are surely looking for her. She feels a stab of shame for causing them yet another problem. She knows they're completely freaking out right now. But then her concern for her parents is replaced by fear for Alby and Nisha.

Did they get hit by the same wave I did? Did they manage to get back to land? Are they still out there?

THE UNCERTAINTY PRINCIPLE

She trudges up the island's one hill to get a better view, and when she rounds a corner, she spots a flash of red on the rocky shore ahead. Her breath catches when she realizes that it's Nisha's Jet Ski. Mia hurries down the slope, dodging calf-high cactuses, but comes to a sudden stop when she spots Nisha and Alby.

They're hugging. And it's not a quick hug. They are holding each other tight, Nisha's head resting on his shoulder intimately, and after all Mia's been through, it's too much.

Mia's mind explodes. Was Nisha plotting this from the beginning, just like Sadie was? Did she and Alby have a thing already? Mia is doubly infuriated after risking her life to save Nisha. It feels like life is repeating itself, like she's back in the cafeteria.

"What the hell?" Mia shouts.

Nisha and Alby separate abruptly and spin, looking for Mia.

Alby starts up the slope toward her. "Hey, are you okay?"

"No, I'm not okay," Mia shouts. "Both of you? Behind my back?"

"Mia, that's not—"

But Mia's too tired, too pissed off, too angry at the world to listen. She turns away, stumbling, tears suddenly welling up and not wanting to have anything to do with anybody anymore.

She makes it to the top of the hill before Alby and Nisha catch up to her. It's not a very big island so it'd be hard to stay away from them for very long.

"Leave me alone!" she shouts.

"Mia, listen, it's not what you think," Nisha says, out of breath from the rush uphill. "Alby saved me."

Nisha's pants are torn and there's a cut across her cheek. "I'm the worst," she says. "I'm just a walking, talking problem."

Mia doesn't say anything. The air is still hazy from the storm and she can only see three or four miles in any direction. There's nothing out there. She looks at her fingers. The sea urchin spines sting but her cuticles don't look as bad as they normally do. She's been so distracted by everything, she's been picking less.

But now there's just the loneliness again. It's even worse than it was when her mom imprisoned her on the boat. Now, she's bonded with two incredible people, lost them, and regained them only to be trapped in some kind of painful farce where nothing works out. And, if all that wasn't bad enough, she's stuck on a desolate island with them as a constant reminder of what a mess everything is. At this point, Tennessee sounds great.

She digs at a thick piece of cuticle and jerks it out. The blood pools around the edges of her nail. It's painfully familiar.

"That's not going to help," Nisha says quietly.

"Oh yeah?" Mia fires back. "What do you think will help right now? Running off into a storm?"

They all stand there awkwardly for a moment. Mia has decided that Nisha and Alby were not hooking up but she's still angry at Nisha for acting like a baby. And, now that she thinks about it, she's angry at herself for following Nisha blindly. She's even angry at Alby for his devotion to her, which only makes her feel less worthy of it given that it's led them here.

"Well look," Alby says, trying to focus on the immediate problem. "We need to figure a way to call for help, so let's build a signal fire or something."

"How are we going to start a fire?" Mia says, letting her frustration out. "We have nothing."

"You're the scientist," he says with an edge, and Mia realizes that he's also angry that she ignored his warnings and followed Nisha into the storm. His anger makes her feel worse and she lashes out.

"Ask Moses to help," she fires back. "Let's see what that does."

She glares at him, challenging him, her bravado thinly masking her hurt.

"I've been praying from the moment you headed into the storm," he says, his jaw clenched.

"Hey, hey," Nisha cuts in. "This isn't helping."

They stand in miserable silence.

Alby starts gathering rocks and trudges uphill.

"Where are you going?" Nisha asks.

"I'm building a rock signal," he says, not turning around.

Nisha looks at Mia. Neither of them says anything and, after a moment, Nisha starts gathering rocks and follows after Alby.

"I like it here," Lene says, looking around and stretching her arms up lazily. She conveniently disappeared during the storm and now doesn't look shipwrecked at all in her blazer, turtleneck, and slacks.

"Shouldn't you be helping me figure out how to get off this damn island?"

"I am helping you," Lene says. "When you don't have anyone else to tell you what to do, you have me."

"Yeah, but you give bad advice," Mia grouses.

"It's something solid to hold on to though, right?" Lene says, proud of herself.

Mia realizes that it's true. Lene gives her some certainty when everything else is uncertain. She's always there with a fast, easy explanation, a way of seeing things that makes sense of the world, though it's often wrong. But Mia also knows that sometimes there aren't fast or easy explanations.

And with that realization, she knows with a hundred percent certainty what she has to do.

Chapter 36

"**Is this really** going to work?" Alby asks, holding Mia's pool-noodle antenna above his head.

"Definitely not going to work," Lene says.

"Be quiet," Mia snaps.

"Sorry," Alby says, hurt and not understanding that Mia was talking to Lene.

While Alby and Nisha spent the day building a large X out of rocks to signal any passing planes (which never came), Mia sat in the dirt and repaired her radio. The ziplock kept it dry but the system was still messed up from the short circuit. Luckily, it didn't damage the radio itself and the cactuses proved useful. She used a spine to pick off the plastic insulation on the cables and rewired the system. Surprisingly, squeezed cactus juice also turned out to be a good replacement for the leaked berry solvent in the damaged solar cell.

Now, she presses the power button and feels a burst of pride when the system lights up.

"I told you the cactus would do the trick," Mia tells Lene.

"You did?" Alby says.

Nisha shushes him. "She's talking to Lene," she says.

"Who?"

"I guess you don't know everything about her, do you?" Nisha says, an eyebrow raised.

"The cactus was a good idea," Lene admits.

THE UNCERTAINTY PRINCIPLE

Mia looks at her two friends. They are both beat up after surviving a night at sea and now a day in the full sun. Alby ripped his T-shirt into pieces to use as bandages on Nisha's cuts and then tied the leftover piece around his head as a makeshift hat. They look like proper shipwreck survivors. She feels a stab of doubt. She created this whole mess. Can she really figure out how to get them out?

"I don't actually know any phone numbers so hopefully you do," Nisha says.

"Just hold the solar cells toward the sun," Mia says, determined. She hands Nisha the array and shows her how to position the glass faces. She holds Nisha's hands to tilt the cells up more and it's the first time they've touched since the dinner on her dad's yacht. Nisha smiles.

"Like this?" Nisha asks, deliberately pointing the cells toward the ground so that Mia has to correct her again.

"No, like this," Mia says, not noticing Nisha's little game.

"Are you really flirting with her right now?" Alby asks, immediately catching on. "We are literally stranded on a desert island."

"Okay, okay, no flirting," Nisha says, chastened. She aims the array at the sun.

Mia walks to Alby. "You're going to point the antenna at the horizon and slowly move like this," she says, holding his arm and arcing it over the sky. It's another intimate moment, standing close to him, touching him. Alby looks at Mia and smiles.

"Hey, hey," Nisha says, wagging her finger. "You said no flirting."

"I tell you what," Mia says, laughing. "Let's just try making a call, okay?"

Nisha and Alby nod, eyeing each other, while Mia sits down with her handset.

"Okay, aim the antenna that way," Mia says, pointing to the horizon. Alby does and Mia starts whistling. In a minute, she hears her whistling come back to her. Without thinking, she quickly punches a series of numbers and the radio emits a burst of static. Then, they hear a phone start ringing and someone picks up.

"Hello?" Sadie says.

Mia's heart is racing. Months ago, she didn't understand why she was so angry at her friend. She didn't understand why she screamed and threw stuff and sobbed.

"Is anybody there?" Sadie says.

"It's me," Mia says finally. "It's Mia."

"Oh," Sadie says cautiously. "What's up?"

"I've got two things to say," Mia says quickly. "First, I need you to call the coast guard on the island of Saint Barth and tell them to look for me on an island downwind of the storm that just passed them."

"Are you trying to mess with me again? Because it's not going to work."

"Sadie, listen very carefully. I am shipwrecked and I need you to call the coast guard. And second, I don't need you or anyone to tell me what to do anymore. I freaked out in the cafeteria because you lied to me and that really hurt because I had a crush on you, not Leif. I wanted to be close to you because you always seemed to know what to do and I was insecure and we were friends."

Mia feels the tears well up and streak down her face. Out of the corner of her eye, she sees Alby tracking the satellite across the sky and Nisha holding up the solar array. The part of her that isn't overwhelmed can feel them supporting her.

"But you were mean to me," Mia goes on and the words tumble out. "You don't seem to like who I am but you know what? It's actually okay if I'm a little weird. This is who I am."

Mia lets go of the talk button and it feels like she's letting go of something more.

THE UNCERTAINTY PRINCIPLE

There's a burst of static and the connection drops before Sadie can respond but Mia already feels different. If Sadie doesn't call the coast guard, they can always pick up another satellite and call someone else. But Mia said what she needed to say and she feels more at ease than she ever has.

She wipes the tears and starts to laugh. She's stranded on an island with her two current crushes and she just called her ex-crush. Despite it all, she feels pretty great. Lene is so happy, she breaks into one of her awkward dances and Mia giggles.

"You okay?" Alby asks gently.

Nisha and Alby are both looking at her questioningly. Behind them, Lene continues to dance, if you can call it that. She's flapping her arms and jumping around like a bird trying to fly.

Mia raises an arm to the sky.

"You need something?" Nisha asks.

And then Mia starts flapping her arms and jumping up and down like Lene, a joyous, hopeful, flailing dance that says exactly what she's feeling. That she's free of something that was holding her down.

"Oh my god, she's having some kind of breakdown," Nisha says to Alby.

Mia spins, feeling the embrace of the water all around them. For the first time, she feels like these six painful, agonizing months were what she needed after all. She had to leave the world behind, sail over the horizon, and get a new perspective. She needed to be isolated so she could learn to listen, to discover what had been paved over and smoothed down by Sadie, the demands of high school, and her mother's nagging. It feels like the winds have just shifted and she's going to have to readjust her sails.

Chapter 37

The sleek Agusta helicopter lands on the aft deck of the *Alfa Nero* five hours later. Izzy rushes to the helicopter, and when Mia steps out, her mother pulls her into a fierce hug. Her dad is right behind and wraps them both in his arms, the rotor wash whipping their hair and making it impossible to hear anything.

Alby's parents and Darshan are there as well and the ship's crew usher them all inside, out of the blasting wind.

"Do you realize how much money it cost to mount a rescue mission?" Darshan asks Nisha when they get inside, his eyebrows raised. They're surrounded by zebra-print chairs in one of the ship's carpeted living rooms. Nisha looks down, ashamed and hurt that he thinks she's not worth it. But then Darshan pulls her into a tight hug. "It wasn't that much, actually, particularly since I got my daughter back and two semirandom teenagers.

"Don't do it again, though," he says, trying not to sound emotional. "I was scared."

Nisha hugs him back, something she hasn't done in years.

A nurse takes Mia's blood pressure in the ship's sick bay. The room looks like a doctor's office mixed with a candy store; there are glass jars filled with tongue depressors, cotton balls, and, oddly, a jumble of fake plastic eyeballs. It seems like the space was

THE UNCERTAINTY PRINCIPLE

put together by an interior designer, not a medical professional. Everything is pristine, like it's never been used. Izzy sits in the corner watching the nurse work. There's not enough room for Ethan and Kaden.

"Why are there plastic eyeballs?" Mia asks, nervous that her mom is going to start yelling at her if no one else is talking.

"I have no idea," the nurse says, focusing on the blood pressure machine.

"And isn't it a bad idea to have glass jars in a sick bay on a boat?"

"Yes, now be quiet and relax your arm."

The blood pressure cuff inflates, squeezing Mia's arm more and more. The tick-tick-tick of the machine in the otherwise quiet room is nerve-racking.

"Can I take one of those?" Mia asks, pointing at the cotton balls.

"Sure," the nurse says, handing her one from the jar.

Mia starts to pull the ball apart, unnerved by her mother's silent presence.

"She's a little dehydrated," the nurse concludes. "And she's got sea urchin spines in her hands." The nurse uncaps a bottle of white vinegar and pours it into a stainless-steel bowl, filling the room with a pungent smell. "Let's get your hands in there."

Mia puts the cotton ball down and submerges her hands in the bowl. It stings a little.

"The vinegar will dissolve the spines but we'll have to watch for infection," the nurse says. "Other than that and a sunburn, you're doing okay so I'll go check on the others."

The nurse walks out, leaving Mia and Izzy alone. Mia looks at her mom warily, ready for criticism.

Izzy exhales as if she's been holding her breath for a while.

"That was really, really poor decision-making," Izzy says.

"I know," Mia says quickly, defensively.

"But I'm proud of you," Izzy says, a catch in her throat. "For so many reasons."

Izzy looks at her daughter with a sad smile. "I think you're growing up and we can do things differently from here on out. I don't need to tell you what to do anymore. If you can connect to a satellite with some cactus juice, you can handle yourself anywhere. Even Tennessee."

Mia laughs. "I think Tennessee will be pretty easy in comparison."

Izzy nods and looks at the floor. She clearly wants to say something more. Mia lets her take her time.

"I know you think I've gotten better on the boat," Izzy says after a minute. "But I'm still struggling. You pick your fingers to deal with your feelings. I've just gotten smarter about it. I bite the inside of my cheek. That way no one can see that I'm hurting. They can't see the cuts."

Mia blinks. Her mother's issues have always been the dominant factor in the family but they never talk about it like this. Calmly. Honestly.

"I think we need to find a way to get help," her mom goes on. "We can't just deal with it on our own anymore. When you get to Tennessee, I'm going to ask Uncle Paul to pay for a therapist."

"What about you?" Mia asks.

"I don't know," Izzy says, sounding defeated.

Mia walks over to her mom and hugs her even though it's a little awkward since Mia is standing and Izzy is sitting. But Izzy hugs her back and buries her face in Mia's stomach. It feels different, like Izzy is the kid and Mia is the adult.

"The truth is, you'll probably be better off without me," Izzy says.

This is not how Mia thought her time at sea was going to end. She imagined she'd rage away in a huff of righteous indignation, her anger toward her mom fueling her transition back to regular high school. She

THE UNCERTAINTY PRINCIPLE

was motivated to succeed in Tennessee just to prove that her mom was wrong about everything.

"Before you leave, I just want to say I love you," Izzy says, holding back tears. "I'll miss you every day and I'll beat myself up for not paying more attention to you when you were here."

Mia takes a sharp breath in. For the first time, she senses the tantalizing, maddening possibility that their relationship could be repaired. And it's happening just at the moment that she's leaving.

~~~

Mia and Izzy walk into the *Alfa Nero*'s expansive living room, and everyone stands up. Alby's right forearm is wrapped in gauze and Nisha has a bandage on her cheek.

"So what's going on?" Nisha asks nervously. "Where are you headed?"

"Wherever you go, we can go too," Alby announces. "Tennessee is up the Mississippi, right? I bet we could sail there."

"Or she could come stay with us for a while in California," Nisha says, walking over to her dad and poking him. "My dad could build a giant lab for all your experiments, right?"

"One thousand percent," Darshan says, swatting away Nisha's pokes.

"We could sail to California too," Alby says, glancing at his parents with a hint of desperation. "Might take us a minute to get through the Panama Canal and up through Central America, but we could meet you there."

"You know, there's another option," Izzy says. "We could just get rid of the *Graceland* and move back to Duluth. Whatever you want to do, we can do."

They all look at Mia and this time, instead of feeling the burn of the attention, she feels the warm glow of everyone's love.

257

Chapter 38

Kaden turns the *Graceland* into the wind and the mainsail flaps loudly. Wordlessly, Ethan drops the sail and ties it to the boom as Izzy starts the engine. It chugs to life and Kaden turns the boat to starboard, aiming them for the harbor in Cádiz.

They move toward the Spanish coastal town at an easy five knots. It was a long six-week crossing from the Caribbean, but summer was coming, and they needed to get out of the Caribbean before hurricane season.

The passage seems to have changed Kaden. His hair is longer now and windswept. Standing at the wheel, he doesn't look so young anymore. Without his sister on deck to boss him around, he has an added air of maturity.

Kaden eases up on the throttle as they approach the ancient stone fort that guards the entrance to the town. It looks like something out of a fairy tale, with battlements rising out of the water and waves crashing all around. A long stone bridge leads into town, which lines a beautiful beach filled with white umbrellas and a summer crowd.

"People," Kaden says, glancing at his mom.

Izzy nods, her eyes squinting warily behind her sunglasses. She takes over the helm as they approach the marina. "Tie us off," she tells Kaden.

Ethan throws the plastic fenders over the side to protect the boat and Izzy pulls the *Graceland* up to the hammerhead dock. Kaden leaps off the bow with a rope, tying them to a cleat. Izzy throws the motor in

THE UNCERTAINTY PRINCIPLE

reverse, pulling the boat close in, enough for Ethan to step off the stern with a line and pull the stern snug. The fenders squeeze against the concrete dock with a satisfying cushioning sound.

"Mia would have done it better," Izzy admits. "But we got the job done."

"Always feels wild," Kaden says, holding his arms out and wobbling. After weeks at sea, the ground underneath seems like it is swaying beneath him.

A few locals walk the docks, preparing sparkling motorboats for a day on the water. They look over at the *Graceland* as if travelers from another dimension just arrived. The boat's rails are strapped with five-gallon red plastic jugs, two bicycles, and a buzzing windmill. The paint on the hull is blotchy and dotted with barnacles and seagrass. They look like they came from underwater, not over the water.

Below deck, in her bunk, Mia opens her eyes. She smells the scent of juniper trees and fried food coming off the beach and her mouth starts to water. Five weeks at sea—with a five-day rest on the Portuguese island of Madeira—has whetted her appetite for land. It whetted her appetite for everything.

She climbs up on deck and blinks in the bright Mediterranean light. It was a long night. She captained the final overnight leg and went to sleep at sunrise.

"Here you go," Izzy says, handing her a thermos of coffee. Since they left Saint Barth, and Mia decided to stay, her parents have treated her differently. They seem to recognize that something has changed.

"Thanks," Mia says, screwing off the top and sipping the coffee. The smell mixes with the mildew on the boat and a hint of seaweed.

It smells like home now.

She hops down onto the dock and smiles. She's never been to Europe but now that her feet have touched the dock, she's arrived. Before she left Duluth, she'd never been outside the United States. Now, she's a proper explorer who's sailed from the West Indies to Spain with the Mediterranean lying ahead. There's so much to see.

Down the dock, Mia spots Lene. She's walking purposefully away, headed into the old town on her own. The guidebook says it's one of the oldest continuously inhabited cities in Europe and Columbus set sail from here on two of his voyages to the Americas. Mia knows Lene is excited to check it out.

"There's Wi-Fi," Kaden says, coming back from a chat with the boaters nearby. He hands Mia a piece of paper with the code. She's got her old cell phone in her pocket. In Madeira she got emails from both Alby and Nisha. They each said they were excited for her, that they understood her decision to keep sailing. But neither of them really seemed to understand why she didn't choose them.

She tried to explain. She wrote that they each helped her learn so much about herself and she loved them both, but she needed time to explore it all. Now that she can connect to the internet again, she's sure they're going to flood her with more questions. They're going to ask when they can see her. She tenses up.

She pulls a cotton ball out of her pocket and starts plucking. The skin around her cuticles has healed but it's not like the urge to pick went away. She's just learned to live with it.

She looks at her phone. She could log in and try to explain herself again. But then she'd be staring at a screen and not looking up at Europe. She leaves the phone in her pocket.

"I'm going to clear customs and go for a walk," she tells her parents.

"Can I come?" Kaden asks.

"Sure," she says, taking his hand. "We can storm the castle together."

Acknowledgments

Kal Kini-Davis

Many of the people who inspired this book are nameless. The old sailors on battered boats, shirtless in the morning sun, hauling up anchor and heading out to sea. The fancy people on their megayachts, unaware of anyone around them, particularly not me studying them.

Then there are many people I know well, whom I have grown up with and grown with. Thank you to everyone who has provided feedback on this book throughout its many drafts: Nana, Grammie, Delilah Roller, Maya Kini, Shamus Roller, Eva Bogan, Danielle Davis, G Ammondson, Zee Zakheim, Mackenzie Fargo, Aaron Dixon, and Sarah Pledger. Your edits and notes are forever appreciated.

High school was a tough time for me, just as it was for Mia. But I am lucky to have had teachers who helped make it better along the way. Thank you to Alex Myers for giving me space to talk and encouraging me to write. And thank you to Tara Siegel for supporting me in my projects, both at school and away.

Bérénice Diveu and Simon Favaud taught me to sail when I was thirteen in the French West Indies, where much of this book takes place. They took a tough love approach, often motoring past my small boat at full speed to create a wake that tipped me over. As a result, I learned to be comfortable alone on the water. They taught me not to fear the ocean but to see it as a place of magic and adventure. Thank you for your constant shouting, coaching, and joking. I don't know where I would be without you.

When I was sixteen, I walked into the boat shop at the Dolphin Club in San Francisco and was welcomed by master builders Jon Bielinski and Julia Hechanova. They introduced me to the world of wooden boats and inspired me to apply to the Northwest School of Wooden Boatbuilding. I was accepted, and now, every weekday, I wake up excited to learn about the properties of different wood species or how to plank a boat. Thank you to Jon and Julia for showing me the way here.

And finally, I want to thank my family. For reading draft after draft, for giving us time and space to write this book, and for your unwavering love and support. Thank you, Mama. Thank you, Kirin. And thank you, Papa, for putting up with me throughout this whole process and for sticking with this book. It was a pain and a joy.

Joshua Davis

The main person I want to thank is my son, Kal. We began this project five years ago, when he was thirteen. In many ways, he grew up writing this book. With each new draft, Kal would gain some fresh insight into the characters and himself. It has been one of the most profound experiences of my life to watch him mature as a person and writer.

When I was ten years old, I went on my first big sailing trip. Francoise Kirkland and Pamela Bennett, two of my dad's ex-girlfriends, had become friends after splitting with him, and they decided to explore Tahiti together by boat. They offered to take me with them. My father and mother, who were divorced, agreed to send me along for the summer.

ACKNOWLEDGMENTS

It was a beautiful and strange trip. The year was 1984 and radio was our only form of communication with the outside world. The experience left an indelible impression, and I want to thank Francoise and Pamela for taking me on such an adventure.

My father got seasick easily, but he saw my love of the sea. In 1985, he bought an old dinghy and rented a rack for it at Marina del Rey in Los Angeles. He'd drop me in the morning and come back at sundown. I spent the days sailing and, on one memorable occasion, my father agreed to go out with me. He weighed nearly two hundred pounds, overwhelming the little dinghy, and water flooded in. We had to paddle the half-sunk boat to shore. My dad has passed now, but I think of him often and know that he was always there for me, even when we were sinking.

I'd like to thank our wise agent, Bonnie Nadell, with whom I've worked for twenty years now. Joshuah Bearman, Arthur Spector, and Kiana Moore at *Epic Magazine* have been my friends and creative sounding boards for a decade. Elizabeth Lee, our editor at Penguin, has done a masterful job helping us refine this book, as have executive production editor Shara Hardeson and copy editor Michelle Lippold.

Elayna Carausu and Riley Whitelum of *La Vagabonde*, Behan and Jamie Gifford of *Totem*, Liz Clark of *Swell*, Brian Trautman and Karin Syrén of *Delos*, and Cole Brauer of *First Light* have inspired and thrilled us with their bravery and humanity. Thank you for sharing your experiences with the world.

We are indebted to Lin and Larry Pardey, whose *Self Sufficient Sailor* helped us think about living aboard a boat in a new way. Similarly, our copy of Rick Page's *Get Real, Get Gone* is well worn. For bringing the sea into our home every month, we want to thank Andrew Parkinson of *Cruising World*, John Arndt at *Latitude 38*, and Joe Cline at *48° North*.

ACKNOWLEDGMENTS

I'd like to thank Martin Roscheisen for his guidance on Grätzel cells, as well as Arbor Scientific for equipping Kal with a dye-sensitized solar cell kit so we could explore the reality of Mia's experiments. Allan Cameron advised us on radio matters and Gregory Bearman and Saswato Das consulted on the physics. Moulie Vidas gave feedback on scripture. Rebecca Prosino shared her stories of sailing the Caribbean as a teenager. Pierre Lord fine-tuned our Australian slang.

During one of the intense phases of writing this book, we lived and sailed in the French West Indies with Greg, Anja, Alexei, and Alia Manuel, and I couldn't ask for better shipmates. We are indebted to Steve Hilton and Rachel Whetstone, who took us to Scrub Island in 2020. Deborah Calmeyer and Robert Breen also provided safe harbor in the Caribbean. Patrick Wachsberger has been a dear friend and creative sounding board for decades. He introduced us to Mark Shanker and Lee Wheeler, who became part of our extended family while we were writing this book in the islands. My mother, Janet Niemi, instilled in me an early love of reading and writing. She read multiple drafts of this book, providing constant support.

Finally, I'd like to thank my wife, Tara, for listening to the rest of her family talk about the sea all the time. And then, when we proposed months-long sailing expeditions, she signed on with enthusiasm. Thank you for your support of our whole family and of this book.